THE GIRL AND THE LIES

A.J. RIVERS

PROLOGUE

S HE WAS IN THE MIDDLE OF A DREAM.

Fragments of it lingered with her as a sharp sound cut through, jostling Sabrina into that phase between sleep and wakefulness where everything and nothing seems real. The sound came again as the feeling of floating was replaced by the sensation of soft, white cotton sheets and her pillow beneath her head. She wasn't sure if it was actually happening or just part of the dream that hadn't dissipated yet when she heard her husband's voice.

"Hey, Mom... Wait, what? What happened...? I'm on my way."

By the time she realized Ander had answered his phone, she'd forgotten the dream. He tossed the blankets off his legs, the movement familiar even with her eyes still closed, and leaned across the bed to kiss her forehead.

"What's wrong?" she asked, opening her eyes in time to see her husband pulling a pair of pants from the large cherry dresser on the far wall.

The dresser had been a wedding gift from her parents, and every time she looked at it, she thought of the happy days leading up to the wedding when they moved the bedroom furniture into the house. They had been living together for years already but in an apartment too small even to be cozy. This was their first house, with the swing on the front porch, the extra bedrooms with all the possibilities, and the huge bedroom with new cherry furniture.

"Something's going on at Mom's house. She says she needs me to come," he said, shaking off his shirt and tossing it to the hamper.

She still liked looking at him without his shirt. His job kept him fit, and a little smile crossed her lips as he dropped a fresh shirt over his head.

"Do you want me to go with you?" Sabrina asked.

She stretched out against the sheets and rolled to her side to follow his progress across the room. Ander shook his head while he put on his shoes.

"No, it's still early. You stay here. I'll come home before going to work," he said.

Sabrina was relieved. She would have gone with him if he asked her to, but she hadn't been able to sleep for a few nights. She'd finally gotten a decent sleep last night and was hoping to sink back into it for a while longer.

"Are you sure?" she asked, her head already back on the pillow and her eyes fluttering closed.

"I'm sure," he said. "I'll see you in a bit."

He started out of the room, but Sabrina lifted her head from the pillow.

"Hey," she said.

Ander smiled at her and came back for another kiss, patting her hip through the sheet.

"Get some sleep," he said.

Sabrina smiled and settled back into the bed, willing the sleep and the dream to come back as she listened to the sound of her husband leaving the house. She lay there for a while, drifting somewhere near sleep but not really ever getting all the way back into it. She rolled over and tried to shield her eyes from the sunlight now coming through the big windows. It wasn't happening. She'd woken up, and there was no getting back to sleep this morning. She decided there was no point in continuing to toss around in the bed. There were things to do, and she needed to get a head start to her day.

Reluctantly leaving the comfortable cocoon of the sheets and blanket, Sabrina sighed and stretched, trying to completely wake herself up. She made the bed, smoothing out the sheets and fluffing the pillows until they looked perfect. It was her turn to go to the cherry dresser and take out clothes. She brought them with her into the bathroom and showered.

The hot water helped to get her blood pumping and clear away the fog. She stood beneath it, washing her wavy blond hair and going over the list in her head of everything she wanted to accomplish that day. She and Ander had plans to go out later that evening after he came home from work, so she wanted to get everything done early enough to relax a little before getting ready. She was shaving her legs when a sound downstairs startled her. She hissed as the razor nicked her ankle and she rinsed it, watching the diluted blood streak across her foot and head for the drain.

Another sound came from downstairs, and Sabrina felt her pulse in her temples. No one else should have been in the house. Only the two of them lived there. Nothing should have been making any noise anywhere in the house. Fear crept up the back of her neck, but then she realized it might have been Ander. Maybe whatever was going on with his mother got fixed before he got there and he was able to come back home. The sounds seemed to be coming from the kitchen area, which would make sense if he decided to make one of the big breakfasts he adored but rarely got to have on mornings when he was expected at work.

Sabrina slid the glass door of the shower open and leaned her head out.

"Ander?" she called. "Babe?"

There was no response, and the frightened feeling came back, but for another reason. Her husband was in great shape now, but he had experienced some health problems in the past, and she was constantly worried about him. She was terrified he was going to experience a sudden emergency like his father and not make it through. Maybe he wasn't responding because something serious had happened and he needed help.

She finished rinsing off and got out of the shower, reaching for one of the towels hanging on the bar on the wall.

"Babe?" she called again. "Are you all right?"

Still no response. She quickly dried off and threw on her bathrobe. Rushing out of the bathroom, she continued to call for her husband, concern growing the longer she went without hearing his voice calling back to her. She went down the stairs and turned toward the kitchen. They were the last steps she would take before everything changed.

Just as one foot hit the tile floor, something hard hit her in the back of the head, and she felt herself stumble forward. Crying out with the pain that rushed through her skull and down the back of her neck, she tried to turn around to see what was happening, but she felt someone wrap their arms firmly around her from behind.

Sabrina fought hard against the grip, struggling to free herself from the person dragging her backward down the hallway. Remembering something she'd heard on a late-night show she watched one night she couldn't sleep, she stopped fighting and instead went completely limp, dropping all her weight down toward the floor. The strategy worked to throw her assailant off guard, and the hold on her released just enough for her to get away.

She thought about running for the door, but her attacker stood between it and her, making it unlikely she'd be able to get to it. The back door in the kitchen was closer, but it had to be unlocked with a key. There was no way she could get to the drawer where the key was kept and take it out. She screamed for help, hoping one of her neighbors might be outside and would hear her. A hard object hit her across the side of the head, and she dropped heavily to the ground. Crawling, she tried to get back to the kitchen, still forcing her voice through the taste of blood in desperation for someone to come and save her.

Somewhere above her, she heard ringing. Her phone was in the bathroom where she'd left it while she was showering. The ache in her heart told her that it was Ander calling her. She needed to get to the phone. If she could get to the steps, she could get to the bedroom and lock herself in. She'd be able to get to her phone and call the police.

Filled with determination to survive, not just for herself, she flipped over onto her back and planted a hard kick into the gut of the person coming down on her. They were wearing a ski mask, and for a brief second, the image struck her as absurd. It didn't seem real. This happened on TV and in movies. Not in real life. Not when she was still wet from the shower and only wearing her bathrobe.

The kick was enough to push the person away from her, and Sabrina scrambled to her feet. Dizzy from the blows to her head, she stumbled toward the back steps that led up to the second floor from the kitchen. She couldn't get to the main stairwell, but if she could reach the ones in the kitchen, she would be able to get up to the far end of the upstairs hallway and then run for her bedroom. She could make it. She had to. This was for them.

She only made it as far as the bottom of the steps. The third blow was enough to drop her to the floor, and she didn't move again through the others that rained down on her.

Her assailant left her there and took out a black permanent marker. There was no need to rush the messages written on the walls. No one else was around to see them being written. Upstairs, the phone kept ringing. The backdoor opened and closed almost silently. The privacy fence Ander put in place just last summer did its job. The house went still.

Two weeks earlier…

Tracy Ellis was in rare form tonight.

Every time she spoke to an audience, she got riled up and the presentation turned from speaking to shouting, but tonight there was extra fire in her voice. She stalked back and forth across the stage, gesturing wildly as she raged about the horrific death of Terrence Brooks. The beloved church leader had been found dead in brutal, gruesome circumstances, and though many thought it was just a bizarre suicide of a man obviously grappling with his own hidden demons no one knew about, Tracy refused to believe it. Not someone like him. Not a man who dedicated himself to the church and to leading vulnerable youth to try to protect them from the darkness of the world.

Something evil had befallen Terrence Brooks. Someone overcome with the vileness of sin and a searing hatred for those trying to bring good back into the world had taken the bright, compassionate, driven man away from all those who loved him.

And she couldn't tolerate it for a second.

Right offstage, Ander Ward listened to the famed televangelist rant about the death and the downfall of society, whipping up the rapt audience into a fervor. It was exactly what she wanted. It was what she always wanted. Quiet and subdued didn't get attention. It didn't make waves. When she spoke, Tracy craved the reaction. To her, it meant that people were being moved by her words and galvanized to act. There was nothing demure about Tracy Ellis or the way that she latched on to the topics that fueled her presentations.

But unlike Terrence Brooks, who had become the centerpiece of her raving because of his own dedication to faith and her perception of his death as an assault on everyone who claimed to live that way, Tracy would not frequently bring to mind the world *beloved*. There were many who followed her ravenously, attending her gatherings and watching the videos she regularly released online, but they were drawn to her incendiary words and palpable passion that cemented their own views, giving them justification for the thoughts that bubbled up in their own minds. They might say they did, but Ander knew they didn't love her. They loved what she said and the self-perceived justified fury it made them feel. If they felt that, they were righteous. They were higher.

But he also knew that was not the way everyone saw her. Tracy didn't just draw the attention of those who lapped up what she said and carried it out into the world. She also attracted the intense ire of many others. That was why he was standing there, watching the crowd intently, making sure no one seemed to be making any moves toward the stage. It had happened before. He wasn't just a showpiece meant to display her importance. He and the others assigned to protect her had been called to stave off infuriated attackers before. Some had come after her while walking to and from her car; others had tried to storm the stage during her presentations. They'd been subdued, handed over to the police, and disappeared into memory. They often showed up in her next presentation.

Tonight Ander felt particularly vigilant. The special presentation about Terrence Brooks had drawn a huge crowd, but he'd seen the comments online. He knew some people were angry that she was dragging the youth leader's death into her world and using it for her own devices. He stood ready to defend her if he needed to, his eyes flickering over the captive audience and his ears tingling waiting to hear anything from the other guards standing at the ready at other points throughout the venue.

The presentation ended the way most of them did, with loud singing and a defiant call to action from Tracy, who then gave a deep bow and walked off the stage waving and smiling. The expression was always jarring, standing in stark contrast to the intensity she had just shown in her speech. She said these presentations filled her with the spirit, refreshed and emboldened her. In the shielded recesses of his own mind, Ander wondered if the smile came from that or from the applause that lingered long after she was off the stage.

As soon as Tracy was backstage, Ander followed her. Her assistant was already taking her microphone pack off her and chattering about how successful the talk had been. It was hard to hear her over the cheering of the crowd, and Ander knew it was going to be one of those nights. She wouldn't leave the building while the audience was flowing out. They would wait until the people had thinned and then get her out through the back entrance. Because this was a last-minute gathering, it wasn't one of the larger venues with the private parking decks that kept her fully shielded from the moment she got out of her car until she was back in it again. She would have to go to the small employee parking lot and contend with whatever intrepid fans had had her car staked out.

They moved from the backstage area to a small room to greet those attendees who had paid extra for the privilege of shaking her hand and taking a picture of her. Ander stood at one door watching and waiting for everyone to move through the greeting line and get their thirty seconds of glowing exposure. When it was finally over, Tracy went to her dressing room and emerged more than an hour later, changed and ready to leave. Ander stood at the door the entire time. Silent. Waiting. Watching. Her assistant would deal with everything she'd left behind in the dressing room and with any finalities with the venue. Now it was time for Tracy to go home.

Ander brought her out through the back and to her waiting car. The driver took off almost the instant the door was closed. Ander radioed to the other guards to let them know that she was safely on her way. Relieved that his duties were finally done, Ander walked through the now-quiet night toward his own car. He noticed the piece of paper under the windshield wiper when he was still several yards away.

His stomach tightened. This wasn't the first time he'd seen something like this. He knew it wasn't a ticket or an advertisement. He looked around as he snatched the paper from the windshield. No one was around. He unfolded the note and stared down at it. His fingers twitched with the thought of calling one of the other guards or any of the employees of Tracy's company who would still be at the venue. But he stopped himself. He'd hear later if he was the only one who got one.

He looked at the note again:

How could you protect her? It's like protecting the devil himself.

Ander balled the note up and got in his car. Tossing the paper onto the passenger seat, he started the engine and drove home where he knew his wife would still be up waiting for him.

CHAPTER ONE

I LOOK DOWN AT THE CHECK IN MY HAND, THEN THE NOTE I HOLD beneath it. The signature on it is illegible, just a tangle of strokes in blue ink that looks like it shook out of a trembling pen. But I know what it says:

Terrence Brooks

Knowing that, I can almost decipher the first letters of each of the names, but the rest seems to have been purposely scribbled so that it can't be easily read. It isn't the name that has my primary focus though. It's the tiny symbol etched just beneath the name, almost lost in the jumbled letters. The same symbol that was carved into Terrence's body when it was found. The sign of the person now known as the Game Master.

The chilling message sent to the Ashbury Police Department is still fresh in my mind. Detective Melton gave me the letter that arrived at the station when I returned to the town where Terrence Brooks lived and died, and I have it with the rest of the investigation into his horrific and mysterious death.

When you speak of me, know me as the Game Master. Player selection has begun.

It means there could be more. Other victims. Other horrors I can't yet fathom because I don't understand who this person is or what they are doing. All I know is Terrence Brooks was selected as a player, and he ended up dead after weeks of what those closest to him described as "strange behavior." Now I'm scrambling to figure out what happened to him and who this person is.

But it wasn't just the police department that received a note mentioning the Game Master and claiming a connection to the Terrence Brooks death investigation. The media has gone wild with notes they received claiming responsibility, signed with the strange symbol I've yet to decipher. Echoes of notorious killers from the past, sensationalized names like the Zodiac, have the heat turned up on the investigation as people start to panic about what it all means.

I hate that my investigation has been corrupted like this. There are always details I want to keep to myself to protect the integrity of the investigation, but this time they've been stolen from me and splashed all over the evening news. Images of the symbol on the note have been posted alongside pictures of Terrence Brooks smiling during better times. Speculation has given way to full-blown rumors, and people are in an uproar.

The one good thing that has come of the media getting ahold of the story and running with it was the Ashbury Children's Hospital getting in touch with me to tell me that they had something I needed to see. It's what brought me to the hospital as I now sit in the director's office and look at the sizable canceled check signed by the dead man.

"You received this after his death?" I ask the director.

Mary Billings looks at me through emotion-filled eyes. She nods. "He must have put it in the mail just before he died. No one was able to read the signature, and there wasn't a name or return address on the envelope. It's not the first time we've received a donation that couldn't be attributed to a sender, but never something this large. We were trying to figure out who sent it so that we could properly thank them, but it wasn't until I saw the news and heard about the symbol that I put it together."

Her eyes suddenly look worried, as if she thinks she might have done something to upset me.

"I could be wrong. I still can't really read the signature, so I don't know for sure if it says 'Terrence Brooks.' It could be something else. Or someone else. I just saw the symbol on it, and I thought…"

I hold up a hand to quiet her.

"I believe you're right," I say. "The signature isn't very clear, but it shouldn't be hard to confirm that he purchased the cashier's check. And you're right about the symbol. That is the one that was used on the communications that went to the police department and to the media."

"The news said that they were … on his body," Mary says, hesitating as she speaks, like she intended to elaborate more but decided against it.

I don't let my face show any change. "I can't discuss the details of the case," I tell her. "I can only confirm that this symbol is linked to Terrence Brooks and his death investigation. I really appreciate you bringing it to my attention."

"There's something else," she says hurriedly.

I was starting to stand, ready to leave the meeting and go back to my investigation, but I stop.

"What is it?" I ask.

Her eyes move back and forth, like she is making sure no one else is in the room even though she knows it's only us and the door is closed. There's a hesitant energy around her, something that says she doesn't want to talk about what she's bringing up but feels like she has to.

"We received several threats before that check came," she says.

"Threats?" I ask. "What kind of threats?"

"We received letters in the mail as well as phone calls threatening to bomb the hospital, destroy the power grid, and stage a mass shooting. We reported them to the police, but since they weren't able to trace them to anyone, nothing was done. The day after the check arrived, another letter came."

She reaches into the drawer of her desk and pulls out a folder. She slides it across the desk to me. I open it and find a single sheet of paper with a typed one-word message:

Released

Beneath the word, in the corner of the paper, a tiny version of the mysterious symbol is etched in pencil.

"We haven't gotten any threats since. I can't guarantee they have anything to do with each other. None of the threatening letters had the symbol on them, and the caller never said anything that connects them conclusively, but I thought it was strange and wanted to bring it up to you," Mary tells me.

"Thank you," I tell her. "Do you mind if I take this with me?"

She shakes her head. "Go ahead."

"Thanks. Again, I appreciate you getting in touch with me and telling me about this. It is very useful."

I stand and reach for her hand. She shakes mine as she stands, and I head for the door.

Walking through the hospital has a different feeling now that I know about the threats. I look at the children being led around by doctors and nurses, some riding little cars in lieu of wheelchairs, others attached to IVs and wearing gowns. I see the parents following behind or waiting in seating areas, their expressions a combination of fear and hope. They are all so invested in what the children are going through that they can't think of anything else. They feel safe in the hospital, protected by the cheerful decorations and dedicated staff. They don't know the threats that haunt Mary Billings and the rest of the administration.

The thought of someone planning to bring any harm to a place like this makes my blood boil. There's no reason for it—nothing that could possibly justify, even in the most twisted mind, wanting to destroy a place like this and all the vulnerable, innocent people in it.

As I continue toward the exit, I hear my name and turn toward it. Mary is coming after me, and I pause to wait for her.

"I'm sorry, I know you were leaving, but I was wondering if you might be willing to do a favor for me. For the hospital, actually," she says.

"What is it?" I ask.

"Every month we have a birthday party for all the kids whose birthdays are that month so that they will have a chance to celebrate even if they are stuck in the hospital during it. We are hosting one today, and one of the children who is celebrating his birthday heard that there was an FBI agent in the hospital. He dreams of joining the Bureau when he grows up." Her eyes soften and fill with emotion at that comment. "I was hoping that you might go to the party and meet him. Maybe talk to him a little bit about what you do. I know you're busy, and I understand if you can't do it, but it would mean a lot to him and to us."

I smile. "Of course, I can absolutely do that."

She grins. "Thank you so much. The party starts in twenty minutes in the dayroom. I'll see you there."

I decide to pass the time before the party by going to the cafeteria for a cup of coffee. I know Sam is expecting me back in Sherwood later, so I call him to let him know I'm going to be starting back later than I thought.

"Hey, babe," I say when he answers. "I just want to let you know that I haven't left yet. I'm going to be getting home a little later than I thought. I didn't want you to worry."

"What's going on? Is everything all right?" he asks.

It's always his first instinct to assume something is probably wrong when I tell him that plans have changed in one way or another. Considering everything that has happened, it's not necessarily an inexplicable response, but I still hate to hear the automatic spike of worry in his voice. I know how protective he is of me and how frustrating it is to him that there is frequently nothing he can do to keep me out of dangerous situations. He knows my dedication to my career and that I will do what I need to do. But at least in this situation, I can assuage his fears pretty easily.

"Everything is fine," I tell him. "I'm at the hospital, and they asked me to stay to go to a birthday party they're having for the kids. One of them wants to be an FBI agent, and they thought he might like to meet me."

"A birthday party?" Sam asks with a chuckle. "Agent Emma Griffin, Make-a-Wish granter."

I can't help the laugh that tumbles out of me. "Yeah, it should be fun for the kids," I say. "I don't know how long it's going to last, but it shouldn't be too much longer."

"All right. Well, you have a good time, and I'll see you when you get home," he says.

We end the call, and I sip my coffee as I make my way back to the main floor so I can find the dayroom. The doors are closed, and pieces of colorful tissue paper have been put up over the windows to preserve some of the surprise for the children who are already gathered out in the hallway excited about the party. I look at them and can't help but wonder how many of these parties some of them have been to in the time they've been in the hospital.

The door opens slightly, and Mary looks out. She smiles when she sees me.

"There you are. Come on in."

She opens the door enough for me to slip through, telling the children they have to wait just a little longer. I step into the room and see people scurrying around hanging decorations and organizing cupcakes on a long table. There are games set up and little goodie bags in a basket in the corner. It's obvious how much care and attention has gone into putting this event on for the patients, and it makes my heart feel warm to see it.

"This looks great," I tell Mary. "I'm sure the kids love it."

"They really do," she says. "We try to make each one a little different so that it's not the same event every month. This month we're going for a beach theme." She looks across the room and waves. I follow her gaze and see a woman coming toward us. "There are a couple of people I'd like you to meet."

The woman comes up to us and extends her hand to me. "Connie Stinson," she says.

"This is Agent Emma Griffin," Mary says, gesturing toward me. "She's the agent handling the Terrence Brooks case."

The words seem to have an impact on Connie, who nods. "That whole situation is horrible."

"It is," I agree.

"Connie is part of the Hearts of the Community Foundation, the charitable organization that makes so much of what we do for the children here possible. They sponsor the birthday parties as well as holiday events and activities throughout the year and help with supporting the families of patients when they need it," Mary says.

"That's a wonderful cause," I tell her.

"Thank you," she says. "The foundation is involved in a lot throughout the community, but our work with the children's hospital is my favorite." She looks to the side as the door opens and gestures toward a man who slipped in with an armful of grocery bags. "That's the head of the foundation, Mike Morris."

"Connie and Mike also sit on the board," Mary explains. "They know about …"—she hesitates, her eyes sliding over to the other volunteers getting the party ready—"what we talked about earlier."

I nod my understanding. "I'll be adding that into my investigation."

Mike walks over, and Mary introduces us.

"Nice to meet you," he says. "I'm glad to hear things are being taken seriously."

"It's time to start the party," another volunteer says.

"Go ahead and open the doors," Mary tells her.

Opening the doors releases a deluge of children into the room, all excitedly *ooh*ing and *ahh*ing as they take in the sights gleefully. I can almost see the gears churning in their little heads as they try to decide what they want to do first.

"Everybody, take a seat," Mary instructs them.

The children who are able flop down to sit on the floor while those in wheelchairs are brought up close beside them. I step back to watch as Mary introduces the party and describes what the children will be doing. She gives the usual gentle admonishments to make sure that they all behave and give everyone a chance to enjoy everything, then throws her arms up in the air.

"Go have fun!"

13

I can't help but smile at the sight of the children running to the games and giggling over the decorations. Mike steps up beside me to organize some extra snacks and treats on one of the tables, and I smile at him.

"This is really amazing," I say. "They look like they're having a blast."

"I look forward to the party every month," he says. "The hospital has a really special place in my heart. My brother spent a lot of time here when it was still the old facility. They took really good care of him, and they tried to do as many special things as they could for all the kids. I knew I wanted to help make being here easier and more fun for them."

"Agent Griffin?"

Mary is coming toward me with her hand on the back of a boy I'd place at nine or ten years old. He's wearing cotton lounge pants and a baggy T-shirt with socks, and I notice a port in his arm.

"Hi," I say.

"This is Lucas Potter. He's really excited to meet you."

Mike smiles at me and moves away to join in the fun of the party while I talk to Lucas. We chat for a while, his enthusiasm glowing in big brown eyes that defy his surroundings and circumstances. By the time he rejoins the party, I am filled with emotion and even more dedicated to finding out who is at once targeting the hospital with horrifying threats and forcing Terrence Brooks to make a large donation with the mark of the Game Master.

CHAPTER TWO

I call Sam while I'm on the drive back to Sherwood from Ashbury so he knows I'm on the way.

"How was the party? Did you tell the kids all about the glamorous life of an FBI agent?"

"I… skimped on some of the more grisly details," I admit. "But that didn't stop Lucas. He wanted everything. He was a little disappointed when I told him it's a lot more paperwork than in the movies though. Good kid."

"Are you hungry?" he asks. "I'll order some food from the Thai place."

"That sounds amazing," I tell him. "I didn't even stop for lunch today."

"Don't tell Xavier that, you'll end up with another emergency pack of snacks and water stuffed in your back seat," he says.

"That was actually really useful," I tell him. "The chocolate coating on the protein bars might not survive the summer heat as well as they did in the winter, but I got good use out of those during a few investigations last winter. Especially when my tire went flat during that storm and I had to wait for roadside assistance."

Sam laughs. "I think you would prefer your noodles."

"I would always prefer my noodles."

"I'll see you when you get home."

The drive from Ashbury isn't very long, but it gives me enough time to churn the new developments through my mind, trying to piece the new details together with what we already know about Terrence Brooks's death.

I'm still bouncing thoughts around when I get home and pull in behind Sam's car in the driveway. The long summer evenings mean the sun hasn't set yet, but the front light is already on. It's a comforting, welcoming sight that makes me relax into the feeling of being home.

I grab my bag and the papers I got from Mary Billings and head inside.

"Hey, babe," I call out when I open the door. "I'm home."

Sam places something down with a clatter, then emerges out of the kitchen with a dishtowel over his shoulder and comes over to me for a kiss.

"Glad you're back," he says.

"What are you doing in there?" I ask.

"Cleaning out the refrigerator. There were some things in there I think we've forgotten about for a few weeks."

I shudder. "That's not a pleasant thought."

"Not particularly," he says.

I bring everything into my office and put them down, then join Sam in the kitchen. He's at the sink washing pans I'm sure once held leftovers that never saw the light of day again. I try not to mourn the loss of whatever it was and drop down into one of the chairs at the table.

"How did it go?" he asks.

I tell him about the donation and the threats against the hospital.

"Remember when Terrence's friends told me that he suddenly started selling off just about everything he owned not too long before he died?" I ask.

"Yeah," Sam says.

"I think that's what funded the donation. That's why he did it. For some reason, the Game Master required him to make that donation, and he had to sell everything he possibly could to get enough money together to do it," I say.

"But why would this guy want Brooks to donate to the children's hospital after threatening them?" Sam asks.

"I don't know. The name that he chose for himself clearly shows that he thinks of this as a game. But it's not making any sense. I don't understand why someone would target a youth church leader whom everyone seemed to love and force him to make a donation to a hospital before killing himself. Though I'm still torn about whether his death was really the intended end or if it just turned out that way because no one found him," I say. "That symbol showing up is important. He didn't just do these things to the person he chose, he's forcing people to recognize that it was done because of him. He wants people to know the pieces of the game, but not really know what's going on."

"He's not telling anybody the rules," Sam says.

"Something like that." I let out a sigh. "I'm going to put on something more comfortable."

"You're putting on pajamas already?" he asks.

There's something suspicious in his voice, and I'm not sure what to think about it.

"I was just going to throw on some leggings and a tank top," I tell him. "I don't want to be in my work clothes anymore. What's going on?"

"Nothing," he says. "I just thought it was a little early for you to already be packing it in."

"No," I tell him. "The children didn't exhaust me that much."

"Good to hear."

I go up to the bedroom and change into a more comfortable, cooler outfit and put my hair into a ponytail to get it off my neck. Feeling a bit more refreshed, I head back down the stairs. I've just gotten into the living room where Sam has taken up residence on his favorite chair when I hear a knock on the front door. I look at Sam quizzically.

"Are you expecting someone?" I ask.

He shrugs. "Must be the food."

"The food?" I ask, heading toward the door. "Since when does the Thai place deliver?"

I peer through the peephole and am confused when I see Eric standing on the porch with two large, brown paper bags in his hands. Throwing the dead bolt out of place, I open the door and look out at him.

"Hey," I say. "What are you doing?"

He lifts the bags. "Dinner delivery. Tell Xavier they threw in some extra peanut sauce for him."

"Xavier isn't here," I say, starting to feel like I'm the only one who doesn't know something.

"He isn't?" Eric asks, trying to sound genuinely befuddled but coming across like a bad actor. "That's strange. Well, I guess we're just going to have to bring it over to him."

"We are?" I ask. I look back at Sam. "Are Xavier and Dean in town? I thought they were still in Harlan."

Sam shrugs. "I guess we'll just have to go find out. Put your shoes on. We'll take a walk over there."

I go put my shoes on, curious about what these two have up their sleeves. Eric doesn't just show up at the house, especially without Bellamy and Bebe. It's not that he's not welcome to come whenever he wants; it's that the drive and their careers keep them from just popping by spontaneously. There are always calls and plans involved when they are coming to visit, and we don't have anything set for at least a few weeks.

"I know you two have something going on," I say as I rejoin them in the living room.

"What do you mean?" Sam asks, herding me toward the door.

"I can't just pick up dinner for you?" Eric asks innocently.

"You can't drive a couple of hours and happen to get to the restaurant on time and get dinner for someone who doesn't live with me?" I ask. "Whyever would I think that?"

We walk out into the mercifully cooling evening and start our walk over to Dean and Xavier's house—the house that we lived in until only a very short time ago. It's just a couple of blocks, and the walk is so familiar my feet could do it without me even thinking about it. This is the same walk I used to do when I visited Sam when I was younger and with my grandparents. I walked, jogged, and rode my bike along these roads more times than I could possibly count. Every time I do it, I'm grateful the houses are still with us and I still have the opportunity to walk between them to see people I love.

We get to the house, and I notice an extra car in the driveway. It's unmistakably Cupcake's, with its pink custom paint and vanity tags proclaiming her name. There's nothing subtle about her arrival anywhere, one of the things I've come to adore about her. The small, bubbly confection of a woman knows full well that she's not everyone's cup of tea, but she's not going to back down or try to minimize herself to make them more comfortable. She's herself unapologetically and without reservation.

"Oh, look, Cupcake is here," Eric says, his voice still stilted like he's trying far too hard to sound surprised by the circumstances. "I guess that's why there's so much food."

I climb up onto the front porch and knock.

"Come in," Dean calls from inside.

I use my key to open the door and step into an explosion of primary colors and helium balloons.

"Surprise!" several voices shout out at me as people burst out from various makeshift hiding places throughout the living room.

I turn around to look at Sam and Eric, who are coming in behind me.

"What's all this?" I ask.

Suddenly a puff of confetti flutters around my head.

"Happy birthday!"

I turn around and see Xavier wearing a red cone hat strapped around his chin with a strand of elastic and carrying a party horn. He blows the horn at me.

"Um, my birthday isn't for a few more weeks," I point out.

"That's what makes it a surprise," he says, tossing another handful of confetti at me.

"We know you don't like to make a big deal out of your birthday and figured you would find some way to be busy that day so we couldn't celebrate you," Bellamy says as she and Bebe step out from behind the wall between the living room and dining room. "So we thought we would give you a surprise early."

"Well, I'm definitely surprised," I say. I look at Vance Armand, a friend of Dean's, who emerged from behind the curtains when I came into the house. "Where did you even park?"

"Down the street," he says. "I got some looks from the neighbors as I walked here with the balloons."

"I'm sure you did," I say.

I look around at the copious twisted crepe paper and floating balloons. It looks like a party from when I was a child, and I can't help but laugh and shake my head.

"This looks great." I realize it's the same thing I said about the party at the hospital, and I look at Sam. "You let me talk about going to the birthday party at the children's hospital when you *knew* this was going on, and you didn't say anything?"

"I know. For once, I managed to keep a secret," he says. "I couldn't believe it when you said they wanted you to stay for a birthday party for the kids. We were already setting everything up."

"Thank you for this," I tell him. "You're right, I don't usually want to celebrate my birthday, but this is perfect."

"I'm glad you said that, because I would have felt really dumb wearing this thing if you didn't like it," Dean's son, Owen, says, coming out of the kitchen wearing a blue cone hat and carrying a vegetable tray.

He sets it down as I cross the room to hug him.

"Owen," I say. "It's so good to see you. How is your sister?"

"She's good," he says. "Getting better every day, I think."

"I'm glad to hear it."

"Let's eat," Dean says. "Xavier wouldn't let us eat anything until you got here."

"There's all kinds of stuff in the kitchen," Bellamy says.

"And we have this," Eric announces, holding up the bags of Thai food. "I really did go pick up the food order. And, Xavier… extra peanut sauce."

"Excellent," he says calmly. I start for the kitchen, but he stops me. "Wait, Emma. You're not ready yet."

"I'm not?"

He picks up a yellow party hat and plops it down on my head.

"Proceed."

We go into the kitchen, and everyone fills plates with food, which we bring into the dining room and living room to eat. I can't believe they pulled this off. I don't know how they managed to keep the secret from me. It's a good thing nothing more serious happened while I was in Ashbury keeping me there.

We're finishing up when Cupcake lifts her hands up in the air to get everyone's attention.

"Time for games!" she says.

"Games?" I ask.

"Of course," she says. "You can't have a classic birthday party without some classic birthday party games. I hope you are ready to pin the tail on the donkey!"

I do not by any means feel ready to pin the tail on the donkey. But she is so excited I can't turn her down.

It turns out they have planned an entire party that would have been the highlight of the year for any six-year-old—complete with games, goodie bags, and cake and ice cream. We discover a competitive streak in Xavier as he aggressively tries to get the tail in the precise right position and it looks like the anxiety is going to get the most of him as we play musical chairs. Bebe is having the time of her life.

"I made it for you," Cupcake announces as I'm opening gifts. "I hope you like it."

I reach into the gift bag sitting on my lap and pull out a large, plush crocheted cinnamon roll with big eyes and a smile.

I laugh. "It's amazing. Thank you, Cupcake."

"It's scented," she tells me.

I bury my nose in the plush and breathe in the smell of cinnamon.

"She's been so excited to give that to you she almost ruined the surprise," Xavier says.

Cupcake giggles and rests her head on his shoulder. He leans his head over to rest on hers for a moment, and I feel my heart squeeze.

The party wears on until well after Bebe has fallen asleep on the couch. Eventually, Eric scoops her into his arms to carry her back to my house. Sam already invited them to stay with us for the night and got the guest room ready without me knowing, so Bellamy takes the little girl from her father's arms and carries her the rest of the way to the bed when we get to the house.

"I'm going to grab a shower and put on some pajamas," I tell Eric. "You going to be up for a little while?"

"Yeah, there's actually something I wanted to show you if you're up for it," he says. "I know we just had your birthday party, but if you're willing to think about work again, it might interest you."

"Sure," I say. "I'll be right back."

When I've showered and am in my favorite summertime pajamas, I go to the kitchen to make some tea and bring it with me into the living room. Eric is watching TV when I get there, but he grabs the remote and mutes it when he sees me. He picks up his tablet from where it was sitting on the coffee table, and I sit down beside him.

"Have you ever heard of Tracy Ellis?" he asks.

"No," I say. "Who is that?"

"She calls herself a faith-based inspirational speaker and writer. Essentially a multimedia televangelist. She's pretty controversial. A lot of people don't like her style or the kinds of messages that she preaches. But there are others who think that she's the greatest spiritual voice of our time."

"That's always a good division," I say.

"Yeah, no problems could come out of that," he says, swiping through screens on the tablet until he settles on one. "She did a talk recently that I thought you would be interested in hearing. It's pretty long, so I'm not going to play the entire thing, but here's a particularly interesting section."

He presses Play, and the image of a woman with dark hair tightly curled to her shoulders and thick glasses standing on a stage appears on the screen. It's obvious she is already well into her speech; she looks riled up as she paces back and forth across the stage.

"The death of Terrence Brooks is a sign," she intones. "Mark my words, it's a sign. Society is degrading rapidly, and it's trying to drag all of us down with it. There are forces in power now that will bring an end to this world if we don't stand up and fight. Terrence, a man of the Word, a committed walker of faith, was brought down by evil. He was destroyed by the very forces we must battle against in order to save ourselves and all the souls of this world!"

I'm stunned by the intensity in the woman's voice as she continues to rant about Terrence Brooks's death, drawing parallels that don't exist and crafting ways to make the death seem even more heinous than it already is.

"What the hell is this?" I ask. "She's trying to say that he was murdered in some sort of religious hate crime."

"She's not trying to say it," Eric points out. "She *is* saying it. She wants people to believe that the religious community is under siege and is turning Terrence Brooks into a poster child for it."

"This investigation has already been compromised enough with the media latching on to it the way it has and publicizing the messages they got from the Game Master." My lips involuntarily curl up at the feeling of the words coming through them. "I hate even saying that. It feels like I'm playing right into what he wants."

"You are," Eric says. "But you don't have much of a choice. There's nothing else to call him. Besides, it's important to remember how messed up this person actually is. He's playing a game that might have started with Terrence Brooks, but it isn't over."

The message is ominous. Terrence was the first to fall victim to the one who calls himself the Game Master, but he made himself clear. There are other players being selected. I don't know what he has planned for them, and I don't want to give him the chance to show me.

CHAPTER THREE

THE SUMMER HEAT IS INTENSE ENOUGH TO LURE SAM AND ME TO the Sherwood Community Center's pool that weekend. The newly reopened pool has drawn much of the town to get a respite from the searing temperatures, and I am happy to grab two loungers beneath a large umbrella that keeps us both out of the glaring sunlight. I drop my tote bag onto the deck and slip out of my cover-up, rolling up a towel to put under my head on the chair. Despite me telling him that he should do it before we leave the house the way I do, Sam stands off to the side slathering himself in sunscreen.

"You know that's not going to be effective for a while, right?" I ask, tilting my sunglasses down to get a better look at him.

"It'll be fine," he says.

Famous last words. I have a strong feeling I'm going to be following up this slathering with my own version featuring aloe gel and lidocaine. I kick off my flip-flops and feel the heat of the cement deck sizzle into the bottom of my feet. The familiar, nostalgic feeling makes me think of my father and the long afternoons spent at the waterpark in Florida before my mother's death. I immediately crave salty French fries.

Sitting down, I swing my legs up on the chaise lounge and lean back, taking a breath as I close my eyes. The reclined position doesn't last long. It's just too hot for me to sit here like this. Leaving my cover-up draped across the lounger to stake my claim on it, I go to the pool and walk down the cement steps into the shallow end. The chill of the water instantly cools me, and I brace myself before dipping all the way down into it. A few laps bring my temperature down, and I'm floating around enjoying the relief when I hear Sam calling me.

"Emma, Eric's on the phone," he says.

There's a note in his voice that says this isn't a social call. I climb out of the water and dry off with a towel from my bag before taking the phone from Sam's hand. I smooth my towel across the chair and sit down as I answer.

"Hey, Eric," I say.

"You're at the pool?" he asks.

"Yeah, it's so hot Sam and I decided it would be nice to take a dip. The community center looks amazing since it was rebuilt," I tell him.

"Yeah, Sam was telling me," he says. "I'm sorry to interrupt, but I have a new case for you."

"A new case?" I ask, continuing to dry off my legs then pulling my sunglasses out of my bag so I can put them on.

"Yeah. Remember when I showed you the video of Tracy Ellis?" he asks.

"Of course," I tell him. "Did something happen to her?"

"Not her, but a man who worked for her was murdered last night. There's a lot more. I need you to get here as soon as you can," he says.

"All right," I say. "I'll be there soon."

Sam looks over at me with a disappointed expression on his face, but he nods and starts packing up our stuff. I stuff my phone back in my bag and shrug into my cover-up.

"I'm sorry," I tell him.

"It's all right," he says. "I'm guessing there's something serious happening."

"I don't know any details yet," I tell him, "but he said that there's been a murder and there's a lot more to it, so he needs me there as soon as I can get there."

We're barely away from the chairs when other poolgoers swoop in to score them. As soon as Sam and I get home, I run upstairs to take a fast shower and get dressed. Tossing a few things into a bag in case I'll be away from home for a couple of days, I fill a bottle with iced water and a storage container with some fresh fruit for the drive. I kiss Sam and point to the batch of cinnamon rolls rising on the counter.

"Don't forget to bake those," I tell him. "The icing is already ready in the refrigerator. I'll call you later when I know what's going on. I love you."

"Love you. Be safe."

He walks me to the front door and watches as I jog to my car and jump inside.

The drive to headquarters gives me plenty of time to think about what might be happening. It wouldn't have surprised me to find out that something happened to the controversial figure, but I'm intrigued by the death of someone working for her. Without any other context yet, I don't know what happened or why we would be called in to handle it.

Eric is waiting for me in his office when I arrive at headquarters. He offers me coffee, and I accept despite the heat. I've finished my water, but ice cubes still survive inside my cup, so I pour the coffee down over the ice and swirl it around to cool. Eric watches me and lifts his eyebrow when I look up at him.

"Classy," he says.

"It's hot as a skillet out there," I tell him. "I'm not going to turn down coffee, but I can't do a hot beverage right now."

"Fair enough," he says.

I sit down across from him. "So I'm here. What's going on?"

"The victim is Gideon Bell. He was stabbed to death in his apartment last night. His roommate, Jesse Kristoff, wasn't home when the attack started, but he interrupted it and was injured," he tells me.

"You said there was a lot more," I say. "What's going on?"

"Apparently, several people within the company, including Gideon, have been receiving threats over the last several weeks," he says.

"What kind of threats?" I ask, immediately thinking about the Game Master and his vile messages to the children's hospital.

"Someone has been threatening employees of the company if they continue to work for Tracy Ellis," Eric says. "Some of them reported the threats to the police, but they were told there was nothing they could do about them because they didn't know who sent them. The detective assigned to the case is Liam Fuller. He's waiting for you to get in touch with him."

He hands me a business card for the detective, and I see that he's from a department about half an hour away.

"You can stay at our place if you want," he says.

"I don't want to be in the way," I tell him.

"You know you're never in the way," he argues. "And Bellamy was just saying we haven't spent enough time together recently."

"That's true," I tell him.

"Then it's settled. You go talk to the detective and come over whenever you're done," he says. "It's better than another hotel. Unless Bebe gets to be too much for you. Then you can get a hotel."

I laugh as I stand up. "She's never too much for me. But I'll keep that in mind."

He laughs and hands a folder over to me. "Go. I'll see you later."

I call Detective Fuller as I'm leaving the building to let him know that I'm on my way. He's waiting for me when I get to the department and immediately ushers me back to a conference room already set up with all the materials they have on Gideon Bell's murder.

"How familiar are you with Tracy Ellis?" he asks as he closes the door behind us.

"Not very," I admit. "I've only seen a small clip of her speech about Terrence Brooks. I'm sure you know that I'm handling that death investigation."

"Which is why I was particularly interested in working with you on this case," he says. "Ellis is a highly controversial public figure, but her recent coverage of the Brooks death has been especially incendiary."

"Agent Martinez told me about threats employees of her company have received. It sounds like they have been coming since before Terrence Brooks died," I say.

"Yes," Detective Fuller says. "They've been reported for several weeks. They've come as letters being left on cars and arriving at the houses of multiple employees of the company. They are why I wanted to call in the assistance of the Bureau. With the intensity of the feelings toward Ellis and these threats, this situation could be far more serious than just this single murder."

"I'll need the contact information for Bell's family so I can talk to them," I say.

"He has no family," Fuller tells me. "The closest thing we've been able to find to a next of kin is his roommate. He was given official notification of the death."

"He interrupted the attack?" I ask, remembering what Eric told me about the murder.

"Gideon was already dead by the time he arrived home," Fuller says. "The door was broken open when he got home, and he went inside to find out what was happening. He reported seeing a figure writing on the walls of Gideon's bedroom with a permanent marker. The assailant came after him and gashed his back before he was able to get into his bedroom and get his gun. He shot at the killer but missed him while he was running out of the apartment."

"Writing on the walls?" I ask. "What was written?"

"The message wasn't completed because Jesse Kristoff interrupted him," he says, opening a file and turning a crime scene photo toward me.

I pick up the photo and examine the words written in thick, black letters across the wall:

Defender of the vile, protector of —

There's a streak on the wall where the marker slipped, likely when the killer was startled by the arrival of Gideon's roommate. I reach for the folder with the rest of the crime scene photos. Gideon's body is stretched across his bed like he was sleeping when he was attacked and didn't have a chance to fight back.

"It doesn't look like there were many knife wounds," I point out.

"No," Fuller says. "Whoever did this knew what they were doing. It was a fast kill."

"This wasn't spontaneous. He was targeted specifically. Whoever sent the threats fulfilled them with him," I say. "Has the scene been processed?"

"Yes. Very little was found other than a few synthetic hair fibers," he says.

"Synthetic hair. Wig fibers," I say.

"Exactly."

"All right. I need to talk to Jesse Kristoff. Has he been released from the hospital?" I ask.

"He's being held for observation," Detective Fuller says. "He gave a preliminary statement when the first responders arrived, but he hasn't been formally interviewed yet."

He gives me the information about the hospital where Jesse is being treated for his injuries, and I take that, along with the notes about the investigation so far, and return to my car. I call Sam on the drive to the hospital to let him know that I'll be staying at Eric and Bellamy's house for the next couple of days.

"I'll miss you," he says.

"I'll miss you too," I tell him. "I'll be back as soon as I can."

"Do what you need to do. But be safe," he says.

"I'll do my best."

CHAPTER FOUR

GET OFF THE PHONE AS I'M PULLING INTO THE HOSPITAL PARKING lot. I park at the main entrance and head inside to the fifth floor where Detective Fuller said I'd be able to find Jesse. A man in pale-green scrubs looks up at me from a desk when I reach the floor, and I show him my shield.

"Agent Emma Griffin, FBI," I say. "I'm here to see Jesse Kristoff."

"I'll get the doctor," he says.

I step to the side to wait while he walks out from behind the desk and goes further into the floor, disappearing into a room. He emerges a few seconds later with a doctor right behind him. She walks up to me and shakes my hand.

"Dr. Zachary," she says. "You're here to see Jesse Kristoff?"

"Yes," I say. "I'm investigating his roommate's murder and his attack. I need to speak with him. Is he in a condition that he can speak with me?"

"Yes. He has been given considerable painkillers, so he might be tired. He might not be able to speak with you for long."

"I understand," I say.

"Come with me."

We walk down the hallway, and she knocks on a closed door.

"Come in," a voice calls from inside.

She opens the door partially and sticks her head in.

"Jesse, there's someone here to speak with you. She's investigating what happened," she says.

"Okay." He sounds slightly hesitant, but the doctor opens the door the rest of the way and gestures for me to go inside.

I smile as I walk into the room, hoping to put Jesse at ease. After what he went through, it's understandable for him to be on edge, but I need him to be as comfortable as possible so he's willing to speak to me about what happened.

"Hi, Jesse," I say. "I'm Agent Emma Griffin. I'm with the FBI. We're working with Detective Fuller and the rest of the team to investigate what happened last night. I just need to talk to you about it."

He nods. "All right."

"Thank you," I say.

I glance over at the doctor, who seems to realize she's not needed for the conversation and starts toward the door.

"I'll be back to check on you later," she says to Jesse. "Use your Call button to let the nurses know if you need anything."

He nods, and the door closes behind Dr. Zachary. I step up closer to the bed.

"I want to say first that I'm so sorry for your loss. You and Gideon were close?" I ask.

"Yes," he says. "He was my best friend."

"I'm sorry. I know this is a very difficult time for you, and I really appreciate you being willing to talk to me about it. I'm sure this doesn't seem like the best time, considering," I say, glancing around the room to indicate him being in the hospital. "But it's really important to talk to you while everything is as fresh in your mind as possible so we can hopefully get the information we need to find out who is responsible for this."

"I understand," he says. "I already gave a statement to the police."

"I know. But I'd like to hear from you myself. And maybe now that you are a little bit separated from the situation, more will come up. How are you feeling, by the way?" I ask.

"As good as can be expected, I guess," he tells me. "They have me on pain meds for the cut on my back, so I'm not feeling much of anything."

"I'm glad to hear that," I say. "Let's start with you just telling me what happened last night. Just in your own words, tell me what you did and what you saw."

I sit down in a chair near the bed and take out my notepad and pen so I can jot down anything significant that Jesse might say.

"I was out late with some friends. We were bowling for one of their birthdays and ended up going to a bar afterward. I figured Gideon would already be in bed by the time I got home because he has to get up earlier for work than I do, but when I pulled into the parking lot, I noticed that the lights in the living room were on. His bedroom has a window that faces out to the parking lot, and I noticed the shadow of someone moving in there, so I thought maybe he couldn't sleep. But then I got to the door and saw that it had been pried or broken open. The doors on the apartments aren't great, so it wouldn't have taken a lot of force. Since I wasn't home, he hadn't put the chain lock on.

"I probably should have just called the police when I saw the door like that, but I was worried about Gideon, so I went inside. I went to his bedroom and saw him on the bed first. There was blood, and he wasn't moving. Then I noticed the person writing on the wall. They were wearing a ski mask and dark clothes. I didn't get much of a look at them because I went running for my bedroom. They caught up to me, and that's when they slashed me in the back. But I was able to get to my room and grab my gun. I got a shot off but missed them. It was enough to make them run, and I barricaded myself in the bedroom and called the police. I stayed there until they got there and knocked on my door to tell me they were officers. I really wanted to check on Gideon and see if he was all right, but I didn't know if the person was going to come back or if there was someone else, so I stayed in my bedroom."

"You did the right thing," I assure him.

"But if I had gone to his room," he says, a note of desperation in his voice, "maybe there's something I could have done for him."

I shake my head. "No, there's nothing you could have done. You can't let yourself think that way. You did what you needed to do by protecting yourself. That's why you're sitting here talking to me. You have to remember that."

He nods, briefly looking down at his lap to gather himself. "I wish I'd gotten a better look at them," he says.

"You said they were wearing a ski mask," I say.

"Yes," he says. "I couldn't see their face."

"The crime scene investigation team found wig fibers in the apartment. Do you own a wig, or did Gideon?" I ask.

He shakes his head, looking vaguely confused. "Wig fibers? I don't know why they would be in the apartment."

"I know you say you couldn't see the person's face or anything, but based on size and movements, do you think it's likely that they were a man or a woman?"

"I would think a man," he says.

"All right," I say. "And you couldn't see their hands or any other skin?"

"No, they were wearing gloves."

"When you got to the apartment, none of your neighbors were outside or anything? It didn't seem like any of them noticed what was going on?" I ask.

"No," he says. "I didn't see anyone until after the police got there. Either they didn't hear anything or they did and didn't want to get involved."

I make a mental note to make sure I talk to the neighbors closest to their apartment so I can find out which of those scenarios is true.

"I know you said that you saw the person writing on the wall of Gideon's bedroom. Did you get a chance to see what they had written?" I ask.

"No," he says.

I take out the crime scene photo that shows the message written on the wall with a permanent marker and hand it to him. Jesse takes the picture and looks at it, his breath catching in his throat as he looks at the scene.

"Does that mean anything to you?" I ask.

"I have to guess that it's referring to Tracy Ellis, the woman Gideon worked for," Jesse says. "He was one of the people in her entourage, I guess you'd say. Officially, he was security, so he did protect her."

"This is pretty strong language," I say. "Does it seem to you that someone would call Tracy Ellis 'vile'?"

"Absolutely," he says without hesitation. "She is one of the most divisive people I've ever heard of. I worked for her company really briefly a couple of years ago, but then I found something else. Even in the short time that I was working there, I saw so much controversy and negativity. Then Gideon talked about the things he experienced when they would do appearances and travel for presentations and guest speaking gigs. There are a lot of people who can't stand that woman or any of what she apparently stands for. I think that's why Gideon didn't take the threats very seriously."

"Did he talk to you about getting the threats?" I ask.

"Yeah. He showed them to me when he got them. I thought he should call the police about them, but he said they weren't that big of a deal and he was used to hearing threats against Ellis because of the things that she preached and talked about. He said he didn't think they were anything to really worry about because they were so much like ones that he'd heard of Ellis getting before and nothing ever happened to her. He didn't think that anyone would go after him just because he was one of her security team. I pointed out that some of the threats came in the mail, which meant that they knew where he lived, but he still wouldn't think too much about it. After getting a couple of them, he did bring them to Tracy's attention so that she at least knew what was going on."

"Did he tell you how she reacted to that?" I ask.

"Pretty much how I would have expected her to. She blew it off and told him that he was doing righteous work by working with her so he didn't need to be afraid. Getting the threats was just a sign that what she was saying was being heard and it was affecting people, which was exactly what she wanted," he tells me.

He continues, "That's the thing about her. There's no middle ground with Tracy Ellis. People are either absolutely obsessed with her teaching and everything she says, or they despise her and completely condemn what she stands for. But it doesn't really matter to her. She likes being fawned over by the people who all but worship her, but she is just as fine with the people who hate her. She might even like them more because they tend to talk about her more and get other people to listen to her just out of sheer curiosity and wanting to know what has offended other people so much. Hate-watching is definitely a thing. And she doesn't really care as long as she's getting the attention. The whole 'all publicity is good publicity' thing."

"Have there been any specific people whom Gideon ever encountered who you think would want to cause him harm? Anyone he was specifically afraid of?" I ask.

"No. None of the threats he ever got or that ever came into the company were signed. He's encountered people who were threatening to hurt Tracy Ellis while on her appearances, but they never mentioned wanting to go after security, and they were always easily subdued. The vast majority of the time when people speak out against people like Tracy and claim they were going to do something about them, it was all talk. They weren't actually going to take any action. They just wanted people to hear them talking because they thought it was going to make a difference if they sounded like they were vehemently against the things that were pissing so many people off," he says.

"A messed-up version of virtue signaling," I say. "I'm unfortunately very familiar. Do you know if he kept any of the threatening notes?"

"I don't think so. I'm pretty sure he threw them all away," Jesse says. "If there are any, they would be at the apartment."

"Are you going back there after you are discharged?" I ask.

He's only being held for observation, likely to make sure that the wound in his back doesn't get infected and to monitor his mental health after the extreme stress he just endured. But that means he won't be in the hospital very long. He'll likely be discharged within the next few hours and have to face this new normal in life. The thought of him going back to the apartment already is sobering.

"Not yet," he tells me. "The detective told me he would let me know when I'm allowed to go back. I'm going to stay with my parents for a few days anyway. I just don't want to be alone there. I don't know if I ever want to be there again."

"That's perfectly understandable," I say. "I'm going to let you get some rest. Thank you for talking with me. I will likely want to talk to you again." I give him one of my business cards. "If you can think of anything else, don't hesitate to call me. I always have my phone on me."

I leave the room and go back to my car. I call Detective Fuller as I wait for the air-conditioning to kick in.

"I want to go to the apartment and get a look at the crime scene," I tell him.

"The door was replaced, and there's a lockbox on it. I'll send you the code," he says. "Do you want backup to go with you?"

"No, I'll be fine."

"Did you get a chance to talk with Jesse Kristoff?" he asks.

"I did. He didn't have much to tell me about the attack, but he gave me some interesting insights into Tracy Ellis and how people see her. It sounds like this is far from the first time that people associated with her have gotten threats," I say.

"That's probably very true."

We get off the phone, and a few seconds later, a message comes through with the code for the lockbox on the apartment door. I find the address in the file I got from the detective, input it into my GPS, and head there.

CHAPTER FIVE

CRIME SCENE TAPE AND A NOTICE TO KEEP OUT OF THE APARTMENT are still in place on the temporary door fitted to Gideon Bell's apartment. I'm putting the code into the lockbox to get the key when the door across the breezeway opens. I turn to see a young woman carrying a trash bag step out. She eyes the door, concern and sadness etched on her face.

"Are you investigating the guy who died in there?" she asks.

"I am," I tell her. "Agent Emma Griffin. I'm with the FBI."

"FBI. Wow. I thought it was just the detective," she says.

"There are some additional circumstances that made the local department want to seek out the assistance of the Bureau," I tell her. "What's your name?"

"Casey Burgess," she says.

"Did you know your neighbor?" I ask.

"Gideon? Yeah, I knew him. He was a good guy. I can't believe something like this happened to him."

"Did you hear or see anything last night?" I ask.

"I thought I heard something outside pretty late, but I didn't know what it was. I thought maybe somebody had locked their keys in their apartment and were trying to get in or something. It wasn't like there was a lot of loud noise or anything that really made me think that something was seriously wrong. I should have paid better attention or looked through the peephole or something, but I didn't. I was up studying and didn't want to stop. But then I heard the gunshot.

"I thought it was coming from Gideon and Jesse's apartment, but I didn't want to open the front door to my place because I didn't know what was going on. So I looked through the peephole and saw someone running out. I didn't get a very good look at them. They were wearing a mask, but it looked like they had long blond hair. I noticed it because it was sticking out from the bottom of the ski mask, and I thought that was really strange.

"I called the police, but they told me that someone had already called and officers were being dispatched. When they got here, they came and asked me for a statement. They wouldn't tell me what was going on or what had happened, but I saw the paramedics bring Jesse out. Later I watched them bring the gurney out with a body on it, and I knew that Gideon must be dead. Why did Jesse shoot him? I thought they were so close," she says.

"Gideon wasn't shot," I tell her. "At the moment, Jesse isn't a suspect. Since this is an active investigation, I can't divulge details, but we are trying to find out exactly what happened."

"Jesse didn't kill Gideon? I don't know if that's a relief or if it should make me scared because that means someone else killed him," she says.

"Right now, we have no reason to believe that anyone else in the building is at risk," I tell her.

She lets out a sigh. "That's good. I moved into this place because I thought it was going to be a good place to live and I didn't have to be afraid living alone. I can't believe something like this happened right across the hall."

"Thanks for your time," I tell her.

She nods and heads down the stairs with her trash. Rather than going inside, I go to the next neighbor's apartment and knock. I don't get an answer, so I move on to the one next door to Gideon's. An older woman answers. She isn't able to give me any new information. According to her, Gideon was a nice young man who always helped her with her groceries or packages when he saw her coming up the stairs, and Jesse was always sweet and friendly, but she didn't spend a lot of time with either of them. She was asleep during the attack and only woke up to the sound of the gunshot but stayed inside her apartment until the police came to get a statement from her. She didn't see anything else.

I go back to the door and put the code into the lockbox to get the key. Ducking down under the tape, I enter the apartment. There's nothing suggesting that any kind of struggle happened in the living room or dining areas, which further confirms to me that Gideon was asleep when he was attacked. Whoever did it was able to get inside the apartment without waking him up, killed him in his bed, and then turned the lights on so that they could see while they were writing on the wall, not knowing the light would catch Jesse's attention when he got home.

Without a warrant, I can't do any digging through the apartment looking for copies of the threats that Gideon received, so I look at all the papers and mail I can find just sitting out. I don't see anything threatening and wonder if Jesse was right that Gideon just threw the threatening letters away because he didn't take them seriously. Moving further into the apartment, I notice an evidence marker on the wall and see the bullet hole from where Jesse shot at the attacker.

I follow the hallway to the back part of the apartment and find Gideon's room. There's lingering evidence of the crime scene investigation unit processing the scene, and the bedding has been removed from the bed. I look at the message written across the wall and notice the handwriting. It's stark block print, written very deliberately as if in an effort to prevent anyone from recognizing any characteristics of their handwriting. It would take longer to write something like that, which might be why Jesse was able to interrupt the process. I see a laptop sitting on the dresser and make a note to get a warrant for access to the contents of the computer and his email.

Touring the apartment didn't really give me any new information, so I lock the door and leave. I want to talk to Tracy Ellis about the situation, but I know she wouldn't be in the office on a Sunday, so I postpone speaking with her until tomorrow morning. Instead, I head for Eric and Bellamy's house.

By the time I get there, I've put in requests for the computer and Gideon's email as well as his phone records. There may be further communications that might be valuable to the investigation. As much as the threats to the people throughout the company are hanging over the heads of everyone investigating the case, there hasn't been anything that confirms that's actually what's happening. It's important to keep all possibilities open this early in an investigation, which means considering the chance that this was personal.

Bellamy is home when I get to the house, and she lets me in with a tight hug.

"I know I just saw you for your birthday party, but I still feel like I never get to see you anymore," she says.

"I know. We need to do better about that," I tell her. "I need to come here more often."

"Yes, you do," she says. "Come on and get something cold to drink. It's blazing out there. You can tell me what you can about the case. Eric said it has something to do with that televangelist woman, Tracy something."

"Tracy Ellis," I tell her, following her into the kitchen. "Where's Bebe?"

I know that both of the little girl's parents work with the Bureau, and she likely overhears conversations about cases, but I'm always cautious about talking about any of the gruesome details of what I investigate anywhere where her little ears might pick it up. When she was just a baby, it wasn't as pressing, but now that she's getting older, it's more important to protect her from the harsh realities of the things we face every day.

"She's in her room coloring," Bellamy says. "We played in the sprinkler earlier, and I think all that sun and everything just wiped her out."

"I can definitely understand that. I was actually at the pool when Eric called me this morning," I say.

"He told me." She reaches into the refrigerator and pulls out a pitcher of iced tea while I go to the cabinet to get glasses. "He was saying that he just showed you the presentation that woman did about Terrence Brooks."

"Yeah," I say. "After my party, he showed it to me because he thought it might make an impact on the investigation. Neither of us saw this coming."

"Have you found out anything?" she asks.

"So far not much. I talked to Gideon's roommate, Jesse, who got attacked when he interrupted the killer but was able to scare him off by shooting at him. He said that Gideon wasn't very concerned about the threats that he was getting because it's just something that happens when you work for a person like Tracy Ellis."

"I can see that," she says.

"The detective told me that the investigators found wig fibers when they were processing the scene, and one of the neighbors said that when they saw the killer, he had long blond hair sticking out of his ski mask," I say. "That struck me as really odd. Why go to the effort of wearing a wig if you're going to wear a ski mask, unless it's so that the wig is visible? It could mean that they knew they were going to be seen and wanted to have a recognizable feature that would throw people off," I say.

"I'm curious how this person knew where Gideon lives," Bellamy says.

"Apparently, several people in the company have gotten threatening letters delivered to their homes, so all of their addresses are known somehow. It could be as simple as they were followed, but there could also be a data breach situation," I say.

The conversation shifts to other things as we sip our tea and relax. When my temperature has cooled and I feel like I've stepped out of work mode for the day, at least as much as I ever do, we start making dinner so it will be ready when Eric gets home. The rest of the evening is spent relaxing and talking, catching up on everything having not seen each other nearly as often as we used to for a long time. When we're sprawled around the living room watching TV in the dark after Bebe has fallen asleep, I look at my two best friends and wonder at how much things have changed.

For years we lived within a few minutes of each other and saw each other virtually every day. For a long time, Eric and Bellamy had a contentious relationship that essentially put me in the middle and left things tense when we did happen to all be together in the same space. But that frostiness thawed considerably during my first ill-fated undercover job in Feathered Nest, and over time the two fell in love. I rediscovered Sam, and we were suddenly not just three individuals anymore. I moved, our little chosen family expanded, and things shifted so much our lives are nearly unrecognizable. But we're still together. Even if we don't have the chance to just pop over and see each other on a whim and working at the Bureau together has taken on some new meaning, these are still some of the most important people in my life, and I feel grateful for the chance to spend time with them. Even with the heaviness of the circumstances hanging over me.

CHAPTER SIX

THE NEXT MORNING I ARRIVE AT THE SMALL HEADQUARTERS building for Tracy Ellis Ministry and walk up to the reception desk. An older woman with a warm, genuine smile greets me as I approach.

"Can I help you?" she asks.

"Yes," I tell her, showing her my shield. "I'm Agent Emma Griffin with the FBI. I need to speak with Tracy Ellis. Is she in the office today?"

The woman's face drops, and an expression of concern goes across her eyes. She picks up a phone beside her and hits a button.

"Ms. Ellis, there's an FBI agent here who wants to speak with you," she says.

She pauses and listens to the other end of the call. A slightly less enthusiastic smile returns to her face as she hangs up.

"She says you can go on through to her office. It's at the end of the hallway." She gestures behind her to a hallway leading away from the lobby area, and I nod.

"Thank you."

The doors to the office are closed, and a man wearing dark slacks and a branded polo stands outside, his hands clasped in front of him. I show him my shield and tell him that Ellis is expecting me. He knocks on the door and opens it just slightly so he can look inside without letting me see into the office.

"There's someone here to see you," he says. "Should I let her in?"

"Yes, Ander. Thank you," a familiar voice I recognize as a less intense version of the one from the video says.

He pushes the door the rest of the way open, and I walk past him inside. He follows me, and I think of what Jesse said about Tracy Ellis having a security team. Regardless of what he said about her not taking the threats seriously, she clearly feels the need to have protection near her at all times.

"Ms. Ellis?" I ask.

"Tracy please," she says. "Come in. This is Ander Ward, my head bodyguard. Thank you, Ander. I'll be out in just a few minutes."

Ander says nothing but nods and steps out of the office, closing the door behind himself. Tracy gestures at a seating arrangement to one side of the office, and I go to it.

"Can I get you something to drink?" she asks.

"No, I'm all right, thank you," I say.

She pours herself a cup of tea from a set sitting on a table near the window and brings it over to sit in a high-backed leather chair diagonal from the settee I chose.

"What can I do for you?" she asks. "Estelle said you are an FBI agent? I assume this has to do with Gideon Bell's death." She is straightforward and to the point, not wanting to dance around the topic at hand. I appreciate that.

"Yes," I tell her. "I am heading up the investigation into his death and the attack on his roommate, as well as the threats that have been received by employees of your company. I'd like to talk to you about the situation."

"I'm happy to speak with you, but I'm afraid I don't have the time right now. I've called a company-wide meeting that will be starting in just a few minutes. I'll actually be addressing this situation there. If you'd like to come to the meeting, you'd be more than welcome. Then we can speak more if you'd like," she says.

"That would be fine," I tell her.

She sips her tea and gives an emphatic nod, like we've just come to a firm business agreement. With another few sips of the tea down, she stands up, checks the diamond-encrusted watch on her wrist, and returns to the small table to set the teacup down where she got it.

"The meeting is being held in the conference room upstairs," she says.

Without any further invitation or instruction, she heads for the door. I follow behind her and notice Ander step into place beside her as we pass by him without acknowledgment. He looks back toward me, a motion that isn't lost on Tracy.

"Agent Griffin will be accompanying us to the meeting, Ander," she says. "Then we'll be back in the office."

He nods again, still not speaking. I wonder if that is a personality trait or a requirement of the position, feeling both are equally possible. We step into an elevator that brings us up to the second floor of the building, and Tracy leads us to a large conference room already filled with people. I stop in the back of the room, and she continues on to stand behind a lectern on a small podium that lifts her up above the rest of those sitting in folding chairs beside a table laid out with refreshments.

"Good morning, everyone," she says with a heavily rehearsed smile and slow swing of her head so she can make eye contact with as many people in the room as possible. "Thank you for joining me here. I hope you're enjoying breakfast. Unfortunately, as many of you already know, the reason for this meeting is not a pleasant one. You'll see we've been joined by a guest this morning." She gestures toward me standing behind everyone at the back of the room. "That is Agent Griffin from the FBI. She's here under very serious circumstances." Her expression goes dark, and her hands tighten around the sides of the podium.

"Last night, one of our own, a member of my security team, Gideon Bell, was murdered. His roommate, a former employee of the company, was also attacked but mercifully survived."

Gasps and whispers ripple through the audience, and Tracy nods along with them. She lets them continue for a few seconds before holding up her hands to get their attention again.

"This death is a shock and a tragedy for all of us. You may know that it follows several weeks of threats that have been received by several people within the company. These threats have been received by members of my security staff as well as others throughout the company and have been very pointed in their declaration that the recipient should turn their back on me and the ministry. We have lost two employees due to these threats, and there have been suggestions that I cancel my upcoming appearances because of them.

41

"I stand before you this morning to tell you that I have no intention of making any changes to my schedule or letting this situation control me or my work. I will not bow down to the whims of a mere human when those whims are to end my battle against the evils and darkness that have taken over our society and are trying to bring us down. Every day we face more reminders of the degradation of what our world should be, all the ways that society is falling victim to the evils of Satan and all of his temptations. They try to force us to consume their poison and be like them, but I refuse."

Her voice is getting louder, and I recognize her starting to slip into the persona I saw on the video recording of her talking about Terrence Brooks.

"I will not be seen as weak and malleable. We are in a battle here. A war with darkness and sin. A war for salvation and deliverance. We can't allow ourselves to be taken down from the rock on which we've placed our feet. This is not the time to sink back and be broken. Now is the time to show complete and unshakable faith. I stand before you now saying, 'Listen to the words we have been taught.' Do not be afraid. If I am to show fear or hesitation in the face of this, if I am to change my schedule, let down the people who want to hear me speak, bend to the will of this mere human, then I am questioning my faith. I am failing in what I teach, and those who look to me will think that I do not practice and believe what I tell them. I can't have that happen. This is a test, and I intend to pass it."

A hand goes up and a woman speaks.

"But doesn't this show that the threats are real? Gideon got a few of them, and now he's been murdered. Are we supposed to just pretend that his death doesn't mean anything?" she asks.

A few people mutter responses and support, and I can see anger building on Tracy's face. She doesn't like being questioned.

"I would never ask that the loss of a human life be ignored. Gideon's life, like all lives, was precious and cherished, and it being ripped away does absolutely matter. But I will not run and hide because of it. I will not show weakness. Not as a Follower. Not as a woman. I will be seen with the strength I speak about, the power that comes to me through my faith and dedication. I am calling on all of you to share that strength. We must create a unified front. Be defiant in the face of these threats and push even harder to spread our message. Again, this is a test. Those who choose to live what has been shared with so many will be rewarded, and we will all have the chance to touch more people. Isn't that what we want?

"I never said and will never say that being righteous and spreading the truth to the world would be easy and comfortable. In fact, I guarantee it won't be. The darkness fights hard to stop it. The world is in the clutches of self-indulgence, wrath, and the loss of our true meaning and being. Pushing against that and fighting for what is real and right and true is the hardest battle that will ever be fought, but it is a worthy one. You must be willing to put on the armor of faith, take up your sword, and go into battle, or all is lost. I tell you now, I will not stand by and let this stop me. I will not give in. I will not give pleasure and satisfaction to the one who destroys the light. I will press on, and I tell you, those who will stay with me will do the same. Now I ask that we all take a moment to honor Gideon with a moment of silence."

She bows her head, and I look around the room at the members of her company gathered in front of her. I can see on their faces that many, if not most, of them do not share the same zeal she's showing. They aren't filled with the fiery enthusiasm this has sparked in her. I see fear in their eyes and hesitation in their expressions. I see some lean toward each other, whispering. Suddenly, the same woman who spoke earlier stands up.

"I'm sorry," she says. "I don't want to disrespect Gideon, but I can't do this. I got one of the threats on my car, and I've been terrified ever since. This just makes it worse. I can't let my family be at risk. I need to leave."

Tracy stands in chilly silence for a few seconds, staring at the woman. It brings the eyes of everyone else in the room toward her, and the woman starts to turn pink, but she doesn't back down.

"Well, Dawn," Tracy says in a slower, calmer voice, "if that's how you feel, I can't argue with you. I can't force anyone to do something they don't believe in. If you are truly ready to walk away, then I can't stand in your path. If anyone else is ready to make this declaration, please, go with her now."

Two others stand up, and they all move to the door. One makes eye contact with me as she leaves the room. I dip out of the room as Tracy launches back into her speech, lamenting the loss of faith and the fear that has shaken their foundation.

"Excuse me," I call after the three.

They stop and come back toward me.

"I'm Agent Griffin. As Tracy said, I'm investigating Gideon's death and the threats that have been sent to the people working for the company. I know what you just did was really difficult, but before you go, do you mind telling me a bit about it?"

They glance at one another and nod.

"I've been thinking about it for a few weeks," the woman Tracy referred to as Dawn starts. "At first I didn't really think much of the threats because things like that have happened before, but then more people started getting them. Then I got one, and it really scared me. It was left on my car while I was at the grocery store. I had my daughter with me, and I've never felt quite so helpless. Now with what happened to Gideon…" Her voice trails off, and she shakes her head. "I just can't do it. The job isn't worth feeling like I'm putting my daughter in harm's way."

"How about you?" I ask the other two. "Did either of you get threats?"

They both shake their heads.

"No," the man says. "I didn't get one myself, but I know a couple people who did, and it's really unnerving. I just feel like something should have been done. More than just calling the police and talking about it at company meetings. I know that the police can't really do anything because they don't know who sent them, but Tracy should be doing something to protect the people working for her. She mentioned that someone suggested she change her schedule and not do the appearances she has soon. That was me. I put in an anonymous note and said that I thought it would be better if she laid low for a while, at least until all the heat she caused recently calms down a bit. I just think she needs to stop making herself, and the ministry, so blatantly visible with all this going on."

"I feel the same way," the other woman says. "I think it's really irresponsible for her to take something like this and use it as a rallying cry to put herself, and all of us, out there even more. She's putting all of us, not just the ones that actually got the threats, in danger. And I'm not going to stick around and wait to find out what else is going to happen because of it."

"Does any of you have any ideas of who might be behind this? Is there something different about these threats than the other ones you've heard of?" I ask.

"Before the threats came to the company itself," Dawn says. "Sometimes if we were out at an event or something, we might hear people yelling things at us, but this is the first time I know of where anything has actually gone to people's homes. That's what really scares me. They know where people live. They can get to them."

"You should look into Marcus Kelsey," the man tells me. "He used to work for the company but was fired a few months back. I know he had some really pointed words for Tracy and the ministry when he was leaving."

"Do you think he would be capable of doing something like this?" I ask.

"I didn't know him well," the man says. "But what I did know about him wasn't good. He was a favorite of Tracy's because he met her intensity. There were even times when he was more zealous and aggressive than she was, to the point that he could be legitimately frightening."

"Then how did he end up fired?" I ask.

"No one is completely sure," Dawn says. "All Tracy said about it after it happened was that she found out he was not who he was presenting himself to be and she couldn't have any of that among the people she kept closest to her. It sounded like he had betrayed her in some way, but it wasn't advertised to the whole company."

"Which really surprised me," the other woman said. "Tracy is never above making an example out of people when she feels like she can put a spin on it and turn it into something that's going to get her more loyalty."

"All right. Thank you for talking to me." I give each of them business cards. "Call me if you can think of anything else that you think might be important."

The three leave, and I go back into the room just as Tracy is coming down off the podium to the applause of the audience. The clapping certainly isn't universal across everyone in attendance, and I have a feeling the three I just spoke to are the beginning of an exodus.

I fall into step with Ander and Tracy as they leave the room. We get back on the elevator, and she glances at me, dabbing at the sweat on her forehead with an expensive-looking handkerchief. There's expectation in her eyes, like she's waiting for me to tell her what I was doing when I stepped out of the room. I'm positive she noticed. The whole time I was listening to her talk, her eyes were flickering to me at the back of the room. I was a new listener, a new person she could attempt to impress and sway with her fervor. Maybe that's what she's waiting for. Confirmation that she has captured me and I'm going to be one of her dedicated followers. Or that she has repelled me and I'm going to still garner her more attention with my complaints.

She's not going to get any of that from me. I'm here for only one reason, and that's to talk about what happened to Gideon Bell and the threatening messages her employees have been receiving.

CHAPTER SEVEN

RACY GOES DIRECTLY FOR HER TEAPOT AGAIN WHEN WE GET BACK
into her office. She pours more into the cup that she left behind and
doesn't add anything before taking a sip. Looking over at me again,
she lifts the cup to indicate it.

"Are you sure I can't get you something?" she asks.

"I'm fine," I tell her. "Thank you."

"All right," she says, bringing the cup over to the seating area and
settling into the same spot as before. "I saw you step out of the room.
Did I say something to offend you?"

It almost feels like a challenge, but I don't let anything show on my
face. I can absolutely see how this woman has gotten the reputation that
she has. She's undeniably compelling and charismatic, but there's also
something about her that doesn't sit well with me. Other than what was
said in the brief clip I watched about Terrence Brooks, I don't know
enough about her ministry or what she preaches for it to have an effect
on me, but I am still bothered by the way that she talked about him.

I have a feeling that other issues she takes up aren't handled with any more of a deft hand. But there's more to it than that. It's the woman herself that I'm not responding to.

She has all the hallmarks of someone caring and welcoming. Offering tea alone shows that she puts importance on hospitality and knows how far such a gesture could go in earning the loyalty of the people she interacts with. But there's an undercurrent of something in her that I can feel. Something that fuels the raving and that has obviously pushed away people who once numbered themselves among her committed employees and possibly even followers.

"I wanted to speak with the people who left the meeting," I tell her. "Getting as many perspectives on this situation as possible will be helpful to the investigation."

"Did they have anything interesting to say?" she asks.

"They offered me some insights," I say. "What can you tell me about Marcus Kelsey?"

Her eyes darken slightly. "Marcus Kelsey? Why would you ask about him?"

"I heard he was fired from the ministry," I say, purposely not answering her question.

"He was," she says matter-of-factly. "He used to be a member of my outreach team. He was extremely committed to the ministry and one of the most, perhaps *the* most, fervent of my flock."

"He was a follower," I say.

She chuckles slightly and gives me a look that borders on chastising. "I don't have followers," she says. "I'm not a prophet or a cult leader. I'm just a teacher. I have people who listen to me and those who choose to follow the word I'm teaching, but they aren't following me."

It sounds like a brochure response, and I don't believe it for an instant. She knows that people are following her, and that is what she wants.

"If he was so committed to you and what you teach, what happened between you two?" I ask.

"I thought that he was truly committed. I thought he believed in what I teach, in what we are trying to bring to the world as a way of fighting for the salvation of our community and all who live in it. Then I found out that he was not living up to the principles the way that he should have. He was indulging in temptations that brought him too far away from the path. He wouldn't be honest with me about it until I confronted him with irrefutable proof, so I removed him from my circle," she says.

"I thought there was supposed to be forgiveness and redemption," I say. "Isn't that a core tenant of your faith?"

Tracy goes quiet again, the same veil of control coming over her that did when Dawn spoke out. She stares at me for several long seconds before giving a slight nod.

"I can forgive without being willing to have those influences around me, and redemption only happens when someone does something to redeem themselves. I can't have disloyal, dishonest people around me. I can't allow the serpent into the nest, so to speak," she finally says. "I won't allow myself to be vulnerable to the influences that have destroyed so many." She relaxes her face, pulling back on the intensity. "But I thought you were here to talk about Gideon Bell."

"I am," I tell her. "In the meeting, you said that people are trying to get you to change your schedule and not do the appearances you have planned. Even in light of Gideon's death, you seem adamant that you aren't going to do that."

"I am adamant," Tracy says. "Agent Griffin, what I do is not for the faint of heart. I don't have the faith that I do and teach the things that I teach because they are easy. I find great joy in the truth that I carry in my heart, but that joy also comes with deep pain and sorrow as I watch the world around me fall to evil, misinformation, and darkness. I know that I'm not popular with everyone. I can't be. If I were popular with everyone, it would mean that everyone believed as I did, knew as I did, and did what was right. And of course, that would mean there would be no need for me to teach, wouldn't it?

"I call this a battle, a war, because that's what it is. I'm fighting for the souls of all those in this world. It's so easy to look at things around us that have become the norm, the mainstream, even the trendy and beloved, and think that they are good, normal, and true. It's easy to tell ourselves that they wouldn't exist if they weren't supposed to, if things weren't made that way. But that's temptation talking. It's evil talking. I can't be weak in the face of that. I have to be stronger now than I ever have been. I will not turn my back on my faith and what that means."

"Have you received any of the threatening messages yourself?" I ask.

"I receive threats all the time," she says. "They don't deter me."

I give a tight smile. "Obviously not. I know Gideon spoke to you about the threats he received. Did he have any idea who might have sent them? Anything that he pointed out to you that might indicate who could be responsible?"

"He didn't have anybody in mind that he mentioned to me," she says. "He didn't seem overly worried about getting them. Gideon was quiet. He didn't make waves."

"I need the names of the others who told you they got threatening messages," I say. "I'm going to need to speak with them."

Tracy reaches into her drawer and pulls out a notepad. Getting a pen from the holder on the desk in front of her, she starts writing out names.

"You are welcome to speak with Ander now if you'd like. Though there isn't much time. I am expected at an interview in less than half an hour."

The implication is that he will, of course, be going with her, only further underscoring the question of why, if she doesn't want to show any fear, she insists on having a security detail. I'm sure she has a craftily spun explanation, but I don't want to listen to any more of that right now, so I'm not going to ask. She writes down several names and hands the list over to me.

"I don't know for sure that this is everyone. Others might have gotten them but didn't bring them to my attention," she says.

"Thank you for this," I tell her, standing up. "And thank you for taking the time to speak with me."

"If you need anything else, feel free to come back," she says.

"I will."

I walk out of the office and stop next to Ander. I can't help but wonder if his entire purpose is to stand beside her office all day or if he does other things.

"Tracy just told me that you are among the company employees who have gotten the threats," I say.

He nods and finally speaks, "I have."

"I know that you're working right now and you're getting ready to go with her to an interview, but I need to talk to you about the messages. Can we set up a time to do that?" I ask.

"You can come by my house tonight," he tells me.

I hand him one of my business cards. "Text me the address and time, and I'll be there."

As I'm walking out into the lobby, I stop by the reception desk. The woman I'm assuming is Estelle looks up at me with another smile.

"Can I help you with something else?" she asks.

"Yes, actually," I tell her. "I need the most recent contact information for a former employee. Marcus Kelsey. Can you access the personnel records and get that for me?"

She shakes her head. "I don't have access to that kind of information. You'd have to speak with the staffing director."

"Where would I find them?" I ask.

"The second floor. Her name is Leslie Downing," she tells me.

"Thank you," I say and head for the elevator. As I'm going up, I check the list that Tracy gave me and confirm that Leslie's name is on it.

I know the staffing director could balk at providing me contact information for Marcus Kelsey without a warrant, but I'm hoping she will understand the urgency of the investigation and give it to me. Even if she won't, I need to talk to her about what threatening messages she has gotten. I get to the second floor and read the plaques on the offices and rooms until I find the one that has her name. I knock.

"Come in," she calls from inside.

I open the door and see that she's on the phone. I show her my badge, and she holds a finger up to ask me to wait a moment.

"I'm going to have to call you back and continue this another time. How is your schedule this afternoon…? Perfect. I'll talk to you later." She hangs up and stands to shake my hand. "Leslie Downing."

"Agent Emma Griffin," I tell her.

"I know," she says. "I was in the company meeting earlier when Tracy introduced you to everybody. You're the FBI agent investigating Gideon's murder."

"I am," I tell her.

"What can I do for you?" she asks.

"I need the most recent contact information for Marcus Kelsey," I tell her. "I spoke with Tracy about him, and I'm interested in talking with him."

She nods and goes behind her desk. "I can get that for you. Give me just a second to pull up his personnel file."

"Did you hire Marcus?" I ask as she types commands into her computer.

"I did," she says. "I thought he was going to be a fantastic match for the company. He had a lot of energy and enthusiasm, and his belief system seemed to be in alignment with what Tracy teaches, which is extremely important for the position he was filling."

"Are you familiar with why he ended up being fired?" I ask.

"No. I do the recruiting and hiring for positions that Tracy doesn't handpick people for, but she is the one who handles firing anyone. She says since they are working for her, it's her prerogative to be the one to determine when their usefulness to her has run its course and to have that final conversation with them." She reaches to the corner of her desk

THE GIRL AND THE LIES

for a bright-pink sticky notepad and picks up a pen. "Here you go. This is the last phone number and address we have for him."

She holds the note out to me, and I take it from her.

"Thanks. I also wanted to ask you about the threats. Tracy told me that you have gotten some of them," I say.

Leslie looks uncomfortable, her gaze dropping down to her lap briefly before she looks back at me. There's the distinct impression she was hoping I wasn't going to bring that up.

"Yes," she says. "I have gotten threatening notes."

"Do you still have them?" I ask.

"No, I threw them away after talking to Tracy about them," she says.

"What did they say?" I ask.

"They said I was helping grow the army of the devil and I needed to quit. The other said to hire people who would overthrow Tracy or I would pay," she says.

Leslie swallows hard, and I can see that even talking about the messages upsets her.

"Did you think they were genuine?" I ask.

"Not when I first got them. It just seemed too bizarre for something like that to happen. Especially because it wasn't like there was a specific person or a group or anything mentioned in the notes. No one was taking credit for them or putting anything in them that made them stand out against the rest of the hate mail that comes through here just about every day. The only thing that was different was that they were coming to specific employees rather than just Tracy or the ministry in general. But now that Gideon has been murdered..."

"Are you considering quitting your position?" I ask.

Leslie suddenly straightens up, her spine going stiff and her chin lifting defiantly.

"No. I've been with Tracy since almost the beginning of her ministry. I'm not going to let someone take that away from me because they want to spook us," she says.

I can see this woman is loyal to Tracy Ellis and believes what the speaker said about holding firm and not backing down. There's no point in arguing with her. It won't do any good.

"Please get in touch with me if you receive any other threats or anything does happen," I tell her.

She nods, "I will."

I hold up the sticky note as I stand. "Thank you again for this."

CHAPTER EIGHT

N O ONE IS HOME WHEN I GET BACK TO ERIC AND BELLAMY'S HOUSE, so I let myself in using the spare key they gave me and go straight to the kitchen to make a snack. With a bowl of fresh fruit and another glass of iced tea, I sit down at the kitchen table to call Marcus Kelsey. I'm hoping he'll agree to meet up with me and talk about what happened between him and Tracy Ellis, but after several rings, the voicemail picks up. I hang up and call again, but he still doesn't pick up. I leave Marcus a message introducing myself and asking him to call me back.

Looking at the sticky note that Leslie gave me, I decide I'm not willing to just sit around and wait for Marcus to call me back. I have time before I need to meet with Ander at his house, so I'm going to use the listed address to my advantage and see if I can track Marcus down that way.

I finish my fruit and tea, send Bellamy a text to let her know my plans for the rest of the day, and head back out into the blazingly hot afternoon. Putting on my sunglasses and blasting the air-conditioning to keep me from melting, I input the address into my GPS and start the drive to Marcus Kelsey's house.

Forty-five minutes later, I pull up in front of a small house in a neighborhood that reminds me of the ones built for the soldiers coming home after World War II. There are rows of houses of identical design and only differentiated by details like shutter color and decorations in the flower beds, precise little square yards.

There's no car in the driveway, but there is a garage, so it's possible Marcus is parked in there. I park at the curb in front of the house and walk up the driveway to the sidewalk leading to the front stoop. A "No Soliciting" sign is adhered to the door along with a handwritten note warning that the doorbell is broken and to knock. I follow instructions and wait for Marcus to open the door. I don't hear anything coming from inside, and I knock again. There's still no reaction, and I back up down the steps so I can try to peek in through the living room window. Curtains pulled tightly over it stop me from seeing anything inside the house.

As I'm walking back toward my car, I see the next-door neighbor setting up a sprinkler in the front lawn. I go around the car and down the street to stand in front of their house.

"Excuse me," I say.

The man looks up from what he's doing and notices me. He sets down the sprinkler and walks over.

"Yeah?" he asks. "Something I can do for you?"

I show him my shield and introduce myself. "I was wondering if you know your neighbor, Marcus Kelsey," I say.

The man's eyes swing over to Marcus's house, and he shakes his head. "I don't think we've exchanged ten words total as long as he's lived here," he says. "He's not the type to stop and chat at the mailboxes or come by with a plate of cookies in the holidays, if you know what I mean."

I don't think there's a lot of room for interpretation with that, but I nod anyway.

"All right. Thank you," I say.

I get back in my car and check the time. I still have a couple of hours before the time that Ander sent me, but I don't feel like going through the drive all the way back to Bellamy's house only to turn back around and come out here again later. Instead, I look up the nearest library and head there.

The library is bustling with young families finding respite from the heat, but for the most part, the little children are in the children's area playing with toys and reading picture books. I bypass that area and go to the information desk. A woman who looks like she was plucked out of a vintage movie looks up from the computer when I approach.

"Can I help you?" she asks.

"Are there study rooms I might be able to use?" I ask.

"Sure," she says. "At the back of the library, there are five of them. If one is empty, you're welcome to use it."

"Thank you," I say.

I walk in the direction of her gesture and weave through the stacks until I see the row of glass doors on the far wall. Each leads to a tiny room featuring a table bolted to the wall and a simple office chair with its back to the rest of the library. There are people in three of them, but I duck into the last one on the row and put my bag down on the table. I take out my tablet and prop it up on the table so I can video call Sam.

He's sitting in his office at the sheriff's department when he answers.

"Hey, babe," he says, then looks slightly confused. "Where are you?"

"I'm in a library study room," I tell him. "The investigation is a bit of a drive from Bellamy and Eric's house, so I'm hanging out here while I wait for my next meeting rather than going all the way back to their place."

"That makes sense," he says. "How is it going?"

"It's going," I tell him. "I met with Tracy Ellis this morning."

"How did that go?" he asks. I let out a sigh, and he chuckles. "That well, huh?"

"It was fine," I say. "I got a lot of good insight into her and her company, and I have to say, I really understand now why people might be so upset by her that they would want to threaten her."

"Why is that?" he asks.

I try to describe the way Tracy talks and the fierce intensity she exhibits.

"It's not her faith that bothers me necessarily," I say. "It's just some of the beliefs and perceptions that she has, that she masquerades as being about faith. She weaponizes them and turns them into something divisive and exclusive, even when she's saying that she's trying to spread her message and bring more people into it. She's actually just trying to break people apart even more. She calls herself a teacher and says that she doesn't have followers, but she very clearly puts herself on a pedestal and makes everything all about her and the way she wants things to be.

"I went to a company meeting she had so that she could talk about Gideon Bell's death, and three people walked out of it, ready to quit right there rather than stay with the company and continue to be threatened. One of the women looked like she was ready to pass out just speaking out against what Tracy wanted, and there were other people in that room who looked absolutely terrified at what she was going to do. There are people in her company who wholeheartedly believe the same things she does and are completely loyal to her because they think she's right, but I think that there are far more who are just scared of her and don't want her wrath to come down on them," I say.

"And this woman is supposed to be a spiritual leader?" Sam asks.

"According to her," I say.

"Do you think this murder has anything to do with Terrence Brooks?" he asks.

"No," I tell him, running my fingers back through the front of my hair to try to get some of the wispy pieces at the front to behave themselves in spite of the humidity I just left. "None of the people I've talked to who have actually seen the threatening notes have mentioned seeing the symbol that is on the Game Master communications. The killer wrote on the wall in Gideon Bell's apartment, and it wasn't there either. I don't think that they are connected in any way.

"But that doesn't mean I'm not bothered by the way that Tracy Ellis is talking about him and his death. She's trying to posthumously make him a part of her stance against the world even though there's nothing about him that I've read or heard that sounds like his beliefs were anything like hers. It's almost like she's trying to turn him into a martyr she can point at and scare more people into following what she says.

"Now that Gideon has been murdered, I'm afraid the media is going to latch on to it even more. There's no clear evidence that Terrence Brooks's death had anything to do with his religion or his job, but that's popping up everywhere. It's being called a hate crime, and I've even seen some posts online suggesting some sort of cult or satanic element to his death. I watched some of the coverage of Gideon's death last night, and they mentioned Tracy and Terrence. They're blending the two stories already, and that could have serious implications for the investigation."

I don't say it, but I think about the Game Master and how adamant he is about being recognized through the inclusion of the undecipherable symbol on his communications and on Terrence's body. I don't want to think that Terrence's death being mixed up with Gideon's and turned into something it isn't will further trigger him into action. But it's also about protecting the dignity of both victims. They deserve the truth about their deaths to be understood and their real stories to be told, which means not trying to find parallels and links where there aren't any.

"What is your next meeting?" Sam asks. "You said you were waiting in the library for it."

"I found out that Tracy Ellis's main bodyguard has gotten some of the threats, and I'm going over to his house after he finishes work for the day to talk to him about them," I tell him. "You know, it strikes me as really strange. She went on and on about how she wasn't going to back down to a 'mere human' and that she wasn't going to show any fear just because of what's been going on. But she maintains a robust security detail, including a bodyguard who stands in front of her office and goes with her everywhere. Those two things don't really seem to line up to me."

"Maybe she's worried about being mobbed by all her fans," Sam says.

I laugh. "Yeah, I'm sure that's it." I let out a breath. "How is work for you today? Anything interesting?"

"It's still Sherwood, babe," he says. "Interesting doesn't really happen around here very often. And when it does, we're not happy about it."

That's true. The sleepy little town is not a place where crime runs rampant and the newspapers overflow with stories of intrigue. But there have horrific events in Sherwood, most recently the bombing of the community center with me barely escaping before it detonated. As the trusted sheriff of the town, Sam is looked to for guidance and answers when things like this happen. People want him to protect them and stop the rest of the world from getting into our community. He's been serving in the role for many years, just as his father and grandfather did before him, but now he's planning the next step by running for mayor.

"How are the plans for candidates' night coming?" I ask.

He's been nervous but also looking forward to the first big event of his campaign since announcing his intention to run. The community gathering at the town square will give families of Sherwood the opportunity to come out and enjoy an evening of activities while adults hear from the candidates for the different offices and positions coming up for election. I know Sam wants to make a good impression and show how serious he is about committing himself to the town in this new capacity, but I don't think he needs to be as worried as he is. The people love him and are thrilled about his candidacy.

Though he hasn't said it, I think a lot of the nervousness he's feeling comes from uncertainty about what it will be like to walk away from his role as sheriff. He's served the community in that capacity for so long. It's so much a part of his identity that I don't know if he's fully wrapped his head around the idea that if he's elected, he'll be doing something completely different and someone else will be in his old position.

THE GIRL AND THE LIES

"They look good. The high school band is going to come out to play, so that should be fun. We have the food all lined up. I think that new dessert food truck is even coming out," he says. "The child safety tent is going to be doing fingerprinting and taking pictures of the kids, and Savannah designed a coloring book for them that's getting printed. They're also talking about a whole water play area with bubbles and things because it's going to be really hot."

"That should be fun," I tell him. "Everyone will really like that."

"It should be," he agrees. "I've got to go, babe. Keep me updated."

"All right. I will. Love you."

I end the call and lay the tablet down so I can type on it. It makes me wish I'd brought my laptop with me. Some people seem to be able to use their tablets with the same speed and ease as a computer, but I am much more comfortable with my computer while I'm doing research. I could go out into the library and use one of the public computers, but I'd rather keep the investigation out of the public eye. I don't want anyone at the library reading over my shoulder, even if it's unlikely they would put anything together.

Instead, I use my tablet to search for Marcus Kelsey and the Tracy Ellis Ministry. I want to know more about this man and why he was ousted from the company to which he showed so much enthusiasm and loyalty. My search brings up articles about the ministry and some of the events they hosted during the time that Marcus worked for them. Images come up of Tracy and Marcus posing together, and the articles mention the work Marcus was doing planning outreach events and coordinating with other organizations to broaden the reach of Tracy's message.

I read through the material that I find, but there's nothing about him leaving the company. That is, until I find a forum where people discuss their experiences at their places of work. They post anonymously so there can't be any sort of backlash or retaliation if the company finds the post. I can't see who made any of the comments, but it's obvious Marcus Kelsey's reputation wasn't exactly glowing among those working for the company.

He's even more of a zealot than she is sometimes.

Some of the venues he's chosen for appearances are completely inappropriate. It's offensive.

I never felt comfortable working for him. I always felt like I had to be on edge because I didn't know what he was going to do next.

I quit after hearing some of the conversations that the two of them had. They are a scary pairing.

He doesn't even pretend to be friendly. It's like he thinks that he's too far above other people to be nice to them. Even when he's asking them to do something for him.

I hope he never gets into politics because of the destruction his policies would cause, but he seems like just the type to do it.

A few of the comments express relief that Marcus was finally out of the company but also curiosity about what could have happened to turn Tracy against him. None of the people posting seem to have any idea about what happened.

I can't decide how I feel about the posts and what the assessments of this man might mean for the suspicions against him from the man I talked to earlier. I can understand the ire of a disgruntled former employee, and maybe even rage at having what was really important to him taken away, but I don't know if it corresponds with the threats and the writing on Gideon's wall. I need to keep trying to talk to him and find out what actually happened.

CHAPTER NINE

STAY AT THE LIBRARY TO DO RESEARCH AND LOOK THROUGH MY notes for a while longer before the rumbling of my stomach reminds me that I haven't had an actual lunch today. The fruit at Bellamy's house feels like a long time ago, and I pack up everything to go to a restaurant I saw not too far away so I can grab something to eat before going to Ander's house.

Rather than taking up a table, I slide onto a stool at a lunch counter and smile at the waitress dressed in an old-fashioned pink uniform. She comes over to me with a mug and a pot of coffee, pouring me a cup before even asking if I want it. I guess the majority of people who make their way into this place are on a near-constant stream of caffeine, so she doesn't feel the need to confirm. I wouldn't have ordered the hot coffee if she'd asked, but now that it's sitting in front of me, I'm glad I have it.

She offers me a menu. "My name's Lisa. Let me know when you're ready," she says.

"Thanks."

Lisa smiles and walks away to tend to the others sitting at the lunch counter. They seem like regulars with the way they chat and laugh. I glance over the menu and settle on a simple BLT with a side salad. I call Lisa over to give her my order, and she eyes me curiously.

"You just here alone?" she asks. "No one coming to meet you?"

"No. I'm actually just taking a break from work," I tell her.

"What do you do?" she asks.

"I'm an FBI agent," I say.

She looks something close to impressed and nods as she takes the menu and brings the order to the kitchen. I scroll through my phone as I wait for my food, reading emails that have come in and laughing at pictures Bellamy has posted of Bebe trying to feed a giraffe at the zoo. It only takes a few minutes for my sandwich to come out, and when she sets it in front of me along with a glass of iced water, Lisa has the same curious expression on her face.

"Are you really in the FBI?" she asks.

I nod. "I am."

"You're not from around here, are you?" she asks. "I think I'd recognize you if you'd been in here before."

"No. I'm actually from Sherwood. I'm in town doing an investigation," I say.

Her eyes suddenly go wide. "You're investigating that murder, aren't you? That guy who was stabbed in his apartment. I heard on the news they brought the FBI in for it."

"Yes. His name was Gideon Bell," I tell her. "I'm investigating his murder and the attack on his roommate."

She shudders. "Horrible to think about something like that happening right in your own home. I heard he was sleeping when it happened. I guess that's better. He didn't know what hit him. Just one second he was dreaming, and the next he was in glory. But it's scary to think about not even being safe in your own bed."

"It is," I agree. "What else have you heard about the murder?"

She leans against the counter. "He worked for that Tracy Ellis woman. That's probably why someone went after him."

The comment piques my interest. "Why do you say that?"

"Haven't you ever listened to her? To the people who admire her and think like her, she's some sort of modern-day saint, but for everybody else, she's a nightmare. I've watched her videos a few times just to try to see the draw. I don't get it. Not many people can get that riled up and spew that much hate in the name of faith. I always grew up thinking that church and religion were supposed to be about loving each other and trying to help each other get through life the best they could. She's nothing like that. At least not unless you're one of the tiny population of people she thinks are of any good in life. Or one who wants to be like that. She makes a lot of people very angry with the things she says," Lisa says.

"She's local to the area," I say. "Right?"

Lisa nods. "I'm actually surprised with how popular she's gotten that she's stayed around here. We're not exactly a small town, but I would think that she would be more interested in being in a big city where she could get even more attention."

"I think that being able to say she's from a place like this is part of the persona," I say. "She wants to seem down-to-earth and approachable to everyone rather than like a member of the elite. Have you ever interacted with her?"

"She's come in here," Lisa confirms. "She recorded almost the whole time, but when she didn't have her phone pointed at herself, she was a totally different person. Like you said, she was talking into the camera like she comes in here all the time and is just a good ol' hometown girl. But then when she wasn't recording, she was rude and dismissive of everyone working here. She greeted a few people who were here and had that big, fake smile, but then her bodyguard started shooing people away from her, and she left without saying anything."

Lisa leaves me to eat my lunch, but I'm still thinking about her assessment of Tracy Ellis as I pay and leave. It seems the woman's reputation for being divisive and controversial is very accurate, which only means the list of potential suspects just keeps getting longer.

When it's time to meet with Ander Ward, I drive through a quiet neighborhood of beautifully kept homes on lush lawns that make me thirsty just thinking of all the water needed to keep them that green. I bring my notepad and file of notes with me as I climb the stone steps onto their front porch and ring the bell.

Ander has changed out of his suit and into more casual clothes when he comes to the door to let me in.

"Agent Griffin," he says. "Come in."

"Thank you," I say. "And thank you, again, for letting me come to your home to talk to you."

"Absolutely," he says. "My wife is waiting in the living room. Can I get you something to drink?"

"No, thanks, I'm fine," I say as I follow him through the front of the house to the living room.

There's a pretty blond woman sitting on the couch when I walk in, and Ander gestures at her.

"This is my wife, Sabrina," he says.

I hold my hand out to shake hers. "Agent Emma Griffin."

"Glad to meet you," she says.

"Please sit down and make yourself comfortable. I'm going to get some lemonade," Ander says.

There's a much more comfortable air about him now than there was at the office. He's at ease now that he's out of his suit and in his home, away from the pressures of work. I sit down on a cushy recliner and set my bag at my feet.

"I couldn't believe it when Ander said an FBI agent was coming over to talk about what's been going on," Sabrina says. "I just hate that it had to come to someone being murdered for these threats to be noticed."

"Has Ander been getting them for long?" I ask.

"For a few weeks," he tells me, coming back into the room with a tray holding a pitcher of lemonade and three glasses.

He fills a glass and hands it to Sabrina, then fills one for himself, leaving mine empty but sitting there in case I change my mind about wanting a drink while we're talking. He sits down on the couch beside his wife and rests a hand on her thigh, giving her a thoughtful gaze.

"But to be honest, I didn't really think about them at first because I've seen so much hate mail going to Tracy," he says. "Being her body-guard is nothing short of interesting."

"What is it like?" I ask, urging him to elaborate. "Tell me about working for her."

"I started about five years ago just as one of her lower-level security guards. I was one of the people who hung around the office building in case something happened and went to events and appearances, but I was stationed around the perimeter, not actually with her. It seemed like pretty much any other security job. I'd done some other security work before, and this didn't seem much different other than the types of events I'd gone to.

"To be honest, I barely even knew who Tracy Ellis was when I applied for the job. I just needed work, and there was an opening for security. When I met with the staffing director, she asked me all sorts of questions about the things that Tracy teaches and how I felt about her mission. I was honest and said I didn't know much about it but that I would be willing to learn if that was important to the position. I was willing to say just about anything to land the job," he says.

"And did you learn about it?" I ask.

"Absolutely. I started listening to her presentations the night I was hired. I was really impressed by how devoted and driven she is. She knows exactly what she believes and doesn't care about what anyone else thinks. She's going to talk about it, spread the truth, and do what she can to make the world better, no matter what it takes. It made me really proud to be in the position to protect her," he says.

"So you believe in what she teaches?" I ask. "This isn't just about having a job anymore?"

"Definitely not. I think that she is a true revolutionary and will make more happen than anyone can even start to imagine. That's what got me rising through the ranks until I became her personal bodyguard," he says. "Tracy said she could see the commitment in me and knew she could place her trust in my hands."

He looks at his wife, and they exchange a smile. I can see the pride in Sabrina Ward's eyes, but it's tempered by worry.

"How do you feel about the people who have so much negativity about Tracy Ellis?" I ask.

"I think they just don't understand. They aren't ready to hear the truth and be courageous enough to live it. What she teaches, what she asks of people, isn't easy. It's not something that just happens for a lot of people. It takes dedication and true willingness to shed the self and take up a life of sacrifice and adherence to what is right and real rather than what might seem easy or desirable. She tells us that the world around us will make things look natural and easy so that we'll fall victim to those temptations when what we need to be doing is reminding ourselves of the truth, true nature and reality, and the teachings that show us the way we are meant to live. Those will keep us strong even in the face of temptation."

Ander leans forward and steeples his fingers. "The thing is, Agent Griffin, I get why people might not be receptive to her. She can be difficult to take. Anytime you are faced with something that challenges you and pushes you to grow and change, it can be painful and uncomfortable. People don't like that. People want to be comfortable and have things the way that comes easy to them. They don't want to hold a mirror up to themselves and recognize all the faults and flaws that exist, and that's exactly what Tracy does. She forces people to see these things in themselves so they can take the steps and do the work to make themselves right again. She isn't delicate about it. She isn't warm and fuzzy about it. She can't be. This is far too important for her to be anything but forceful. And that rubs people the wrong way."

I can certainly hear the influence of Tracy Ellis on the way Ander speaks, and I can't help but wonder how much of what he just said came directly from her mouth.

CHAPTER TEN

"WHEN DID YOU START THINKING THE THREATS MIGHT BE something more serious than just a frustrated person who Tracy rubbed the wrong way?" I ask.

"When the first one came to my home," he says. "I had been getting them on my car at work and at events, and a couple were mailed to my name at the office. But then one showed up at my house, and that really made me feel like something could be more serious."

"When did you tell Tracy about them?" I ask.

"She knew I was getting them from the beginning because like I said, some came to the office. She basically told me that I would get used to it like she had and that I didn't need to be afraid. When I told her that one had come to my home and it frightened my wife, she said that I was being tested and I really needed to think hard about what I was going to do in response. I could let the words of this anonymous person bend me, or I could stand firm and show the world what I was really made of. I made the decision that I wasn't going to let these things scare me away from something I really believe in," Ander tells me.

"How did you feel about the threats?" I ask Sabrina.

"They really scare me," she says. "My husband has tried to reassure me and tell me that there's nothing to be afraid of, that I can't show fear or the person has won, but I can't help it. Getting something to our house was really unnerving. And some of the threats talked about destroying his family. It wasn't just about him, they were starting to include me too. It hasn't just been the threats though. There have been a few times when I felt like someone was following me when I was driving, or when I was home alone, I thought someone was trying to get in. It's never turned out to be anything, or at least anything that we could find, but it's really hard. But at the same time, I don't work. Ander is our only income. And I also know how much his job means to him. He loves what he does and feels very strongly about not backing down. I've accepted that he can't just quit because of words on a piece of paper." Her message is determined, but she doesn't sound as convinced as the words convey.

"Have you ever had to defend Tracy from someone who was actively trying to hurt her?" I ask.

"There have been a couple times where people have tried to get to her, but they were always easy to defuse," Ander says. "One time someone showed up at one of her appearances with a gun, but he insisted that he had it because he always carried it and didn't have any intention of using it against her. One other time, there was a person with a gun at a rally where she was speaking, but again, we were able to bring it to a peaceful close without incident."

"I want to talk to you about Gideon Bell," I say.

Sabrina gives a sharp intake of breath, like just the name is difficult for her to hear. Ander takes her hand in his and squeezes it comfortingly.

"He was a good guy," Ander says. "We didn't know each other really well, but we were starting to get to know each other better because he was moving up through the ranks in the security team. Over the last few months, he'd started working closer with me at events and appearances. He was a dedicated worker, never complained about anything, and seemed to fit in with the company really well."

"Did he ever talk to you about getting any of the threats?" I ask.

"No. I know that he did, but only because Tracy mentioned it. He didn't say anything to me about them," he says. "I know he got one of them after a talk Tracy did at the local college. A huge protest broke out, and it got a little hairy between the protestors and the people who came to listen to Tracy speak. Gideon and I worked together for that event and ended up having to subdue several people. The police got involved and everything. Usually, events are a lot more closed off and protected than that, so it was one of the more eventful experiences I've had working for her."

"You said there was police involvement, so the protestors would have been able to find out your names," I say.

"Yes," he says.

I look over the notes I've taken about our conversation and then take out the list of names Tracy gave me.

"Do you know anything about the threatening messages any of these people have gotten?" I ask.

Ander takes the paper from my hand and looks over the list. He points to a name.

"Cameron Sawyer. He came to me after one of the notes showed up on his car. He was really worked up about it. He got really angry when he found out that the only cameras on the building cover the entrances, not the parking lot. I know he went to Tracy about the threats, and she told him the same thing she was telling everybody else. He ended up quitting not too long after he got it. He was the first person to quit because of them," Ander says.

"So he took them seriously right from the beginning," I say.

"Definitely. When he left, he told me he thought it was stupid for anyone who was getting threatened to stay with the company, that it wasn't worth it and he wasn't going to feel bad about anything that happened if people put themselves in that position," he says. "I'm sure he's regretting those words now."

He looks at the list again. "Grant Pruden, Hilary Watts, and Mila Taylor all spoke about the notes they got at one of the company meetings. Grant's threats specifically mentioned his parents, whom he takes care of. The other two, I think, just got the same kind of general notes, asking how they could be willing to be a part of her ministry, demanding they quit or speak out against Tracy. That kind of thing. These two," he says, pointing at the paper, "Marshall and Carla. They're married. Carla actually just put in her notice. Marshall has been saying that he's thinking about quitting, but he hasn't yet. I've known Marshall since I started working at the company. He works on the outreach team."

"Like Marcus Kelsey," I say.

The name makes Ander go still.

"Yes," he says.

"One of the people who walked out of the meeting this morning told me I should look into him as possibly being involved in all this. What can you tell me about him?" I ask.

"Marcus was close to Tracy. She trusted him and thought he was one of her most impactful employees. He's actually the one who made the first contact with the college where the protest happened. They didn't generally have speakers like Tracy, but he convinced them that it would be a meaningful event for the students and the community around the college, so they let her do it. He's like her in a lot of ways. They fed off each other and got more whipped up and intense when they were together. She used to have him talk to everybody during company meetings, and she watched him like he was the one leading the ministry."

"Was there something going on between the two of them?" I ask, wondering if that could be the explanation behind his sudden departure.

"There were some whispers," Ander admits. "With it being the two of them, I don't think many people would have wanted to openly speak out about something like that. It wouldn't fit in with the image that Tracy has with the people who follow her."

"What do you think?" I ask. "You have a position that puts you close to her. You surely would have seen or heard something if they had a romantic relationship."

"Tracy has a gift for discretion," he says. "If she doesn't want someone to know something, they aren't going to know it. I definitely am not close to her on a level that would make me privy to any kind of personal relationships she had going on. But I can say that there were a lot of private meetings between the two of them. Then suddenly he was fired. There was one company meeting where she addressed it, but all she said was that circumstances necessitated he be relieved of his responsibilities and commitments to the company. She didn't give any more details than that, then she didn't talk about him again."

"Does she have anyone else in her inner circle like that now?" I ask.

"No," Ander says, shaking his head.

"Do you think he would be angry enough at her for being fired that he would be willing to send these threats and kill Gideon?" I ask.

"I don't really have an answer for that. I didn't know him personally. I only ever saw him when he was 'on' for work. I remember the day that he was fired and what he looked like when he stormed out of Tracy's office. He looked as angry as I've ever seen a person. I know I thought then that he could be dangerous. But that doesn't mean anything. He had just gotten fired, and he was upset. I don't want to say anything I don't know for sure," he says, quickly trying to cover himself for what he is willing to say.

"You've been very helpful," I say. "If you can think of anything else that you think might be important or you get any other notes, please call me."

"I will."

I shake both of their hands and leave. They stand with their arms wrapped around each other, waving as I get in my car. I look at the mailbox as I pull away, getting an eerie feeling at the thought of the ominous letters appearing there.

Detective Fuller stands up to shake my hand when I walk into the investigation room after leaving Ander and Sabrina's house.

"How's the investigation coming?" he asks.

"I just came from Ander and Sabrina Ward's house," I tell him. "Ander is the personal bodyguard of Tracy Ellis and has gotten some of the threats. At least one of them has specifically mentioned his wife. She told me that she has had a couple of incidents where she called the police thinking that she was being followed or that someone was coming into her house. Can you show me those reports?"

"Sure. Give me just a minute, and I'll get them for you," he says.

He leaves the room and comes back several minutes later with a slim folder in his hand. He offers it out to me with a slight, apologetic shrug.

"There really isn't a lot to go through," he says. "She made four calls over the last couple of months. Two of them were because she was positive that someone was following her while she was driving, one of them because she was home alone and thought someone was coming in, and one of them because she got home and said she felt like someone had been in her house. When officers responded each time, there was no evidence of anything happening. In fact, the time that she called because she was home alone and thought someone was coming in, it turned out to be her husband coming home early from work. He'd locked his keys and phone in the car and was trying to get in using an old key they had hidden but got stuck in the lock.

"She admitted that she was just feeling a little jumpy and was fine by the time the officers left. We haven't heard anything else from her since. While the officers were talking to her, she did report the threats her husband was getting and said she thought they were just getting to her. But he reassured her everything was going to be fine, and she said that she was all right before the officers left."

"There was never any indication of anything in any of the four calls?" I ask.

"Nothing that the officers could pinpoint," he says. "I mean, it's almost impossible to prove that someone was following you unless you have a camera to capture it, but she wasn't able to give any details about the car, the driver, or anything. She said she just felt like there was some-one right behind her and they were driving aggressively."

"So it was probably just someone in a hurry who didn't like that she was following traffic laws, and it spooked her," I say.

"Probably."

I nod and flip the file shut. "All right. Thanks for getting that for me."

I stand up and head for the door.

"Where are you going now?" he asks.

"I have a few other people I want to talk to about these threats. Someone has to know something."

CHAPTER ELEVEN

I CALL LESLIE DOWNING THE NEXT MORNING AND AM ABLE TO GET contact information for everyone on the list. My call to Grant Pruden goes straight to voicemail, so I leave him a message and move on to Hilary Watts and Mila Taylor. Another voicemail for Hilary Watts comes before I finally get ahold of Mila Taylor. She's cooperative and willing to talk to me, but she doesn't have much new information to offer. She tells me essentially the same things I've already heard, including that she doesn't have any idea who might be sending the notes or could have killed Gideon.

I ask her if she is planning on quitting the company, and she hesitates.

"I don't want to. This has been a really great job for me, and I feel like I'm doing something that matters. I feel like this is exactly what Tracy has been telling us. Just a big test of how committed we are and how much we choose to lean into our faith when times are difficult. I don't want to seem like I'm questioning anything or that I'm not dedicated to the ministry. But Gideon's death has really scared me. I don't know what to think anymore," she says.

That is a sentiment that is far from the thoughts of Cameron Sawyer. I meet up with him at a coffee shop during his break from his new job half an hour after I get off the phone with Mila. His hands wrapped around a caramel cold brew, and a mini quiche all but forgotten on a plate beside him, he stares directly into my eyes without any hesitation or signs of reluctance.

"There was no way I was sticking around that place after the threats started coming in," he says.

"You knew that she and the ministry got hate mail all the time though," I say. "Didn't you?"

"Of course I did. Everybody knows about stuff like that. Tracy almost takes pride in it. She'll stand up in front of the whole company and read the letters that she gets, then break them apart and detail exactly what kind of sinner wrote the letter and why it only strengthens her resolve in her ministry. She believes that the more hate she receives, the better she's doing at her mission," he says.

"Then what made these different?" I ask, taking a sip of my own drink and tearing off a chunk of the scone I ordered.

"They weren't going to Tracy or to the ministry in general," he points out. "They were going to specific people, and some of them had details about the families and lives of the people they were sent to. Mine only said that I would pay dearly for loyalty to the devil. It wasn't personalized, but it was enough for me. It was under my windshield wiper blade when I found it, and I thought for sure that there would be enough security around the building that they would at least have an image of who put it there. Then I found out that they don't have cameras covering the parking lots.

"That made me really angry. We were in a work environment that was inherently risky just because of what we were doing and the way people felt about it, yet there wasn't any kind of security in place to make sure we were protected. I went to Tracy about the situation, and she brushed me off. It was the same song-and-dance bullshit about being tested and digging deep into faith to push through. She wanted me to be an example to whoever was sending them that I couldn't be shaken."

"But you weren't willing to do that," I say.

"Hell no. I'm not like the drones working for her. They lap up everything she says and treat it like she wrote the Bible itself. That was never me. I got the job by telling the staffing director that I would adhere to the standards in the contract and be a part of the company culture in all ways visible to anyone else. Essentially, I promised to act like them if I was going to work for the company, but it was never really in me. In fact, I think the way that woman acts and the things she says are bullshit and can cause a lot of harm. Then when the threats started and that was the way the company responded, I decided there was no way I was going to stay working for someone willing to risk my life when I didn't have the personal or spiritual conviction to back it up."

Cameron's words are still with me as I leave the coffee shop and start toward Carla and Marshall Powell's house. I called them while I was waiting for Cameron, and they invited me to come to their house to talk. As I drive, I let what Cameron said roll around in my mind. The other people I've spoken to have expressed great commitment to the ministry and even loyalty to Tracy. Even the three who walked out of the meeting didn't speak out against anything that Tracy teaches or the work of the ministry; they were just unwilling to continue feeling in danger.

But Cameron is openly unmoved by the ministry and critical of Tracy. He said that he acted like he fit in with the company culture while he worked there, but it stands out to me that he received the threats along with true devotees. It makes me wonder why the killer chose the recipients that they did. They obviously knew them well enough to know their address and their cars, but they either missed or didn't care about the level of devotion that they felt for the ministry.

I pull into the driveway of the Powell house and walk up a flower-lined sidewalk to the large front porch. A cat looks at me through the narrow windows on either side of the front door, and I am finger-waving at it when a man I'm assuming is Marshall opens the door in response to my knock.

He smiles as I straighten. "Tabitha gets all the attention," he says. "She likes to just sit there and bask in it."

"She's beautiful," I say as the sleek, black cat stands and walks away, flicking her tail lightly through the air as she goes. "And I think she knows it."

"She certainly does. I'm Marshall Powell."

"Agent Emma Griffin," I tell him. "Thank you for letting me come talk to you."

"Of course, please come in. My wife isn't here at the moment. She had to run out, but she should be back soon," he says.

We walk down the front hallway into the living room, and he gestures for me to sit down.

"This shouldn't take too long. I just wanted to talk to you about what's been going on at the Tracy Ellis Ministry and the death of Gideon Bell," I say. "Tracy gave me your name when I asked about her employees who have received the threatening messages."

Marshall nods and sits down. "Yes. My wife and I have both gotten them," he says.

"What did you think when you first got one?" I ask.

"I thought it was someone Tracy had offended, and they were trying to make a point," he says.

"That's a pretty common sentiment," I tell him.

"Unfortunately, she has a tendency to make enemies," he says. "She has a lot of the opposite too, or at least her ministry does. But everywhere she goes, there are people who don't want her there and are angry about what she is saying. You get used to hearing some pretty vulgar, disgusting things come out of people's mouths when they're getting hurled at you every week. It used to shock me. I couldn't believe anyone would think things like that, much less actually say them out loud. But then it just kept happening, and I realized it was just going to be part of the job."

"What changed?" I ask.

"I found out they were going to other people and some of them were getting really specific and pointed. It felt like this was something different," he says.

The front door opens, and a second later, a woman comes bustling in with her arms laden with grocery bags.

"I'm sorry," she says. "The lines were all the way to the back of the store. You would think they would have more than two cash registers open. It was ridiculous. I was just trying to pick up a few things for dinner, and it took me almost two hours."

"It's all right, honey," Marshall says. "Agent Griffin and I were just talking."

She looks at me, and her cheeks go pink. "I'm sorry… Yes, Marshall told me you would be coming by."

"Not a problem," I tell her.

"I'm Carla," she says, crossing from the open-concept kitchen into the living room area to shake my hand. "Marshall told me that Tracy introduced you to the company yesterday morning. Give me just a second to put these things away, and I'll be right in."

She hurries back over to the kitchen and starts pulling things out of the grocery bags she put on the island.

"How would you describe your feelings toward the ministry?" I ask Marshall.

"My feelings toward it?" he asks. "Like do I believe everything that Tracy stands for?" His eyes slide up slightly, like he's trying to see the thoughts going through his mind and searching for the right words to answer me. "I believe that she believes it. I believe that she thinks that she is doing something good and what she is supposed to be doing. There are elements of what she teaches that I believe, but over time, she has gotten more aggressive about things that I can't align myself with fully."

"Does it cause problems for you within the company that you aren't fully sold on everything that she says?" I ask.

"No, I don't talk about it with anyone within the company. But it is a big part of why I'm leaving it," he says.

"You're planning on quitting?" I ask. "I heard that Carla put in her notice."

"And I'm taking all my accrued vacation time to fill out the last two weeks so I don't have to go back," she says, coming into the room with us. "That's why I wasn't at the meeting. I have no interest in working there for another second. We are ready to move on."

"You said it was in part because of how you feel about the ministry. Does that mean it isn't because of the threats?" I ask.

The couple looks at each other as Carla settles into her husband's arm on the couch.

"We started talking about getting a fresh start a few months ago," Marshall says. "We decided to move to be closer to Carla's family and see what kind of new adventures we can get into. Both of us had been questioning how much we really wanted to be working for Tracy Ellis and her ministry, and it just started to fall into place. But we didn't want to rush anything. We wanted to make sure that we had everything settled and were really ready before we quit. Ideally with positions lined up and everything.

"Then the threats started, and it felt like that was the real sign. We both heard Tracy's assertions about the situation, and it didn't sit right with either of us. We knew then that being with the company wasn't right for us anymore. We didn't have it in us to put what we felt like was our lives on the line for the organization, and that was the only thing that would have changed our plans."

"Does Tracy know about your plans?" I ask.

"Yes," Marshall tells me. "I told her so that she wouldn't be blindsided by it. She told me that I should reconsider, that staying here rather than moving would be a bold statement to the coward sending the anonymous messages, and it would make so much of a difference to everyone within the company. She tried really hard to convince me, but it's just not something I can do. I was expecting her to fire me when I turned her down, but I think because I didn't quit on the spot, she still has some hope that I'm going to change my mind and stay. Maybe even shepherd Carla back into the fold."

"Which isn't going to happen," Carla says. "I'm really ready for our new life, and I can't wait for it all to work out. We're just waiting to hear on a couple of positions for Marshall."

"Did you happen to have kept any of the notes that you got?" I ask.

"Yes, actually," Carla says.

She walks out of the room and comes back with a few pieces of paper in her hand.

"I don't know why, but I thought it would be important to hang on to them. I've just been keeping them in the office."

I take the notes and read them.

Turn your back on the vile teachings or be punished

Walk away or lay down your life for the wicked

You work for a wolf in sheep's clothing. Cleanse yourself and be spared.

"Do any of these sound familiar to you for any reason? Have you heard these phrases used before?" I ask.

"They sound vaguely religious," Marshall says. "Like someone is trying to reference Tracy without saying her name and using religious language to make a point. But I don't think I've ever heard these specific messages."

"Neither have I," Carla says.

"How well did you know Gideon Bell?" I ask.

"We've both worked with him for a couple of years," Marshall says. "We've hung out with him in group settings with other people from work, so I'd say we were friends, but we weren't really close. It isn't as easy being friends with someone who isn't married. He was just at a different place in his life."

"I understand," I say. "So he wouldn't have had reason to tell you if he was worried about someone in particular, like if he had suspicions about who might be sending the threats?"

"I don't know if I would say he would have no reason to," Marshall says. "He knew that Carla and I had gotten them too, and if I had suspected someone, I think I would have said something to him about it.

Comparing notes, so to speak. If he did have any suspicions, he never said anything to me."

I notice Carla getting emotional, tears starting to well in her eyes, and she brushes her hand in front of her face like she's embarrassed to be crying.

"I'm sorry," she says.

"There's no reason to say you're sorry," I tell her. "Someone you knew was murdered. That's plenty cause to feel emotional."

"He was just a really good guy," she says. "He was always kind to everyone and tried to help out any way that he could. I don't understand why anyone would want to hurt him. And it just really scares me to think that this person is following through with the threats that they've sent. Does it mean that…"

"Stop, honey," Marshall says, pulling his wife up against his side for a tight hug. "You can't let yourself think that way. I won't let anything happen to you."

She nods tearfully and looks up at him with a soft smile. "I know."

I thank them both for letting me come to the house and give them a business card so they can get in touch with me if they think of anything else. Marshall walks me to the door with a steely look in his eyes.

"My wife is terrified," he says. "She's already quit and won't go anywhere near the offices, but I don't think that's enough. I think I'm going to have to put in my notice so that she will feel more secure."

"You need to do what you feel is right," I tell him. "Whatever is going to make this easier for you. Just know that I'm doing everything in my power to find out who is doing this."

"Thank you."

CHAPTER TWELVE

MAKE IT BACK TO BELLAMY AND ERIC'S HOUSE AS THEY ARE FINISH-
ing eating.

"There's plenty," Bellamy tells me when I walk in. "Grab a plate."

"Thanks," I tell her, breathing in the rich scent of her lasagna as I
drop my bag in the living room and head for the kitchen.

She comes in carrying dishes as I cut a chunk out of the baking dish
and put it on a plate to zap it in the microwave.

"There's a salad in the fridge too," she says. "I made too much, so
you have to eat some of it."

"I will," I assure her.

I grab a bowl from the cabinet and get the salad out of the refrigerator.

"How did it go today?" she asks.

I barely register the words. My mind is in the bag in the living room,
lingering in my notes.

"Hmm?" I say, realizing she said something but not really knowing
what she said.

"I asked how it went today," she says. "You went and talked to more people, right?"

"Yeah," I say. "It went... It went. I still don't feel like I'm on any definite path, but I got some insights that were interesting."

"You're thinking about something," she says.

The microwave dings, and I take my plate of lasagna out. Carrying it and my salad into the dining room, I set them on the table and look back at Bellamy.

"I am," I say.

I go into the living room and get my bag, taking it back to the dining room so I can dig out the notes from my talk with Ander. Deeper in the house, I can hear Bebe giggling as Eric gives her a bath to get her ready for bed. I have a feeling tonight is going to be one of those nights for me. The hard nights when I find myself staring at the ceiling for hours and can't will myself to sleep because my mind is going to too many places. If I were at home, I'd snuggle up beside Sam and try to at least relax, but here I might find myself pacing the guest room until just before I should be getting up.

Spreading my notes out on the table, I scan through them and find what I was looking for.

"Ander Ward, that's Tracy Ellis's primary bodyguard, told me about a protest that broke out during one of Tracy's talks at a local college. It apparently got pretty heated. You've seen some of the protests that have happened on campuses recently. These aren't the little groups holding up signs and chanting like they did when we were in school. These things get violent, and people can get really carried away with them. I wonder if that could have anything to do with what's happening," I say.

"It sounds like something to go after," Bellamy says. "I'll leave you to it. Gotta help get Bebe into bed."

"I'll try to be quiet," I tell her.

"You're fine. That girl sleeps like a rock. She gets it from her father," she says.

She leaves to do the bedtime routine, and I grab my phone from my bag. I dial Tracy Ellis, thinking it would go to voicemail and I'll talk to her tomorrow, but she answers.

"This is Agent Griffin," I tell her. "I didn't think you would still be at the office."

"I'm not," she says. "I have my calls transferred to my cell phone when I'm not there to make sure I don't miss anything important. What can I do for you, Agent Griffin?"

"I talked to Ander Ward yesterday evening, and I want to ask you about an incident he described to me," I tell her.

"All right. What incident?" she asks.

"He said that you did a talk at a local college and there was a protest," I say.

She draws in a breath. "Yes. That was just a few months ago. It was just some young people who have been woefully misled in how they see the world lashing out against something they can't understand."

"The way Ander was describing, it seemed much more serious than that," I say. "By the sound of it, things got fairly violent. He said the police had to be called."

"I don't want to sensationalize the actions of those people by talking about them," she says.

"You aren't sensationalizing anything. I need as much information about people who might have a problem with you as I can possibly get. Someone is threatening people who work for you and are now fulfilling that threat with a murder. It's crucial I get your full honesty and openness with me so that I can do my investigation the way it needs to be done."

There's a long pause, as she seems to consider what I've said, then she lets out another breath, slower and softer this time.

"All right," she says again. "That talk was something I was really looking forward to. I believe strongly that our young people are being drawn in the wrong direction by the influences around them, and they need strong leaders to guide them back to the right path."

"Leaders like yourself."

"Well, of course. This was an opportunity for me to show them that there was a truth out there that they could follow, a different life far more fulfilling and meaningful than anything they had ever experienced before. I knew it was going to be a challenge. Like I said, the young people are being pulled away from lives of righteousness and poisoned with all kinds of falsehoods everywhere they look. Even from the kinds of courses they are being taught in their schools now. Things that should never reach their ears are warping their minds and leading them to believe things that are so far removed from what they should be thinking, feeling, and doing… It's tragic. But it's also very difficult to convince them of anything different. I knew I would be facing some difficulty trying to get them to listen to what I had to say.

"It was a thrill when I got there and saw how many students were actually there to hear me speak and excited about what I was saying. It gave me so much hope to see that there were minds that hadn't yet been altered, hearts that were still in the right place, doing the right things. Those are the people who can influence others in the right way, and I couldn't wait to talk to them."

"Can you tell me about what happened?"

"The talk itself was going well. We were outdoors in a courtyard area of the student commons, so most of the people there listening were standing. Suddenly, another group of students rushed in and started shouting and chanting, trying to drown me out. Others who were around joined in. A few of the people there to listen to me argued back with them, and it turned into a physical altercation. Someone even tried to rush up onto the platform where I was standing and get to me. Fortunately, Ander and Gideon were there to bring everything under control, and no one was too seriously hurt," she says.

"Do you remember what they were saying? When they were shouting and chanting, do you remember any of the specific words or phrases they used?" I ask.

"I do remember them calling me the devil," she says. "And saying that my teachings were what were vile, not what I was teaching against."

"They used those words?" I ask, instantly linking them to the threatening notes.

"Yes," she says.

"Can you give me the contact information for the people at the school who arranged the talk?" I ask.

"I'll have to look it up, but I'll send it to you," she says.

"Thank you."

I get off the phone and head for a shower, then change into pajamas, hoping to convince my body to rest. By the time I'm back to the table, I have a message from Tracy with the name and information for the contact at the school, whom I'm assuming Marcus Kelsey went through to get the talk set up. I call the number and leave a voicemail introducing myself and asking Samantha Clark to call me back. I then get my computer and look up the school along with Tracy Ellis's name, wanting to see if any coverage of the protest will pop up.

It doesn't take long for me to get a hit on my search. An article in what looks like the student paper comes up first. There's an image on the front of police officers standing among a group of students in an outdoor area with a caption describing the scene. I read the article and find out the group of protestors was a campus organization that called themselves the Student Action Committee. The vagueness of the name is enough to put me on edge. That's the kind of name a group gives itself when it doesn't want to be clear about what it's actually doing. I jot the name down so that I remember to ask about it tomorrow and keep researching.

There's little news coverage of the incident, and the rest steers away from naming the group, simply referring to them as "protestors" and focusing on the physical assaults that led to the police involvement. One has a close-up picture of Ander standing with one of the officers, and I notice blood trickling down the side of his face. I remember him saying he had to subdue some people, and I see the blood as evidence of just how far it actually went.

I find another article about the incident and look at the picture attached. Rather than being of either of the security guards, the caption reveals that the man in khakis and a polo shirt is Marcus Kelsey. In the picture he's standing close to Tracy Ellis and a police officer. It looks like he's making an angry and agitated gesture. I read through the article wanting more information, but it is largely the same as the other one.

Resigned to the fact that I'm not going to find out anything more tonight, I gather everything back up and bring it to the guest room. It's still early, so I go back out into the living room and find Eric stretched out on the couch with the remote, flipping aimlessly through the channels on the TV.

"Feel like binging some cooking competition shows with me?" I ask.

"Sounds good to me," he says, tossing me the remote.

I curl up in a recliner and flip through on-demand screens until I find the show I want and turn it on.

"I didn't get a chance to ask you how things are going with the investigation," he says. "How is Tracy Ellis in person?"

"She's a lot," I tell him. "What you thought when you watched that video of her talking about Terrence Brooks—yeah, that and then some. I sat in on a company meeting, and she sounded just like she did in that video. Just as worked up and intense, and she was just talking to her employees. It makes me understand even better why people have a problem with her. But also why people would be obsessed with her. She would definitely be the kind of person some people would desperately want to be accepted by. They would want to feel like they were part of the special, exclusive group she creates just by talking about how terrible everything else is."

"That's how people like her end up gaining so much popularity. People really want to feel like they are included in something that others aren't or that they are better than other people in some way," Eric says.

"Even when the whole point is supposedly to reach out to people and make them better," I say bitterly. "Bring them into the truth. That seems like one of her favorite words. Everything is about the truth."

"Convenient when that's exactly what you're trying to find."

I let out a breath. "Yeah."

CHAPTER THIRTEEN

S AMANTHA CLARK CALLS ME BACK WHEN I'M IN THE MIDDLE OF making breakfast the next morning.

"Thank you for getting back to me," I say.

"Sure. What can I help you with, Agent?" she asks.

"I'm working on a case involving the Tracy Ellis Ministry. I heard that she had a talk on campus and you organized it," I say.

"That's right," she says.

"Would I be able to come to your office and speak to you about it?" I ask.

"I have some time this morning," she says.

"Great. Does an hour work for you?" I ask.

"That's fine," she says.

"I'll see you then."

I finish making breakfast and eat as quickly as I can before rushing back to my room to get ready.

"Where are you headed?" Bellamy asks when I rush past her heading into the kitchen.

"The college," I tell her. "I just heard from the woman who organized the talk with Tracy Ellis, and she's willing to talk to me about it. Hopefully, I can find out something more about the protestors."

"When do you think you'll be back?" she asks.

"I don't know." I suddenly feel bad. "I'm sorry I'm just kind of running in and out so much. If you want me to move to a hotel, I really can. It's fine."

"You're not moving to a hotel," she tells me firmly. "Go. I'll see you whenever you get back."

I grab all my notes and hop into my car. The GPS has me getting to the campus with hopefully just enough time to find Samantha Clark's office and be there on time.

Summer means the campus isn't as busy as it will be by the middle of August when all the students return for the regular year. I'm able to look up what building Samantha's office is in and find a parking spot close by, making my walk through the sticky, pre-storm heat mercifully short. I walk into the building and go to the fourth floor where the faculty listing said her office is located. The door is standing open when I find the one with her name on the plaque beside it, and I peek my head inside.

"Ms. Clark?"

A woman with thick, chestnut-colored hair pulled up in a massive bun and delicate silver-rimmed glasses looks up at me from the note she's writing and gestures for me to come inside.

"Please, call me Samantha," she says.

"Thanks for letting me come by," I say. "Like I told you on the phone, I'm investigating a case involving the Tracy Ellis Ministry, and I know that she did a talk here a while back. You organized that talk."

She nods, her expression slightly regretful like she's thinking about how the talk turned out.

"I did," she says. "Someone from her organization got in touch with the school and proposed her coming out here to host a talk with the students."

"Marcus Kelsey," I say.

"Yes, I think that was his name," she says.

"What was your impression of him when you were talking about the possibility of Tracy coming here?" I ask.

"He was insistent. Very driven to get things done. It was obvious he believed very strongly in what he was saying and that he wasn't going to be easy to dissuade. He was compelling," she says.

"Were you familiar with Tracy Ellis when he first got in touch with you?"

"Familiar enough," she says. "I knew of her and the reputation she had, which is why I was hesitant to plan an appearance for her here. This is predominantly a liberal arts college. I knew that a lot of the students weren't going to be receptive to the message she'd be bringing with her."

"Then why did you agree to let her come and speak?" I ask.

"Higher education is about broadening your horizons and being willing to stretch your boundaries. Marcus Kelsey pointed out that statistically speaking, there had to be students on campus whose personal beliefs lined up with, or at least closely resembled, Tracy Ellis's and that they deserved recognition, while at the same time having someone of an opposing belief system speak would give other students the chance to challenge their own thoughts and perceptions. He presented it as a learning experience for everyone and an opportunity to encourage cultural and ideological exchange among the students.

"I have to admit, that convinced me. I've always been of the thought that you can't really say you believe something until you've confronted opposing thoughts with an open willingness to listen, learn, and consider. Holding a mirror up to yourself as the only barometer of truth in your life will never foster a real depth of understanding, and it will definitely never give you the opportunity to influence others.

"So I agreed for her to come and give a talk out in the courtyard. It was advertised throughout campus for a couple of weeks leading up to it, and I got quite a bit of feedback about it from both sides. It seemed like this was going to be something impactful for the campus. As it turned out, it was. Just not in the way I was expecting or hoping for."

"When you say you got feedback from both sides, was there anything especially negative? Any kind of threats or anything like that?"

"We did get a couple of messages saying having her on campus was an insult to the students and that there would be retaliation if the talk wasn't canceled. But they didn't make any specific threat, and when we talked to the students who sent the messages, they insisted that they weren't making threats, they were trying to point out a possible danger they saw happening," Samantha tells me.

"But you decided to carry on with the talk," I say.

"Yes. Again, challenging thoughts and beliefs is part of personal growth. People were told when and where the talk was going to be held, so they had the absolute right to not attend and not listen if they didn't want to. If they made the choice to go and listen to what she had to say, then that was on them. Our students are young adults, Agent Griffin. They are coming into their own—and deserve to be respected enough to make—their own choices. But they also have to learn that the world isn't going to bow down to them and shift everything just because they don't like it. They have to learn to live with all types of people and thoughts," she says.

"I agree," I tell her. "Tell me about what happened at the event itself."

"I was actually surprised at how many people came out to listen to her and that they really seemed genuinely interested in hearing what she had to say. There were a lot of students who seemed excited to have her there, and I thought Marcus had been right about giving representation to a segment of the student body that might not usually be heard as much. Everything was going fairly well. There were some people who were walking by and making snide comments or trying to heckle her, but Tracy Ellis just kept right on going like it didn't affect her at all. I'm assuming she's more than accustomed to that kind of thing happening while she's talking."

"That's safe to say," I say.

"Like I said, everything was going well, and then a large group of students came down the sidewalk toward the people gathered listening to her. They were shouting and chanting, getting louder as they got closer, like they were trying to make it so that no one could hear her anymore. Some faculty and administrators were there, and we tried to get them to move on, but they wouldn't. I'm not sure exactly what happened to start the altercation, but I know that both sides started shouting at each other, and at some point, it turned into a physical situation. Several fights broke out, and her security had to intervene. I remember one of the guards stopping a student who was trying to get to Tracy Ellis and bringing him to the ground. He ended up scratching the side of his head on the pavers in the courtyard. It got really nasty."

"Do you know who called the police?" I ask.

"I did," she says. "As soon as I saw things getting out of hand, I contacted 911, and they sent out several officers to help the security guards get everything back under control. A few students were arrested, and charges were filed."

"I read that the group who protested referred to themselves as the Student Action Committee."

"Yes," Samantha says. "They are a student-led organization here on campus."

"Can you tell me more about them?" I ask.

"Their officially declared purpose is social activism and upholding campus culture."

"That's vague," I say, thinking of my immediate reaction to the name they chose for their group.

"It is," she says. "But I think that is the intention. They want to be able to get involved in the widest possible range of situations and events while still declaring it a part of the organization's official activities. That way it's protected by the school, and they can get funding. This situation isn't flattering for them, but they have gotten involved in other things that have been much more effective."

"Is the leadership of the organization now the same as it was during the protest?" I ask.

"There has been some change, but there are still plenty of members who were there during the incident," she says.

"Can you get me in touch with them?" I ask.

It takes a little more than an hour of sitting in the office waiting for her to hear back from members of the Student Action Committee, but they agree to meet with me in one of the conference rooms of the student commons. I thank Samantha for her help and cross the street to the commons.

Approaching the building from the back, I walk across a large, circular stone area that I realize is the courtyard where the protest happened. Seeing it in person rather than in pictures gives better context and helps me to understand more clearly how the situation unfolded.

The courtyard is right in the middle of what I can imagine is a busy thoroughfare during the regular academic year. Sidewalks lead from surrounding buildings, and the courtyard sits right up against the commons building where students gather to eat, study, attend meetings, and go to activities. This would have put Tracy Ellis right in the middle of everything. As much as Samantha Clark insisted that attending this event would be completely voluntary for the students, it's most likely there were a lot of them who didn't have a choice but to walk past and hear what was going on.

It also meant that the group that gathered to listen was easily accessed from all angles. The Student Action Committee only needed to decide where they were going to gather up, and they had a straight shot to everyone there to listen to Ellis talk, and to Ellis herself.

CHAPTER FOURTEEN

I FOLLOW SAMANTHA'S INSTRUCTIONS TO FIND THE CONFERENCE room where I am meeting with the members of the Student Action Committee. There are already a few of them there when I step into the room.

"I'm Agent Griffin," I introduce myself.

"I'm Lindsey," one says.

"Peter."

"Hope."

"Curt."

"Nice to meet you. Thanks for coming to talk to me. I'm going to get started, and if anyone else shows up, they can just jump in." I close the door. "I'm not sure how much Samantha Clark told you, but I'm an FBI agent investigating a case involving the Tracy Ellis Ministry."

The people sitting in front of me draw in breaths and exchange glances.

"You're investigating that murder," Peter says. "The security guard who was killed in his apartment."

"Yes," I tell him. "That's part of it. What else have you heard about that case?"

"That people working for her have been getting threats," Hope tells me. "Doesn't surprise me."

"Why do you say that?" I ask.

"Have you ever heard her speak?" she asks.

"I have."

"Then you know all she does is spew judgment and hate. After a while, people get tired of that. She can't get away with just hiding behind her screwed-up version of religion and damaging people like that," she says.

"I'm guessing that all of you were present at the protest that happened when Tracy Ellis spoke here," I say.

They all nod.

"Us and some others," Curt says. "That was one event where it wasn't hard to get people willing to be involved."

"Wait...," Lindsey says, looking around at the others again and then meeting my eyes. "Do you think we had something to do with that guy getting killed?"

"He was one of the security guards who were here during the protest. I'm investigating as many leads as I can get, and it's no secret how against her your group is. I'm just trying to find out as much as I can," I say.

"We didn't have anything to do with that," Peter says. "That's not what we do. Where about civil unrest and making our voices heard."

"It's difficult to call it 'civil unrest' when a situation gets as violent as that protest did," I point out. "People were seriously injured. The police had to get involved."

"That wasn't the intention," Hope says. "We just wanted to speak out against what she was saying and make sure the administration knew exactly how we felt about having her on campus. That's the focus of our organization. What happens here in our community."

"Tracy Ellis is a disgusting person, and the things that her so-called ministry teaches are abhorrent," Lindsey says. "But we're not about arbitrary shows of violence. We don't send threats to people."

"It would be pointless to do something like that," Peter points out. "We're about action—taking actual, tangible steps to make a difference in our community. It doesn't do any good to slink around in shadows when you're trying to make a point."

"And ultimately, our focus is on what the campus and the college can accomplish," says Curt. "There's only so much a student organization can do when it comes to the wider world. We just didn't want her here. What she and her group get up to elsewhere isn't really our concern. We have more relevant things to worry about."

I leave the meeting convinced that the students have nothing to do with what is unfolding within the ministry. They obviously have serious qualms against Tracy Ellis and her teachings, but they seem genuinely focused on making changes on the campus and within their own community. Going after the employees of the ministry and killing a security guard because he was present at a protest wouldn't align with that. They want to make an impact and be recognized, not send anonymous notes and commit murder with only his employment as a motive.

I get back in my car and pull out into the street. Almost immediately, I notice a car come up behind me. They pull up close to my back bumper and follow right behind me as I turn to drive away from the academic buildings of the campus and into the surrounding city. The street is more congested away from the main campus, and I keep glancing into my rearview mirror to check the car that seems to be staying far too close to my car. I turn, and it turns with me, inching closer until I'm not even able to see the front of the car.

The driver appears to be a man wearing big sunglasses and a baseball cap. I turn again, and he's right behind me. As we approach a line of cars behind a stoplight, I see he isn't making any moves to slow down. I stop, and he rams into the back of my car, sending me into the car in front of me and making my airbag deploy, hitting me in the face and cutting my lip.

Slightly disoriented, I sit up and see that the man has appeared beside my door. He's glaring at me through the window, and now I recognize him. Marcus Kelsey. Taking off my seat belt, I climb out of the car to confront him.

"What the hell do you think you're doing?" I demand.

"I know who you are," he says. "I know what you're doing."

"What I'm doing is taking your ass down while we wait for the police to get here," I say.

I reach out and grab for him, but he swats my hand away, bouncing on his toes slightly as he backs up away from me. A few quick moves have him down on the ground and my hand clamping his wrists into place.

In the distance, I can already hear sirens.

"I'm going to ask you again. What the hell do you think you're doing?" I snarl.

"Tracy Ellis deserves to be punished," he says. "Everyone around her deserves to be punished. You're on the wrong side."

"I'm on the side of a man who was murdered in his own home," I tell him. "But you've just made me even more interested in having a chat with you down at the police station."

The emergency vehicles arrive, and I release Marcus into the custody of the police, introducing myself and letting them know that I'll be at the station to talk to him. Then I go to the vehicle in front of me to make sure the person inside is all right. The young woman looks upset, and she's holding her head where she apparently hit it on the steering wheel, but there are no signs of any serious injury.

"Are you okay?" I ask her. She nods. "I'm sorry. He hit me from behind."

She nods again. "I know."

The paramedics come up to the car, and I step aside so they can help her out.

One of them looks at me. "Let's get that lip looked at," he says.

"I'm fine," I tell him.

"Probably, but I'd rather clean it up for you while we're here."

I relent and go over to the ambulance with him. He cleans the cut and gives me an ice pack to hold against my mouth while I give the police my statement about what happened.

"You say that you've been in contact with him before?" the officer asks when I try to explain the series of events leading up to this situation.

"Yes," I tell him. "I'm an FBI agent. I'm investigating a case, and his name came up as someone I should look into. I tried to get in contact with him, but he didn't answer his phone and wasn't at his house when I went there. He obviously heard about what I was doing and decided this was the way to make his message known. But now I am even more interested in having a talk with him about the case."

"I'm sure you are," the officer says. "You'll need your car towed to the shop for repairs. But I can give you a ride to the station if you want."

"That would be great, thanks. Just let me get my things out of the car."

I get everything I need from the car and call for a tow truck. They tell me what shop they'll bring it to, and I make a note of the address before climbing into the officer's car. On the way to the station, I call Bellamy.

"Can you come out here and pick me up at the police station?" I ask her.

"What did you get yourself into now?" she asks.

"Thank you for your support. I'm glad to know my best friend is so concerned about my well-being," I counter.

"I'm sorry. Are you okay?"

"I have a cut lip, and I'm pissed off, but I'll be fine," I say.

"All right. Then what did you get yourself into now?" she asks.

"Remember I told you about that Marcus Kelsey guy, the one whom the quitting employee told me I should look into because of the strange way he left the company? The way that no one seems to know about?" I ask.

"Yeah," she says.

"Well, he decided that instead of just giving me a callback, he'd somehow track me down and ram into the back of my car at a stoplight," I tell her. "He got out of his car and started ranting about how Tracy Ellis and everyone around her deserved to be punished. So he's on his way to the station, and I'm on my way to talk to him. But my car is not going to be able to accompany me."

"Got it," she says. "I'll head out there in a bit to give you some time."

"Thanks."

We arrive at the station, and the officer leads me to a small interrogation room where Marcus Kelsey is sitting in handcuffs with a detective. The detective stands up and shakes my hand as I walk into the room.

"Detective Reese," he says.

"Good to meet you. Agent Griffin."

He nods. "I know who you are. What's going on here? All I heard was, there was a minor car collision at a stoplight. Hardly seems reason to haul someone in and get them questioned by the FBI."

"That's not exactly the whole story," I tell him. I look at Kelsey. "Is it?"

"You shouldn't be helping her," he says through gritted teeth. "Do you even know who she is? Do you know the types of things she's capable of?"

"I'm not helping Tracy Ellis," I say. "I'm investigating the murder of Gideon Bell and the series of threats that have been received by the people who work for her. One of whom, I might add, brought your name up specifically as someone I should talk to about what's happening."

"I didn't kill anybody," he hisses at me. "But if they work for Tracy, then they had it coming, and you shouldn't be trying to stop the person giving them the punishment they deserve."

"Why do you say that?" I ask.

"She hurts people," Marcus says. "She knows what she's doing. She pretends that she's all about love and making the world a better place, but she's not. She doesn't care whom she steps on along the way or how much damage she causes, as long as she gets all the attention and can feel like she's better than everyone around her."

"I know that you were fired from the ministry. What led up to that?" I ask.

"Tracy used me up and tossed me aside. Just like she does with anyone else who crosses her path," he huffs.

"I need to know what you were doing the night Gideon Bell was murdered," I say.

A smile crosses Marcus's face, and he sits back. "I was spending some quality time with these fine gentlemen."

"You were in custody?" I ask.

He nods. "I got in a fight at a bar, and the little bitch decided he needed to press charges. So I had a lovely sleepover behind bars. And at no point did they let me out long enough to go kill someone."

I get confirmation that Marcus Kelsey was in custody at the time of Gideon's death and leave the station frustrated after making sure he'll get slapped with extra charges for running into me. Bellamy calls me as I'm walking out of the station, and I turn the corner to see her car with another right behind it. Eric climbs out of the second car and waves.

"We decided you were going to need to be able to get around, so we rented you this," he says. "How bad is the damage to your car?"

"Not too bad," I tell him. "The front and back ends are a little messed up and the airbags deployed. I haven't had a chance to talk to the body shop yet, so I'm not sure how long it will take them to get it fixed. I can't imagine it will be too long though."

Eric tosses me the keys to the sedan they rented for me and climbs into the passenger seat beside Bellamy.

"Thanks," I say, holding up the keys.

"You headed back to the house?" he asks.

"Yep," I tell him.

"All right. See you later."

They drive off, undoubtedly to bring Eric back to work, and I start for their house. I'm not far from the police station when I get a call from Detective Fuller.

"Hey, Agent Griffin," he says. "I wanted to let you know that we got all the information you requested about Gideon Bell. His phone records and everything."

"Great. I'll be there to get them soon," I tell him.

I drive away from one police station and head for the other, hoping something in the records will get me on the right path.

CHAPTER FIFTEEN

I SIT IN THE CONFERENCE ROOM PORING OVER THE PHONE RECORDS, trying to find anything in Gideon's calls or texts that would suggest something going on leading up to his death. There's nothing unusual. No numbers that repeat multiple times. No aggressive or threatening text messages. It isn't until I move on to the information taken from his computer that I find something that seems useful.

Among the various emails that he sent and received, there's one sitting in Draft status that catches my attention. It's addressed to Tracy Ellis and the subject line reads: "Situation Report." The message in the email itself doesn't seem to be finished, but it's enough to put me on the phone with Jesse Kristoff.

I find out he has returned to the apartment that he shared with Gideon, and I head there. He opens the door with a concerned, confused expression on his face.

"Agent Griffin," he says. "What's going on?"

"Gideon's records came through. Something showed up that I wanted to ask you about," I say. I take out the folder with the records and pull out the printed-out email, handing it to him. "Does this mean anything to you?"

"'Ms. Ellis, I'm writing today to make a report of an inappropriate relationship within the ministry. I have firsthand knowledge of this situation and would be happy to discuss it with you personally,'" he reads, then shakes his head. "I've never seen this."

"It was on Gideon's computer. According to the time stamp, he was working on it the day he died, but he never sent it. Do you have any idea whom he could be talking about?"

"I don't know. If he had suspicions about somebody at work, he didn't talk to me about it. But from what I understand, I think emails like that are pretty common within the ministry," he says.

"What do you mean?" I ask.

"People are encouraged to report anything they think is immoral behavior or that goes against the company culture," he says. "Gideon has mentioned that before."

This piques my interest, and twenty minutes later, I'm at Tracy Ellis's office, showing her the email. She shrugs and hands it back to me.

"He didn't finish it, and I never got a message like that from him, so I really couldn't tell you whom it's about or what it is talking about," she says.

"But the fact that he was writing you an email like this doesn't strike you as unusual," I say.

"Not at all," Tracy says. "This is part of our company culture. I encourage everyone who works for me to feel free to be open and honest with me about what they witness among the others in our community. All of my employees are held to certain morality and behavior standards. They are clearly outlined to them before they are even formally hired to make sure that they are fully informed and can make a confident decision about their ability to adhere to them."

"And you expect everyone to play watchdog for each other," I say.

"I believe very strongly in accountability and responsibility, Agent Griffin," she says. "I believe that when people make a commitment, they should be held to that, not only by their own moral code and desire to show integrity, but also by the people around them who are influenced and affected by their behavior. It's just like when a couple gets married. They aren't standing in front of their friends and family just because they want to share the moment with them. They are asking for witnesses to the vows they are making so that if there comes a time when those vows are compromised, they will be held accountable and encouraged to do better.

"That's what I expect within my company. I desire for everyone to want the best out of not just themselves but everyone else around them. I want them to feel like they are part of something that is truly admirable, and that means being strong and willing to speak up when something isn't going the way it should. And it's not just about making sure that the inappropriate behavior is brought to my attention so I know how to deal with the person who is struggling. I believe that if you know something is wrong and don't say anything, that is a mark against you. Reporting these things to me is a way for my employees to save themselves from that guilt and shame. Gideon obviously knew something about a fellow employee and wanted to unburden himself. He just didn't get the opportunity."

My skin crawls at her words. I understand having standards and specific guidelines for people to adhere to, especially in the kind of work that she does, but this doesn't feel like protecting company culture and maintaining standards. This feels like pitting people against each other.

"It just doesn't sit right with me," I tell Sam later when we're having a video call. "I mean, I get it. They decided to work for a ministry, and according to her, they knew what the expectations were before they signed their contracts to work for her. But there's still something really disturbing about her encouraging them to report on each other when they see anything they deem inappropriate. That just seems rife with potential for exploitation and fear."

"I agree," Sam says. "I imagine if there was harassment or someone committing a crime on the low, it makes sense to bring that up to superiors. But this is another level. This makes it sound like even the smallest slight could be reported and lead to consequences. And that totally depends on what the other people in the company think of as appropriate or not."

"Gideon knew something. He was ready to report an inappropriate relationship, but for some reason, he didn't finish that email and didn't send it. I really want to know who else in the company has been sending those kinds of reports recently."

"And if they might line up with the same people who have been getting threats?" Sam asks.

"It's a strong possibility," I say. I sigh and pull my hair up into a ponytail to get it off my neck. "Anyway, enough about my day at work. How did the candidates' night go tonight?"

"It was good," he says. "It seemed like just about everybody in town showed up. The children's ID stuff was really popular, which was good. I was glad to see how many parents were getting their kids' pictures taken and their fingerprints and everything. I handed out all of the flyers that I had printed up and spent a lot of time talking to people about all the issues and things. I think that was my favorite part. Just getting to hear from people what they want to do to make Sherwood better and how I would be able to help as mayor."

"That does sound interesting," I say. "You're getting to see the town from a different perspective now. You're going to do great as mayor. Everyone already knows and trusts you, and they know that you have the best interests of Sherwood and everyone in it at heart. They'll know that you are going to do everything you can to make the town the very best it can be."

"Well, I think that's true for some people, but Colby Flannigan was still getting his fair share of attention too. I don't want to get myself too comfortable just because I already have a position in the town. He's really well respected, and people might lean toward him more because he's a little older than me."

"I don't think that's going to matter," I say.

Colby throwing his name into the race is a fairly new development. We didn't think Sam was just going to coast right into the position of mayor of Sherwood without any opposition, but we didn't know who was going to also be vying for the position.

"We'll just have to see," Sam says. "But it keeps me focusing on my campaign and making sure that people know I'm running and what I stand for."

"You're doing a great job," I tell him. "For someone who has never been in politics like this before, you're handling it really well. I'm so proud of you."

"Thank you," he says.

"Did everyone else have a good time?" I ask.

I know that Dean and Xavier were in town, and I think Dean mentioned that Owen will be hanging out with him for a couple of weeks as well.

"They seemed to. Cupcake was there. She and Xavier were walking around holding hands the whole time," Sam says.

"How did he look?" I ask.

"Happy," he says. "Really happy. A little more confident, a little more focused. He even schmoozed a bit with the other attendees and didn't scare anyone off."

It's exactly what I want to hear. Cupcake came into our lives unexpectedly but has effectively made her place with us. She clearly adores Xavier for everything that he is and doesn't want or expect him to be anything else, which is just the way it should be. But it's Xavier's reaction to her and to their gradually blooming relationship that has been more difficult. I know he is still settling into the idea of her, trying to get used to the thought of having another person in his life in that way after losing Lila at such a young age.

Learning about the girl he adored so deeply and lost when he was only a teenager was just another part of Xavier that none of us knew, something that he'd kept locked inside him until the moment he knew he needed to share it. It was heartbreaking, but it helped me understand him a little bit better. I know Cupcake is good for him, and it makes me happy to hear that he is letting himself learn to feel this again.

The sound of my phone ringing on the kitchen table the next morning pulls me away from the cinnamon rolls I'm making to tuck away in Bellamy's freezer as a thank-you for letting me stay with them throughout this investigation. I'm planning on making the drive back to Sherwood to visit Sam and want them to have something delicious while I'm gone. Wiping my hands off on my apron, I go to the table and see it's Detective Fuller calling.

"Hey, Detective," I say, putting the phone between my ear and shoulder so I can go back to the dough while we talk.

"What are you doing?" he asks.

"I'm making cinnamon rolls," I tell him, immediately struck by the tone of his voice. "Why? What's wrong?"

"You need to get to Ander Ward's house as fast as possible," he says.

"What happened?" I ask, my stomach already sinking.

"Sabrina Ward is dead."

CHAPTER SIXTEEN

T HE WARD HOUSE IS SURROUNDED BY EMERGENCY VEHICLES AND blocked off from the road with crime scene tape when I arrive. Curious neighbors stand on the opposite side of the street, watching over the shoulders of officers positioned to hold them back. I park behind one of the cars and pull out my shield so I can show it to the officer standing close to the crime scene tape.

"FBI," I tell him.

He lifts the tape for me, and I duck beneath it, rushing toward the open front door.

"Detective Fuller?" I say to an officer who's standing just inside the house.

"He's in the kitchen," he says.

I nod and move deeper into the house to get to the kitchen. I see the detective as soon as I get into the room.

"Agent Griffin," he says, coming toward me.

"What happened?" I ask.

"Her husband was called away with a family emergency this morning, and when he came back, he found her."

"Is the body still here?" I ask.

"Right over here."

He leads me around a partial wall at the back of the room to a set of back steps leading up to the second floor. Sabrina Ward's body is sprawled on the steps, blood soaking her head and the top of the bathrobe she's wearing. One arm is stretched out above her, and I notice a gold bracelet with a capsule-shaped cage on it around her wrist.

"Looks like she was bludgeoned," I say. "Was any weapon found?"

"No," Detective Fuller says. "The scene is exactly the way he found it. We're waiting for the crime scene photographer to arrive."

I look around the room and see the stark black permanent marker on the walls just like in Gideon's apartment. The words are written in the same careful block lettering:

May you be haunted by your choice forever

Was it worth it?

To the wicked give their due

"What about the rest of the house?" I ask.

"There are similar messages written on the walls in the living room and the bedroom. Her phone was found in the master bedroom. She missed a couple of calls from her husband. It looks like he was calling while the attack was happening," Detective Fuller says.

"Where was he when this happened? You said there was some kind of family emergency?" I ask.

"His mother had a fire at her house," the detective tells me. "A building on her property caught on fire early this morning, and she called him to help her handle it."

"Where is he now?" I ask.

"He was transferred to the station," he says.

"I'm going to go talk to him. Let me know if anything shows up when the scene is processed," I say.

I take a final look at the body and feel a sick twinge in my belly. I sat with this woman just a couple of days ago right in her own living room. She talked to me about how she felt about the threats and the fear she went through when she thought someone was following her. I listened to her talk and watched her husband wrap his arm around her like he was trying to defend her from some unseen force she felt around her. Now she's lying dead on the stairs, stretched across them like she was trying to escape her assailant but was taken down before she had the chance.

The officers have Ander in a room furnished with a couch and a table rather than in one of the interrogation rooms. He's hunched in one corner of the couch, his hands wrapped around a cup of coffee like what he's just been through has taken away all his warmth and now he's trying to draw it out of the mug. His head lifts when I walk into the room, and I see a flicker of something go across his eyes. The emotion is etched deeply into his face, making him look gray and sunken.

"Agent Griffin," he says.

"Hi, Ander. I'm so sorry for your loss."

"Thank you," he says.

"I know this is really difficult for you, but I need to talk to you about what happened," I say.

He nods. "Go ahead."

I pull a chair up closer to the couch and sit down, taking out my notepad and pen so I can jot down anything significant.

"First, is there anything I can get you? Are you hungry?" I ask.

He lets out a mirthless snort of laughter and shakes his head. "I don't think I'm ever going to want to eat again."

"I can understand that," I tell him. "All right. Just tell me in your own words what happened this morning from the time you woke up."

Ander draws in a breath, his eyes focused somewhere in front of him as if he's looking back into the morning.

"We were asleep. It was still really early, and I heard my phone ringing. I never turn the ringer off or on silent or anything because of Tracy, so I thought maybe something was going on with her. But it was my mother calling. She said that her shed was on fire and needed me to come help her deal with it. She's lived alone since Dad died, so I do a lot for her. She has anxiety about a lot of things and usually calls me if anything goes wrong or if she needs to do something that she's not used to. Like anytime she has a repairman coming over or she has to get her internet fixed, she calls me to be there with her.

"She told me she had already called the fire department, she just wanted me there, so I told her I was on my way. Sabrina woke up while I was talking and offered to come with me, but I told her to stay home and get some more sleep. She's been having a hard time sleeping for a few days, and it finally broke last night. I didn't want her to have to get up so early and come with me when I knew there was nothing she was going to be able to do and it would be better if she just got to sleep some more. I didn't think that the situation at my mother's house was going to take up too much time, so I planned on going into the office after I was done. I told Sabrina I would come home before I went to work."

"Did you tell Tracy what was going on?" I ask.

"I did. She is usually unavailable early in the morning anyway, it's her devotional time, but I left her a message telling her what was going on and that I was going to get into work as soon as I could. I wanted to let her know as soon as possible so she would be able to arrange for a different guard to be with her if she had any appearances this morning," Ander says.

"You don't know her schedule?" I ask.

"Not day-to-day," he tells me. "I know when there are big appearances and events, but I generally find out about local meetings and things first thing in the morning."

"What did you find out when you got to your mother's house?" I ask.

"The police and firefighters were obviously already there when I got there. They told me it looked like someone had purposely lit the building on fire and that there had been a rash of small arsons like that throughout the neighborhood and some surrounding areas over the last few months. They don't know who's doing it, but they say they wouldn't be surprised if it was just some kids being mischievous, which sounds absurd to me. Egging a house is mischief. Lighting somebody's building on fire is destruction."

"I agree," I say. "Was there much damage?"

"Yeah, the building is a total loss. Fortunately, the only things she had in there were gardening tools and some seasonal lawn stuff, so it wasn't a lot of really sentimental things or anything. But it's still really upsetting. Mom was in a really bad state over it, and I thought I was going to have to bring her to the emergency room because she was having such a hard time and said she felt like she was having a heart attack because of it. I called Sabrina to let her know what was going on, but she didn't answer," he says.

"Did you think that was strange?" I ask.

"Not at first. I thought she probably just went back to sleep. But the sound of the phone always wakes her up eventually, so I called her again. I felt bad waking her up, but I thought it was important that she knew what was going on. But she still didn't answer. I kept calling. That's when I started to worry. I just felt like something was wrong. I didn't want to leave Mom until I knew she was going to be all right, but I was also getting really concerned. I ended up asking for paramedics to come and take her in to get looked at just to make sure that she wasn't having a heart attack. I promised to meet her at the hospital and left to go check on Sabrina. When I got home, I noticed a window on the side of the house was open. I don't remember opening it. Sabrina might have, but I can't imagine her not closing it. I don't know… I really don't know."

He puts the coffee down on the table and leans forward to bury his face in his hands.

"It's all right," I tell him. "You don't need to know. Right now I just need you to keep telling me what happened."

Ander wipes his eyes as he sits up and takes a breath to pull himself together.

"I went inside the house and called for Sabrina. She didn't answer. Then I noticed the words written on the walls. I remembered hearing about messages on the walls in Gideon's apartment, and I panicked. I ran upstairs to look for her, but she wasn't there, and I ended up going down the back steps. That's when I found her. I called the police, and …"

"All right," I tell him, releasing him from the need to keep describing the disturbing scene. "Have you been able to contact the hospital and check on your mother?"

"No," he says. "I've just been sitting in here."

"Give me just a second," I tell him.

I walk out of the room and call Detective Fuller.

"I just got Ander Ward's statement. I'm going to release him so that he can go to the hospital and check on his mother. Have you found anything else?"

"Nothing," he says. "There's no evidence of the attack upstairs, so we think it all happened downstairs. She likely heard the killer come inside and went downstairs to find out what the sound was."

"In her bathrobe?" I ask. "She wasn't wearing anything else. If she thought someone she didn't know was coming into the house, she wouldn't have left her phone upstairs and gone down in nothing but her bathrobe. She didn't hear them come in because they came in through an open window on the side of the house. Ander just told me about it."

"Good to know," he says.

"I'm going to talk to the firefighters after this. Get in touch with me if you find anything else," I say.

I get off the phone and go back into the room with Ander.

"I forgot to tell you something," he says. "I'm sorry, my mind is just not all with me right now."

"What is it?" I ask.

"I got another threat yesterday. It was in the mailbox, but there was no stamp or anything. I think that someone just walked up and put it in there," he says.

"What did the note say?"

"That I had to quit by the end of the day or I would be out of time," he says. He shakes his head and puts his face in his hands again. "This is my fault. I caused this."

"Ander," I say, moving to sit down beside him and rest my hand on his back. "I know this is extremely hard. I understand. But you can't let yourself think that way. We need to find out who did this to Sabrina. You said you think that the note was just put into your mailbox."

"Yes," he says. "I got it yesterday after work. I meant to call you about it this morning."

"Do you have cameras on your house?" I ask. "Something that would show the mailbox?"

"I do. I put them up right after the first threats came to make Sabrina feel safer at home," he says, sounding pained at the thought.

"After you go to the hospital to check on your mother, I need that footage," I tell him.

"I'll get it for you," he says.

"Can I give you a ride to the hospital?" I ask.

"Please."

CHAPTER SEVENTEEN

ANDER IS SILENT FOR THE DRIVE FROM THE POLICE STATION TO the hospital. He stares out the window, watching the world go by. It's totally changed for him now. He woke up this morning with a wife, and now, only a few hours later, he's a widower, that wife brutally murdered right in their home. He's going to have to learn to navigate this new reality. It's a heartbreaking thought, but even as I watch him walk up to the entrance to the hospital, my mind is still focused on the investigation.

His mother lives in the next town over, and I go directly to the police department there. I show my shield to the officer at the reception desk.

"There was a fire at a home this morning. A shed burned down. I need to speak with the officers who responded to that," I tell her.

"Give me just a second," she says.

I wait in the lobby area until an officer comes through the doors and extends his hand to shake mine.

"Jody Ferris," he introduces himself.

"Agent Emma Griffin," I say.

"Come on back," he says.

We walk into the back, and he leads me to a room similar to the one Ander was just in. Two more officers are already inside.

"Can I get you something to drink?" Officer Ferris asks.

"No, I'm fine," I tell him. "Thank you."

"This is Officer O'Connell and Officer Alridge. The three of us responded to the fire this morning."

"Then you spoke with Ander Ward, the son of the homeowner?" I ask.

"Yes," Officer Ferris says. "He arrived shortly after we did. The fire was already under control by the time he got there, but Mrs. Ward was frantic. She wouldn't calm down until he got there. He was very calm, so it was a relief to be able to talk to him to let him know what was going on and have him settle her down."

"I'm sure she was upset," I point out. "It was early in the morning, and a building on her property was on fire. That's not something that most people would take in stride." He looks adequately chastised, and I move on. "Ander told me that there were other incidents like this recently."

"Yes," Officer O'Connell says. "There have been reports of several other fires to outbuildings in the surrounding areas over the last few months. No residential structures have been targeted during any of these incidents, but there has been a considerable amount of property damage. We've been hoping that someone would have camera footage that would show who is setting the fires, but so far nothing has come up. It looks like something bored teenagers would do to amuse themselves. They don't realize how serious it actually is."

"Once Ander Ward arrived at the house, was he there the entire time?" I ask.

The officers look at me slightly strangely.

"Yes," Officer O'Connell says. "He went with the firefighters to see the remnants of the shed and then sat with us and his mother while she gave her statement as to what exactly happened. She said that she was up early, like she always is, and was making her coffee when she noticed flickering through the kitchen window. She looked outside, and the shed was on fire. The first thing she did was call 911, but then she called her son. He lives in the next town over, so like I said, things were already pretty well under control by the time he made it there. But she was still frantic and thought she might be having a heart attack because of the stress and shock."

"I need to let you know that the reason I'm asking about all this and why it's so important to get the full information about Ander being there and what he did is that his wife was murdered this morning," I tell them.

"While he was at his mother's house?" Officer Alridge asks, sounding shocked.

"He says that he called her several times while he was there, and that's what made him worried," I say.

"He was on the phone a few times while we were handling the situation," O'Connell confirms. "He told his mother that his wife wasn't answering the phone and that he was concerned. She was still worried about her heart, so he asked that paramedics bring her to the hospital and get her checked out while he went home. He seemed a little nervous, but he told his mother that he was going to meet her at the hospital soon, so I guess he figured everything was going to be all right."

"Well, he went home and found his wife, Sabrina, bludgeoned to death. I need to know the timing of his arrival and when he left as precisely as possible so I can create a timeline," I tell them.

We talk through every step of the morning investigation and start creating a cursory timeline for the events as they unfolded. I'll need to see Ander's phone to get the time that his mother called him compared to the time the emergency team was dispatched as well as when he called for help about Sabrina, but right now it seems like an extremely tight turnaround. He got to his mother's house quickly after she called him, and then there was only a small window of time between when he left to go check on Sabrina and when he called 911 to report finding her body. There wasn't enough time at either point for him to commit the murder, clean up, get rid of a weapon, and then go about what he needed to do.

I leave the police station and return to Ander's neighborhood. Only a couple of police cars remain. By now the body will have been removed and transported to the medical examiner's office. The crime scene investigation unit will be thoroughly processing and recording the scene to make sure every bit of existing evidence is found and can be used later. I notice that Detective Fuller's vehicle is still there, which means he's carefully supervising the entire process.

The neighbors that were lined up along the sidewalk have dissipated for the most part. They've seen the body being taken out of the house and know now for sure that something horrific has happened inside the quiet, serene-looking home. I have no doubts that many of them demanded answers from the police officers but were told they couldn't give out any information. The neighbors will have to wait to watch the news to find out all the details that will be shared.

There's still one woman standing at the edge of the yard across the street, her arms wrapped around herself, watching the house. I jog across the street toward her and introduce myself.

"Did you see anything unusual this morning?" I ask.

"No," the woman who introduced herself to me as Elsie Campano says. "I didn't know anything was happening until I heard the sirens and saw the lights. I was really worried, so I came outside to see what was going on and saw Ander out in the front yard with the police. He looked distraught, so I figured something must have happened to Sabrina."

"How well do you know them?" I ask.

"Ander and Sabrina?" she asks. "Just as neighbors. They are friendly, and we sometimes chat when we are both outside. They brought me some soup when I had a long illness over the winter."

"But you wouldn't say that you know then particularly well?" I say. "You aren't close with them?"

"No," Annette says.

"Have you ever noticed anything about their relationship that should be cause for concern? Heard yelling, seen them fighting, anything like that?" I ask.

She shakes her head. "No, they always seemed perfectly happy when I saw them."

"Do you know of anyone in the neighborhood who does know them better?" I ask.

"I don't know about Ander as much, but I've seen Sabrina spending time with the neighbor next door, Annette Chambers. She might be someone to talk to," she says.

"Thank you. I appreciate your time."

"I just can't believe something like this happened in this neighborhood. It's always been such a quiet place," she says.

"Unfortunately, things like this happen everywhere," I say. "It's just a good reminder to be aware of your surroundings, keep your doors and windows locked. Take care of yourself."

I cross the street again and climb the steps to the front porch Elsie indicated. I ring the bell, and a woman who looks like she has been crying comes to the door.

"Yes?" she says.

"Hi, I'm Special Agent Emma Griffin with the FBI. I need to talk with you for a couple minutes," I say.

She nods and opens the screen door she kept closed between us. "Come in."

I follow her into the blissfully cool house, and she brings me to a sitting room off the main entrance.

"This is about Sabrina, isn't it?" she asks.

"Yes," I tell her. "I heard that the two of you spent time together. Did you know her well?"

"We were friends," she says. "She was such a sweet woman. I can't believe she's gone."

"Tell me what happened this morning," I say.

"I really don't know," she says. "Really early this morning, I thought I heard something like screaming. It woke me up from a really deep sleep, and I couldn't really process where I thought it was coming from. I didn't hear it again and decided it must have been in a dream, so I didn't think anything of it. Then later I was outside drinking my coffee on the porch and saw Ander get home. He barely even waved at me. He just headed right inside the house. A couple minutes later, I heard him shout, and he came running out of the house on the phone shouting about his wife being dead. It happened that fast.

"I went over to him to find out what was wrong, but he was too worked up and pacing around the yard while he talked to the police. He was saying that he found his wife dead on the stairs and it looked like she'd been murdered. I just screamed. He came over to me and demanded I tell him what happened, but I hadn't seen anything. I didn't know. I thought about the sound that woke me up after the police got here and were questioning me." She hangs her head. "I can't believe I didn't do anything. Maybe I could have helped her."

"That's very unlikely," I tell her. "You didn't do anything wrong, and you need to not let yourself think that you did. This is a tragedy, and what we need to focus on right now is finding the person responsible so they can be brought to justice."

"I just wish there was something else I could do. I can't wrap my head around the fact that she's really gone. That I won't see her while I'm gardening and we won't have any more chats over coffee. Everything was looking so bright for her. Just as they were about to start a family," she says.

"Start a family?" I ask.

Annette nods and wipes tears from her eyes. "Sabrina was pregnant. At least, she was very sure that she was. She hadn't been to the doctor yet, but when she told me, she said she knew her body and had no question in her mind that the early test that she took was right. She was so excited. Being a mother has been something she's wanted for years. I don't think I've ever seen a person as happy as she was when she told me. She'd just taken the test and said she just had to say it to somebody or she was going to burst. She was trying to come up with some cute way to tell Ander. They would have been the sweetest family."

"Did Sabrina ever talk to you about being afraid to be home alone or anything that was happening in her life that was scaring her?" I ask, not wanting to give too many leading details.

"You mean the threats Ander was getting from work?" she says. "Yeah, she talked to me about it some. It really unnerved her. For a little while, she was thinking she might ask Ander to quit even though he was the only one working. But then she found out about the baby. He put in cameras to make her feel better, and she said that she felt safe because of them."

"Did you know that she called the police a couple of times because she thought someone was in the house?" I ask.

"I know. She said it made her feel so ridiculous that she panicked over nothing. She did a couple of online sessions with a therapist to help her deal with it, and they convinced her that she was just experiencing anxiety, and the police never found anything. That made her feel a lot calmer, I think. A lot of good that did," she mutters.

CHAPTER EIGHTEEN

AS I'M LEAVING ANNETTE'S HOUSE, I NOTICE A CAR PULL UP IN front of the house, and Ander climbs out of the back seat. He stops a step up into the lawn and stares at the house, not moving past the crime scene tape. I call out to him, and he turns to watch me jog across the lawn toward him.

"How's your mother?" I ask.

"She's doing much better now. She wasn't having a heart attack. They said it was a panic attack, and that can sometimes mimic the symptoms of a heart attack. They gave her some fluids and sedatives to help her calm down then sent her home," he says.

"That's good to hear," I say.

"I was going to get that camera footage for you, but I don't know if I'm allowed to go inside," he says.

"Let me go talk to the detective," I say. "The scene is still being processed, so they likely won't want you to go inside, but I might be able to bring the computer out to you."

"It's in the office," he says.

"I'll be right back."

I duck under the tape and nod at the officer, who lets me through into the house. Detective Fuller is in the living room on the phone when I walk in, but he quickly ends the call and steps up to me.

"Agent Griffin," he says. "Have you found out anything new?"

"I confirmed with the police near Ander's mother's home that he was at the scene very soon after she called him, well within the amount of time they expected it to take for him to travel from here to there, and he was with her the entire time. The calls from him that are on Sabrina's phone were made from his mother's house. The officers saw him make them and then heard him mention to his mother that she wasn't answering and needed to check on her.

"I also spoke with a couple of neighbors. One across the street said that she didn't see anything and didn't have much to say about them as a couple other than that they always seemed happy. The next-door neighbor was friends with Sabrina and told me that she thinks she heard a scream really early this morning, but she can't be sure. She didn't see anything either. She did tell me that Sabrina Ward thought she was pregnant."

"That just adds another layer to the tragedy," he says.

I nod. "Ander Ward just got back here from checking on his mother at the hospital. I know he can't come inside right now, but I asked him to get me the footage from the camera at the front of the house. I'm going to get his laptop from his office and bring it out to him."

"Hopefully, there will be something on it," he says. "Right now all we have is the window that the perpetrator used to get inside, the messages written on the walls, and her body. No fingerprints, no weapon. Nothing."

"We'll find something," I tell him.

I find the office and unplug the laptop, carrying it outside to Ander.

"Thanks," he says. "I don't know if I'll ever be able to go back inside there."

"You will," I tell him. "It will be hard, but you will. Let's sit in my car so we can have some air-conditioning while you pull up the footage."

We get into the car, and I crank the air conditioner as he balances the computer on his lap. He goes through a few screens before eventually pulling up some grainy black-and-white footage of the front porch. The mailbox and street in front of it are just visible at the top of the screen.

"I'm not sure when that note got there, but I know it wasn't there earlier in the day because it was sitting on top of the actual mail. Sabrina had forgotten to check it, which is why I did after work. The note was on top of the mail, that would have gotten there in the afternoon," he says.

He scrolls back through a few hours and then goes forward.

"There," I say when I see a car slide to a stop in front of the mailbox. An arm reaches out of the driver's door to open it and put something inside. "Go back and show that again."

Ander scrolls back, and we watch the car come up again. He moves the footage forward, and it shows a few minutes later when he walks out of the house to go check the mail.

"I was right there," he says. "If I'd gone out just a few minutes earlier…"

"Can you get to this morning?" I ask.

Ander scrolls through the overnight hours and pauses when the camera picks him up racing out through the front door toward the driveway.

"That's when I was leaving for my mom's house," he says.

"Go forward," I tell him.

He slowly scans through the next couple of hours until his car shows up again and he walks into the front door. There's nothing that shows someone approaching the house or going around the side to get to the window.

I grab my bag from the backseat and rummage through it, finally finding a thumb drive that I hand to him.

"Could you save that footage to this for me so I can review it again later?" I ask.

"Sure," he says.

He saves the footage and hands the thumb drive back to me.

"What are you going to do now?" I ask.

He gives a bitter laugh and shakes his head. "I have no idea. I don't even know what I'm supposed to do. The world doesn't make sense anymore."

"You're not going to be able to get back in your house today," I tell him gently. "And it would be best if you weren't alone. I recommend you go stay with your mother for at least a couple of days so that you have someone there for you."

He nods. "I'll probably do that. Helping her fix everything from the fire will be a good distraction." He shakes his head and rubs his forehead with one hand. "How could this happen?"

"I'm going to find out," I tell him. "I can escort you through the house to pack some things to bring with you."

"Thank you."

I go inside first and let the detective and officers know that Ander is coming through the house so they are careful what they say. This is already traumatic enough for him; he doesn't need to overhear any gruesome commentary or theories. I can see his eyes scanning the messages written on the walls and encourage him to try to ignore them and keep going. In the bedroom, he looks around and suddenly breaks into tears, covering his face as his shoulders shake.

I put a reassuring hand on his back. "Let's get you packed."

He takes a duffel bag out of the closet and fills it with clothes, then goes into the bathroom and stops to stare at the towel on the floor. I can almost see the thoughts racing through his head as he thinks about his wife so vulnerable in the shower when the intruder climbed through that window into the house. Ander finishes packing, and we leave the house. I wait until he is in his car and driving away before I go back inside to talk to Detective Fuller.

"The camera on the front of the house has a very limited view. It really only shows the front porch and the street. There's nothing showing the killer getting into the house. But there are time stamps showing when Ander left and when he came back. That bracelet she was wearing looked like a fitness tracker. My best friend has one just like it. The tracker itself is inside the little cage. It will show when her heartbeat stopped. That should give an accurate time of death," I say. "It's a tight timeline. Whoever did this was ready for it to happen."

"We'll keep canvassing the neighbors to see if anybody was up and saw anything," he says.

"I'm going to look at this footage again and see if anything pops out at me. I'll keep in touch."

I leave the house and head back to Bellamy and Eric's house.

Bellamy and Bebe are home, and I greet them before going into the guest room to get my computer and pull up the footage again.

"What did you find?" Bellamy asks, coming into the room.

"Ander Ward installed a camera on the front of his house after he started getting the threatening messages. It doesn't have very much of a field, but it shows enough that he got footage of a note being left in his mailbox yesterday. A car comes up, someone reaches out and puts the note into the mailbox, and they drive away. Less than twelve hours later, his wife was dead. I've already looked at the footage a couple of times, and I didn't notice anything, but I feel like there has to be something."

Bellamy stands behind me and watches as I go through the footage again, watching the car drive up slowly to the mailbox, the arm come out of the window, and the note go into the mailbox. The camera isn't great quality, so the footage isn't particularly clear, and at the distance from the house, it's impossible to get a clear view of the person in the car. I zoom in as much as I can, but the person is sitting back in the seat, almost like they are aware of the possibility of being recorded. I zoom back out, but Bellamy puts her hand on my shoulder.

"What's that?" she asks.

"What?" I ask.

"Zoom out again. There's something on the window."

I move the footage in as far as I can and look at the sticker on the back driver's side window. It looks like a logo for something. It takes me a few seconds, but recognition flashes through my head.

"I've seen that before," I say. "That's the logo for that low-cost car rental company, the one that rents old cars and ones that have been in accidents and stuff," I say. "I saw a commercial for it."

"Rent-a-Heap," Bellamy says. "They aren't too far from here."

"Which means they aren't too far from Ander Ward's house," I say.

CHAPTER NINETEEN

SEARCH FOR THE RENT-A-HEAP RENTAL COMPANY ONLINE AND find the address of the lot. It's about twenty minutes from Bellamy and Eric's house, putting it about fifteen from the Ward house. I isolate a few stills of the footage of the car and print them out so that I can bring them with me to show the people working at the rental company, hoping they might be able to give me some information about the car and who rented it.

The lot is loaded with vehicles that look like they might be nearing their last legs but still have a bit of good in them. Sufficient for a short-term rental or a really tight budget. The cars aren't sparkling and impressively arranged like at other agencies, but at least they offer a variety of options, from big trucks I can see people moving with to the little four-doors like the one in the video.

I park off to the side of the customer lot and go into the small office. A man hops to his feet behind the desk he was sitting at and greets me with a broad smile.

"Hi there," he says. "How can I help you this afternoon? What kind of car are you looking to rent?"

"I'm actually not looking to rent anything," I tell him. "I'm Agent Emma Griffin with the FBI. I'm investigating a case, and I believe that one of your vehicles could be linked to it."

The man's face falls, and he glances out the window beside him like he's wondering which of the cars lined up in the lot was used in a crime. He turns back to me and gestures at the chair across the desk from his.

"Have a seat," he says. "My name is Boris Kemp. I'm the owner. When you say that you think one of my vehicles is linked to a case that you're investigating, what exactly is it that we're talking about?"

"I can't provide all of the details since this is an active investigation, but I can tell you that an item associated with two murders was delivered to a home. The footage taken by the homeowner showed a vehicle pulling up to the mailbox and delivering the item. Inspection of the footage showed that the vehicle had what I believe is your company's logo on the back window. I noticed all the other vehicles in the lot have stickers on the same spot."

I take out the stills that I isolated from the footage and lay them out on the desk in front of Mr. Kemp.

"If you look closely at this image, you can see that the partial license plate is visible as they were pulling away. WD23. That's all that I could decipher from it just looking at it. But does this vehicle look familiar to you?" I ask.

"It does," he says. "This car was rented from the lot the day before yesterday and returned last night. It's the only one of its kind that I have in that color, and the license plate fits, so I know it's the same one."

"Can you tell me who rented it?" I ask.

He turns to his computer and types in a few commands. His eyes scan over the screen.

"This says it was rented by a Nicholas Beamer," he says. "But that's just what's on the registration form."

"What do you mean?" I ask.

"One of the reasons my business model is so appealing to people is that I don't make them jump through a bunch of hoops just to rent a car. In other places, you have to have a credit card and provide all sorts of identification and other information just to get behind the wheel. I understand that sometimes people don't have all of that but still need a means of transportation. So I offer an online do-it-yourself-style rental option for a select number of my vehicles.

"Essentially, people can go online and see what's available and sign up to take whatever they choose. They provide basic identifying information and then pay for the rental up front. Rather than having to come into the office and fill out anything, the keys to the vehicles are kept in a lockbox, and they get the code to their specific box after they make the payment," he says.

"And you don't require any type of proof of identification?" I ask. "No scanning their driver's licenses or providing car insurance?"

"Again," he says, "I understand that there are circumstances that don't always allow for those kinds of provisions."

I can't believe what I'm hearing.

"So essentially, you allow people to rent cars without knowing who they are and without any guarantee that they will return them, much less that they have the proper licensing and insurance to operate a motor vehicle," I say.

"The cars are all outfitted with GPS, so if I need to track one down after it's been rented, I can," he says.

I'm trying to keep my emotions in and not show just how frustrated I am by what he's telling me. Obviously, whoever rented the car—and I have no doubt their name is not Nicholas Beamer—knew about these policies and rented the car with them in mind.

"How did the renter pay for the rental?" I ask.

"It looks like a prepaid debit card," he says.

I take a breath and let it out slowly.

"Has the car been cleaned since it was returned?" I ask.

"Not yet," he says.

"I need to see it," I tell him.

"No problem. I can bring it around to you."

"Has it been moved since it was returned?" I ask.

"No, it's still in the same spot," he says.

"Then I'd rather see it there," I tell him. "The police will need to thoroughly examine it, and I would rather it not be compromised."

Kemp leads me outside and around to the back of the building where there are several parking spots with signs indicating they are for the online rental option. A couple of them look like they are in distinctly worse shape than some of the other vehicles at the front of the lot, but I'm not thinking about those. I zero in on the navy blue four-door in the fourth spot with the license plate that matches the partial tag I saw on the footage. The sticker on the back window is just what Bellamy pointed out to me.

I take out my phone and call Detective Fuller.

"Hey, I'm going to need a team to come out to the Rent-a-Heap car rental lot," I tell him. "The footage that Ander gave me showed a car dropping off a note at his house last night, and I was able to track it down."

"It was a rental?" he asks.

"Yeah. I'm assuming they didn't want their vehicle to be recognized or identified by neighbors, so they rented from here. They have a policy not requiring any form of photo identification or anything for certain cars, and this is one of them. So we can't conclusively identify the renter, but the car hasn't been cleaned, so we might be able to find something. I want it to be searched and fingerprinted and any evidence collected," I say.

"Be there as soon as we can," he says.

I hang up and look over at Boris Kemp again. His face is sullen, and he looks like he might be reconsidering everything about his brilliant business approach. I can appreciate that he recognized a niche in the market for people who need to rent cars but don't have a credit card to use or don't want to go through the hassle of going into the office to fill out the paperwork, but his approach just begs for shady abuse of the system.

I'm eager to open the car and see what might be inside, but I know I have to hold back. Just opening the door could smear fingerprints, and leaning my head inside to see anything could compromise fiber evidence. I have to resign myself to waiting for the team to get here with the proper equipment.

It doesn't take long for them to arrive, and I meet Detective Fuller out front. He looks exhausted. I imagine he didn't get a lot of sleep last night and has been going steadfastly on the Sabrina Ward investigation since this morning. Since the heat and the intense pressure of the case are starting to drag on me, I know he's feeling it. He wipes his brow as he walks up to me.

"I found a neighbor behind the Ward house who was up early with their new baby. They say they saw someone walking out from between two houses and then going down the sidewalk away from her house early this morning. She was looking through an upstairs bedroom window, so she couldn't see anything, but she thinks it was a man with long blond hair, and she noticed he was carrying a bundle that looked like clothing," he says. "We're trying to find other neighbors with doorbell cameras or anything that might have captured him."

"Long blond hair," I say. "Just like the description Jesse Kristoff gave of the person who killed Gideon Bell and attacked him. If it was same the person who killed Sabrina Ward, that bundle he was carrying was likely the overclothes, mask, and gloves he was wearing. He would have taken them off to walk through the neighborhood because that would have caught the attention of anyone who saw him. As it is, he was seen, but if he was wearing all that, it would have been much more of a cause for concern."

"Exactly," Detective Fuller says. "The neighbor didn't really think much of it. She just figured someone was taking a shortcut through the houses. She said they didn't look like they were rushing or anything, just walking down the sidewalk. It didn't occur to her that anything might be off until she heard the sirens and then the officers went to talk to her."

"I hope we can get some clear images of him from something," I say. "Let's take a look at this car."

The team follows me around to the back of the building, and I point out the vehicle. I show Detective Fuller the still from the camera footage and instruct the photographer to take a few shots of the vehicle before they go inside. Boris provided me with the keys to the car, so the first thing we do is have a gloved officer open the trunk. There's nothing inside, and the strong smell of chemical cleaners tells me it's unlikely the trunk has been used in a while.

The officers search for fingerprints on the door handle before opening the car and looking inside. I stand back with the detective while they search, wanting to get in there myself but knowing they need to be allowed to do their job. They process the inside of the car for fingerprints and search for any evidence that might have been left behind. It takes a while, but finally, one of them emerges and comes over to me.

"Everything has been wiped clean. No fingerprints. Not on the steering wheel, the controls for the air-conditioning, the radio, anywhere. Whoever did this was really careful to make sure that they weren't leaving anything identifying. But we did find this."

She displays a pair of tweezers, and in it is a single long fiber. It's thicker than natural hair, and I immediately recognize it.

"Another wig fiber," I say.

"So we're looking for someone who is going to pretty great lengths to conceal their identity," Detective Fuller says. "Where do we go from here?"

"Keep looking," I say. "Try places you don't usually think of. Get me a print, a receipt, something."

"Check the seat adjuster," Boris says, coming around the side of the building again. "I've had some people tell me that the driver's seat in that car is a little tricky, and sometimes it will fall a bit backward so the driver has to use the adjuster to get it back up. They might have done that."

"That's great," I say. "Thank you."

The team checks the lever and comes up with a thumbprint. It's a long shot, considering how many people have driven the car, but it's something.

CHAPTER TWENTY

'M UP EARLY THE NEXT MORNING MISSING MY SHERWOOD NEIGH-
borhood and the predawn jogs I take when I can't sleep. The neighborhood is so still during these hours that the sound of my feet hitting
the sidewalk sounds loud in my ears and I'm sure I'm waking up the
neighbors as I run past. Sometimes I get a chance to wave at a particularly intrepid gardener up before the sun to battle weeds and fight pests
out of the flower beds and away from their kitchen gardens. Usually, it's
just me.

I take a walk around Bellamy's neighborhood, but it doesn't have
the same feeling. I remember when I lived not far from here, in the
house my father still lives in. Back then I couldn't have imagined living anywhere else, much less that I would have found my way back to
Sherwood and been happy to relocate there.

Back at the house, I make coffee and sit on the back porch looking out over the small backyard as I think about the case. The dangling
threads are bothering me. I've found myself on paths that have led

nowhere, but there has to be something there. The fingerprint found in the car at the lot is being run through the databases today. If it belongs to someone who has been arrested before, it will come up, and we'll have a possible suspect. But there's a chance it was left by someone who has never been fingerprinted. Then I'll be in the same place I am now.

Eric comes out with his own coffee and sits down in the chair beside me. We catch up for a little bit, talking about everything but the case as he seems to be trying to give my brain a break from thinking about it, though I know he's very aware it's next to impossible for me to think about anything else when I'm engrossed in a case as intense as this one.

Just as he's getting ready to leave for work, my phone rings. I look at the screen and see Ander Ward's number.

"Hey, Ander," I say. "How are you doing?"

I'm fully aware of how ridiculous the question is. His wife was just murdered, and he's learning to navigate the world as a widower. But as Xavier would describe it, it's one of those things you just have to say.

"Agent Griffin, I don't know what to do," he says. His voice sounds tense, like something is really frightening him.

I pull my feet down off the table in front of me, sitting up straighter.

"What is it? What's wrong?" I ask.

"The media is swarming my mother's house," he says. "I don't know how they found out that I'm here, but the front yard is full of them, and their cars are blocking the road. They've been out there for a while. I need to get out to go to work, but I can't go out there with them there."

"To go to work?" I ask, shocked that he's even considering going into the office twenty-four hours after his wife's brutal death. "Do you really think you should be going to work today?"

"I need to. I wasn't planning on it, but I can't just sit around here. It's driving me crazy. I can't stop thinking about Sabrina, and I can't stand it. I need something that will give me a purpose and take my mind off of all of that. But now I can't get out of the house because of all the reporters and cameramen," he says. "Should I go out there and talk to them?"

"Absolutely not," I tell him. "Hunker down, and do not go outside unless you absolutely have to. If you do, just walk to your car without saying anything. I don't want you making any kind of statement or giving any details about anything. We really need to keep as much information as possible contained, especially this early in the investigation. We don't want details being leaked. We don't want this turned into a sensationalized media circus. That can compromise an investigation and cause serious repercussions."

THE GIRL AND THE LIES

"I won't say anything to them," he says. "But you should know that Tracy plans to."

"What do you mean?" I ask.

"She called me last night to give her condolences and let me know that she wasn't going to have Sabrina's death be glossed over. She has already booked a talk at a local church and was planning on talking about Gideon's death, but now she is going to add Sabrina to it as well."

"Shit," I mutter. "All right. I'm going to have to talk to her about that. You just stay where you are. Let her know that you aren't coming in this morning. Keep the curtains closed, and don't go outside. I'm sorry to ask you to essentially trap yourself and your mother in the house, but right now it's the best thing for both of you. Dealing with the media is a stressor you really don't need right now. If they start getting aggressive, coming to the door or anything, call the police."

"I will," he says.

"I'll talk to you soon."

Eric looks at me strangely as I end the call. "What's going on?"

"That was Ander Ward. He's staying at his mother's house for a little while, and apparently, the media tracked him down. They are surrounding the house and trying to get him to come out and talk about his wife's murder. He was planning on going to work today, but he can't get out of the house. I can't believe he would even be thinking about going to work."

"I can," Eric says. "If something were to happen to Bellamy or Bebe, I wouldn't be able to function without having something specific to do. I go to work every day. It's familiar. It would be my first instinct to just keep with my routine so that I wouldn't sit around the house and completely fall apart. I don't know for sure if I would actually be able to do anything when I got to work, but that would be what I would immediately think of. And you would too."

I know he's right. I've dealt with my fair share of painful losses, and every time, I've found solace in leaning into my work. It gives me a sense of meaning and clarity and helps me to feel like I'm doing something in the world rather than just sitting by and letting it happen to me.

"He just told me that Tracy Ellis is planning on having a talk at a local church about the murders. I need to tell her that she can't do that. The investigation is still far too early for her to be making more speculations that will cause as much chaos as her talking about Terrence Brooks," I say.

He nods. "Agreed. I've got to get going, but call me if you need anything," he says.

"I will."

He heads back into the house, and I dial Tracy Ellis. I'm surprised when she doesn't answer. Deciding that it would be more impactful for her to hear from me in person, I go inside and get dressed. Smoothing my hair up into a bun away from my neck, I put on my usual black slacks and white button-up shirt, opting to leave the jacket off in deference to the steamy heat and humidity promised for later in the afternoon.

When I walk into the lobby, Estelle smiles at me, and I wave.

"I need to speak with Tracy," I tell her. "Is she in her office?"

"She's in a meeting right now," she tells me. "But you are welcome to wait for her."

"Thank you."

I go to Tracy's office, intending to wait outside, but I find the door standing partially open. I step inside and stand, waiting for a few moments, before my eyes fall on a piece of paper sitting on her desk. Bold, block letters spell out, *Destroy the false believers.* I pick up the note and stare down at it.

"Can I help you, Agent Griffin?"

I turn around and see Tracy Ellis standing at the doorway to the office, staring at me with steel in her eyes. I don't back down. I hold up the note.

"When did you get this?" I demand.

"You just decided you can walk into my office without my permission and touch my belongings?" she asks. "This is why I need Ander. He needs to figure out a way to get here."

"Your door was open, and this was sitting in full view on your desk. You can let go of your defensiveness now and answer my question. When did you get this note?"

"I didn't get it," she snaps, walking further into the room with a slight swagger in her step. "I wrote it."

"Excuse me?" I ask.

"I saw some of the notes that were sent to my employees, but I foolishly threw them away without thinking about the value that they hold. People have heard all about these notes and how much fear they are causing. I want the world to see them. To have the visceral reaction of actually seeing what these people have had to face. I am creating a series of them to use as a visual aid for the talk I'll be doing this weekend," she says.

"You won't be using anything like this," I tell her.

She gives me a withering look. "I beg your pardon?"

"This," I say, giving the note a shake for emphasis, "is not yours to show to anyone. You might have written this, but you have no place passing it off as real evidence. Even if you tell the people there that you made it yourself, you do not have authorization to discuss the details of this case and its investigation with uninvolved people. None of the notes have been shared with the media or shown to the public. Doing so could compromise the investigation.

"These are people's lives you are planning on using for entertainment value. They aren't just stories. Two people, real human beings, have been murdered, and others are terrified because they've gotten the threats too. Now is not the time for you to trot them out and cause them more pain and misery by turning them into fodder for one of your performances."

"They are not performances, Agent Griffin," Tracy sneers, obviously angry at the way I'm talking to her. "I'm not playing a part. I am a teacher. I am a voice of guidance and reason for those who are lost."

"And you are also not a member of this investigation. This isn't a teaching moment. This is an active investigation into two murders and multiple threats. The details of the notes are to be kept confidential. You will not be using them as a visual aid for this talk or any other. I hope I make myself clear."

She glares at me like she expects me to back down under the sheer force of her will, but I just stare back. Finally, a bemused smile crosses her face, and she takes a step back, opening her hands out to her sides.

"Fine, Agent Griffin. If you feel that there is something damaging behind telling people the truth in this way, then I will respect that. But you can't stop me from addressing the deaths of these two people when I do my talk. I do still have the right to freedom of speech, and I won't be silenced. The deaths have been covered on the news, and if they are able to talk about them, then so am I."

"As long as you are only talking about things that have been shared with the public and not exposing any information about the victims or their families," I say.

She huffs indignantly. "Fine. Now, if you will excuse me, I really do have work to do."

I leave the office with a tight feeling in my stomach. It seems like Tracy Ellis is almost relishing the deaths and the content it gives her. She's savoring being able to rage about another death, drawing a crowd to hang on every word—and pay for tickets. It's obvious she is eager for all the attention this is bringing to her ministry. It no longer seems like a question of how much she is doing this for the benefit of other people—and how much she is doing this for herself.

CHAPTER TWENTY-ONE

T HAT NIGHT THE HOUSE IS QUIET AFTER BELLAMY AND ERIC HAVE gone to bed, and I'm up still going over my notes as I watch the news. A new report on the murder of Sabrina Ward comes on, and it's obvious it wasn't just his mother's house that the media swarmed. Interspersed with shots of the outside of his mother's house as the media waited for Ander to come out are images of the house he shared with Sabrina. The reporters repeat the same information they shared on the initial story last night, emphasizing that police and FBI were still looking for any leads in the situation.

Just as I feared it would, the coverage is leaning heavily into sensationalism, focusing on the frightening details and regularly repeating the link to the Tracy Ellis Ministry. They artfully weave in a mention of Terrence Brooks, stopping short of saying they think the same perpetrator is responsible for all the deaths but making sure to draw enough dubious parallels that it would be easy to confuse the situations as being tangled up together.

I'm particularly frustrated by the aggressiveness of the reporters when I see the trembling, pale face of Annette show up on screen. She's standing behind her screen door, obviously not thrilled with being seen on camera but likely not willing to just shut her door in the reporter's face. They ask her about Sabrina, and tears immediately start to stream down her face.

"She was always a good friend and such a sweet person. It's devastating to think that someone right at the beginning of their life, happily married, expecting their first child, living their dream, could be wiped away in an instant," she says.

My chest tightens at the words. I purposely had not mentioned the possibility of a pregnancy to Ander. Annette had specifically said Sabrina had been looking for a cute and creative way to reveal the news to her husband, which means he might not have ever gotten to hear about it. I didn't want to reveal that kind of blow to him, and now it's likely he heard about it on the news. The thought is deeply sobering.

The footage is still playing when my phone rings. It's Jesse Kristoff. I'm surprised to see his name on the screen and answer.

"Hello?"

"Are you watching the news?" he asks.

"What?" I ask.

"Are you watching the news?" he repeats, sounding worked up.

"I am," I tell him. "Why?"

"They haven't mentioned Gideon even once," he says. "All of the coverage is about Sabrina. They even talked about Tracy Ellis and Terrence Brooks, but the only mention Gideon got was them saying it was the second murder after the 'death of a man.' 'Death of a man,' Agent Griffin. They didn't say his name or talk about what happened to him. And they didn't mention me getting attacked at all. He's being completely overlooked. Both of us are being forgotten in this investigation."

"Jesse, I know it's frustrating that it doesn't seem like Gideon's death and your attack got as much attention as Sabrina Ward's death. Sometimes the media decides to latch on to certain stories more than others, and as much as no one wants to admit it, the story of a young wife and mother-to-be is more... compelling for the media," I tell him.

"So you're saying that we don't matter as much," he says. "Gideon doesn't matter as much."

"That's not at all what I'm saying. Of course he matters. His murder is equally as important as Sabrina's and is just as much a focus of the investigation as hers," I say calmly. "I am just as determined to bring justice to Gideon and am applying all of the information that I find out about Sabrina's death to his investigation as well. I promise you that I have not forgotten either one of you or what happened. I am just building this investigation with the information as it comes."

"All right," he says, taking a breath and letting it out slowly. "I'm sorry, I didn't mean to yell at you."

"It's fine," I tell him. "I know you're going through a lot right now, and you feel like you have to be the voice for Gideon as well."

"He doesn't have anyone else. I'm the only one who can speak up for him and make sure that he isn't forgotten," Jesse says.

"You aren't the only one," I say. "I will make sure that his name is said and that he is not overlooked. This investigation started for him, and I will continue to fight for him until I find out what happened."

"Thank you, Agent Griffin," he says. "That means a lot to me."

I end the call and set my phone on the coffee table before going into the kitchen to make a snack.

As I'm chopping vegetables as quietly as I can so the sound doesn't reach upstairs to the bedrooms, I hear my phone ringing again in the living room. I hurry back in and grab it, hitting the Answer button and pressing it to my ear without looking to see who is calling.

"Hello?"

"Agent Griffin! Agent Griffin!" The voice coming through the line is so high-pitched and frantic-sounding that I don't immediately recognize it. "I need you!"

It clicks. "Carla? Carla, I need you to calm down. Tell me what's going on."

"It's Marshall," she says. "He was attacked."

"Where are you?" I ask.

"At home. He was here alone, and someone attacked him," she says. "Please come."

"I need you to hang up and call 911," I tell her.

"They're already here," she says. "He was able to call during the attack."

"All right. I'll be there as fast as I can get there, but I'm about half an hour away."

"Meet me at the hospital," she says. "The ambulance is about to leave with Marshall."

"I'll be there," I tell her.

I hang up and rush into the guest bedroom to change clothes. The drive to the hospital feels long as my mind churns with possibilities of what happened to Marshall. He's obviously still alive, but I don't know the extent of what he went through and the injuries he's sustained. But I also have hope that he'll be able to tell me what happened and who did this to him.

When I get to the hospital, I go in through the emergency room entrance and find Carla in the waiting area with two police officers. She immediately hops up from her chair and runs over to me.

"What happened?" I ask.

"I should have been there," she says. "I was supposed to be home tonight, and I wasn't."

I take her by her shoulders and squeeze her gently to try to get her to focus. I look into her eyes. "Carla, look at me. I need you to tell me exactly what happened," I say. "Where were you tonight?"

"I was supposed to be home tonight," she repeats. "But I'm on the planning committee for a charity organization I volunteer with, and there were some problems with an upcoming event that I'm chairing. One of the other ladies called me in a panic because she didn't know what to do to fix the issues, and she wanted me to come and help her. I almost didn't go because it was already getting late when she called, but the organization is really important to me, and this is the first event that I've headed up, so I want to do a good job and make it the best event it can be.

"Marshall and I were trying to catch up on a show we've been watching, and I told him not to watch ahead without me, that I wouldn't be too long. I left, went, and handled the issues, and then went back to the house. When I got there, there were police cars and an ambulance in front of the house. They didn't want to let me inside. I finally convinced them to let me in, and they told me that Marshall had been attacked and was unconscious. They were working on him in the bedroom when I got in there. They say he was beaten but managed to get away from the attacker and get to the bedroom."

The police officers come over and introduce themselves as Officers Massengill and Trammel. I tell them who I am, and they nod their understanding.

"Can you tell me more about what happened tonight?" I ask.

"A call came into dispatch from the Powell residence reporting an intruder. Mr. Powell said that he was being attacked and needed help. The dispatcher heard someone in the background call out for Mrs. Powell, and then the line went dead. Police and an ambulance responded within three minutes and broke through the front door into the house. There was no response to calling for Mr. Powell, and the team found the bedroom door locked. We knocked and announced ourselves, but there was no answer, so we breached the door and went inside. That's when we found Mr. Powell unconscious and bleeding. Mrs. Powell arrived almost immediately after," Officer Massengill says with clinical precision. I can almost imagine the words written out on his paperwork.

"Was there any weapon found at the scene?" I ask.

"No," he replies matter-of-factly.

"You said that someone was shouting for Carla in the background of the call?" I ask.

"Yes," he says. "Dispatch reported that there was a voice shouting out the name 'Carla' and that it was not the person on the phone."

I look at Carla, who looks shocked and rattled by the revelation.

"Who knew you weren't going to be home tonight?" I ask.

"No one except the people at the event," she says. "And Marshall."

"You park in your garage, right?" I ask, remembering parking in the empty driveway when I visited their house.

"Yes," she says.

"So if someone came to the house, they wouldn't immediately know that you weren't there," I say.

"Not if the garage doors were closed, which they were," she says. Her eyes go wide, and what little color was left in her face drains away. "They were coming for me. Just like Sabrina. They weren't there for Marshall, they were there for me."

Her body starts to shake, and I put an arm around her to lead her over to the nearby chairs. I help her sit down and sit beside her. Carla leans forward so her head is between her knees and draws in a few deep breaths. I can feel her still trembling and struggling to get the air in.

"Sit tight," I say. "I'll be right back."

I go to the bathroom and get a paper towel. Soaking it with cold water, I bring it back and rest it on the back of Carla's neck.

"Thank you," she says.

"Are you all right?" I ask. "Do you want to see a doctor?"

She shakes her head and sits up. "No, I'm sorry… I'm fine."

"Have you heard anything about Marshall's condition?" I ask.

"No," Carla says. "They just brought him back, and I've been waiting for someone to come out and tell me something."

Almost as though her words beckoned him, a doctor comes out of the back of the emergency room and comes over to us.

"Mrs. Powell?" he asks.

"That's me," she says.

"I'd like to speak to you privately for a moment," he says.

She looks like she doesn't want to stand up, but eventually, she pushes herself out of the chair and follows him into the back. Too filled with adrenaline to sit, I stand and start pacing the waiting area.

CHAPTER TWENTY-TWO

"I THINK THAT WE'VE GOT ENOUGH FOR TONIGHT," OFFICER Trammel says. "We'll talk to Mrs. Powell more tomorrow."

They leave, and as I watch them walk out the door, I'm shocked to see Tracy Ellis come in. I stalk over to her.

"What are you doing here?" I ask.

"Something has happened to a member of my company, and I am here to provide spiritual support," she says.

"Where were you and your spiritual support when Gideon and Sabrina were murdered?" I ask.

"I didn't have the opportunity to be there for their loved ones when I should have been, and I regret that, but I'm here now, and I want to know what happened," she says.

"How do you even know that something happened?" I ask, briefly wondering if Marshall called her after dropping the call with police dispatch.

"Another employee, Miles Kaufman, lives on the same street as Marshall and Carla Powell. When he saw the police cars and ambulance go to their house, he called me to let me know that there was an emergency and my prayers were gravely needed. Please, Agent Griffin, I know we haven't seen eye to eye in some parts of this investigation, but you need to understand how important this is. I'm here to bring peace and comfort. I need to know what happened. Miles said he saw Carla run into the house. Does that mean something happened to Marshall?" Tracy asks.

"I'm not going to give you any information about what happened tonight. This is an emerging situation, and I don't need your interference," I say. "You need to leave."

"I have just as much right to be here as you do," she says. "If something happened to Marshall, Carla is going to need support and guidance. I know she recently strayed from the flock, but I am still here to be a prayer warrior with her and keep vigil over Marshall."

"She didn't stray from a flock. She quit your company because she wants a new life for herself and her husband," I say. "And it's up to her if she wants you to know anything about what's happening or if she wants you here. You can't decide that for her."

"And neither can you," she shoots back icily.

I glance over at the door again and notice a figure standing just outside. He shifts, moving his weight to one foot, but he doesn't turn around to look inside.

"Is that Ander?" I ask.

"Yes, I called him when I decided to come here. I thought it might be a good idea for me to have security with me considering the situation," she says.

"I thought you said not to be afraid and that you weren't going to back down or show any fear in the face of a mere human," I point out.

Her face goes red as she obviously struggles to come up with reasoning.

We fall into an icy silence and stay that way for several minutes as I wait for Carla to come back from talking to the doctor. Out of the corner of my eye, I notice people gathering outside the doors. Ander holds his arm out to stop them from going any further. I can hear the muffled sound of them shouting, but the thick glass of the doors stops the words from coming through. I start toward the door to find out what's happening, but I turn around when I hear Carla's voice.

"What's going on? Tracy, what are you doing here?" she asks.

I walk over to her, putting myself between the two women as Tracy rushes forward like she's going to grab on to her.

"Oh, dear, I had to come be here for you in your time of crisis," Tracy says around me. "Please tell me that Marshall is all right."

"How did you even find out about this?" she demands, the gaze she gives me filled with the question of whether I might have called her to tell her about the attack.

"Someone deeply concerned about the two of you and aware of your need for spiritual guidance and strength at this time called me," she says.

"Miles," Carla says with a note of disdain in her voice. "I can't believe he thought it was his place to call you and tell you anything."

Tracy contorts her face into a hurt expression. "I thought you would be glad that I was here. There are so many people praying for you right now. Don't you know that? So many people holding you in their hearts and lifting you up as you walk through this trial."

My eyes narrow. "What are you talking about?"

The doors slide open as someone comes into the hospital, and I can hear a snippet of the shouting from outside. I catch Tracy's name and immediately turn my attention to what is unfolding right outside.

"Something is going on out there," the man who just came in says to the nurse behind the registration desk. "You might want to do something about it."

I see Ander standing directly in front of the doors with his arms fully outstretched, shifting his weight back and forth as he tries to contain the growing group of people gathering on the sidewalk.

The nurse walks out from behind the desk, and the doors slide open as she steps in front of them. I hear the shouting again, and a few more words get to me. The people are clearly furious.

"What's happening?" Carla asks.

I put my hands on her shoulders and gently move her backward further away from the doors.

"Stay here," I say. "I'm going to go find out."

I walk over to the doors and step out into the pool of light illuminating the entrance in the late-night darkness.

"Where is she?" one of the people demands. "She's in there, isn't she?"

"She should be locked up!" another shouts.

"FBI," I call out over the clamor to get their attention. "Someone tell me what's going on here."

"Tracy Ellis should be ashamed of herself," someone says. "This is her fault, and she's trying to get even more notoriety with it."

"All she wants is attention, and it's disgusting."

"What are you talking about?" I ask.

"She went live to announce that someone else in her company was attacked."

"She went live?" I gasp.

"On her social media channel," someone explains. "She was standing in front of the person's house showing the police cars and then announced that she was going to go to the hospital. Then she put up a QR code asking for donations. It's revolting what she's doing."

Rage rushes up inside me, and without another word, I turn and go back into the waiting area. Tracy is standing close to Carla, who looks uncomfortable and keeps glancing over at the door. I stalk up to Tracy, who turns to me just as I get within a couple of steps of her.

"What the hell do you think you're doing making a live post about this attack?" I demand.

"You announced Marshall's attack on a live post?" Carla asks in disbelief. "Who do you think you are?"

"I was gathering prayer warriors to surround you with their light and strength," Tracy says in a cloying tone meant to manipulate Carla into accepting the massive violation.

"What you did was report a crime that had not been released to the public and make speculations you have no right to make," I growl. "You didn't know what happened at that house or who might have been involved. You only assumed that it had something to do with the other attacks and decided that you were going to spread that to whoever would listen, then try to profit off it."

Tracy raises herself to her full height, seemingly unbothered by my obvious fury. "My viewers frequently ask me how they can support the ministry and ensure I can continue to spread the truth and encourage those finding their path. I don't see the problem with providing them that avenue."

"You're going to take down that video," I say.

"I don't have to do anything. I didn't break any laws by talking about something that was visibly happening right in front of the entire neighborhood. Anyone would have the same grave concerns I did when I heard what was happening. I just decided to be proactive about it and let it be known. People deserve to know what's happening," she argues.

"No one deserves to know my business," Carla says. "Including you."

"You're going to take down the video, or Carla will have strong grounds for legal action, which I will actively support," I tell her. "You've already caused enough difficulty."

Tracy glares at me, but she takes out her phone.

"Fine," she says.

As she's deleting the video, I hear the nurse gasp and look up to see the crowd outside erupting into chaos. I run to the door in time to see Ander tackling one of the protestors to the ground. I watch as the man on the ground bucks up to force the security guard off him and plants a punch directly into Ander's face. Ander comes down on him with a return punch, and the man forces him off, shoving him onto his back on the ground.

The rest of the group scatters back as the men grapple on the ground, forcefully shoving each other into the concrete and delivering blows to wherever they can plant their fists.

"Stop it!" I shout.

I push past one of the protestors and reach down to grab the man who has gotten the upper hand again. Getting a handful of the back of his shirt, I wrench him away from Ander and force him to the side. He looks up at me like he's going to lash out at whoever ended the fight, but he stops when he meets my eyes. Ander gets to his feet as the sound of sirens fills the air and two police cars zoom into the parking lot.

Several of the protestors scurry away, but I point directly at the man who was just fighting with Ander.

"Neither of you move," I say.

I stare at Ander, who has the back of one hand pressed to his swelling cheekbone. That fight was completely unnecessary. I don't know what triggered the first blow, but nothing I saw happening when I was outside was enough to cause that kind of reaction.

The same two officers who were here with Carla before Tracy arrived get out of their cars and jog over to us.

"What's going on here?" Massengill asks loudly. He catches my eye. "Agent Griffin. What is this?"

"These people came to protest Tracy Ellis," I tell the officers. "She showed up here not long after you left and apparently had done a live segment on her social media speculating on the attack on Marshall Powell."

"She has to be stopped," one of the protestors says. "She's costing lives."

The officer holds up his hand. "What she says is protected by free speech. She has the right to have whatever opinions and thoughts she wants to have and express them within reason."

"Within reason," the protestor emphasizes.

"If she isn't violating the rules and standards of whatever platform she chooses, then it is within reason," he points out. "Just like you expect to be able to speak out against her, she has the right to speak about whatever she wants to."

"And we have the right to protest it."

"You don't have the right to block the public entrance to a hospital and engage in a physical altercation," he points out.

"I didn't even do anything," the man who fought with Ander insists. "I was just standing there, and all I said was that the murders and attacks are Tracy Ellis's fault. It's her hate and backward thinking that are causing all this. Then all of a sudden, he came at me. I barely even knew what was happening. All I did was defend myself."

I expect Ander to argue, to say something to warrant the apparently unprovoked fight. But he stays silent, brooding as she glares at the officers.

"Ander is Tracy's bodyguard," I explain to the officers.

Massengill gestures at the group. "You all need to leave. Break this up right now. I want you gone."

There are grumbles and mutters of the officers abusing their power and pushing them around, but the group disbands without further incident, and soon it's just Ander and the man he fought standing with the officers giving their statements. I go back into the hospital and walk up to Tracy forcefully.

"You need to leave," I tell her. "You need to go home and keep quiet. Ander is out there talking to the police because he just tried to beat the hell out of one of the protestors. Fortunately, the guy was able to hold his own, but Ander is going to be really lucky if he doesn't get arrested and face charges for it. Carla clearly does not want you here, and you have only made a very difficult situation worse. It's time for you to go."

Tracy looks almost stunned by my words, but she takes a step backward away from Carla.

"I was only trying to help," she says.

Turning on her heel, she walks out of the hospital. I see her pause briefly with the officers and Ander before disappearing into the parking lot.

CHAPTER TWENTY-THREE

I SIGH AND RUN MY FINGERS BACK THROUGH MY HAIR AS I TURN BACK to Carla.

"I'm sorry you're having to deal with all this while you're already facing such a hard situation," I tell her.

"I appreciate you standing up for me," she says. "I'm not exactly in a position right now to do it for myself."

The doors open, and Officer Massengill comes inside.

"Agent Griffin, I wanted to let you know we decided to release both men on their own recognizance. It sounds like this was a mutual combat situation. Ander admits to being the aggressor, but he says he felt provoked, and Mr. Pauley admits to fighting back. They've both agreed to leave the premises without further incident," he says.

"Thank you," I say.

He walks back out of the hospital, and I see Ander heading into the parking lot. Part of me is shocked by his actions, but at the same time, I know he is under a tremendous amount of pressure. He has only just faced the murder of his wife and made the decision to return to work immediately. Whether he thinks it was the right choice for his coping or not, it obviously pushed him past his own control. Lashing out at the protestor was his way of reacting to the intense emotions and turmoil he's going through.

Turning back to Carla, I see her wrap her arms around herself and sway slightly on her feet. She's clearly exhausted.

"What did the doctor say?" I ask her.

"Um," she runs her hand over her face and back over her hair. "He said Marshall likely has internal injuries as well as that his head was hit several times." Her phone rings in her pocket, but she ignores it. "They are going to run some additional tests to see the extent of the damage, but right now they have him sedated and are admitting him. They don't know how long he's going to have to be here."

Her phone rings again, and she pulls it out of her pocket, looks at the screen, then shoves it away without answering.

"You really should go home and get some rest," I tell her. "You're running on pure adrenaline right now, and it's going to run out soon enough. Marshall is in good hands, and they will take care of him. You need to take care of yourself."

"I don't want to leave him."

"I know you don't, but you can't just keep going endlessly after what you've been through. Go home, and get some sleep. Everything will seem clearer in the morning, and you'll be able to come back and get some more answers," I say.

"I guess you're right," she says.

"Do you want me to drive you home?" I ask.

She shakes her head. "No. They wouldn't let me ride in the ambulance with him because they needed to work on him, so I have my car. But thank you. I'll call you tomorrow and let you know what else I find out."

"Thank you," I say. "I'll walk out with you."

She goes to the registration desk to tell the nurse that she's leaving and makes sure they have her contact information so they can get in touch with her if anything changes with Marshall. We walk out into the now-quiet night, and I escort her directly to her car.

"Thank you again," she says.

"I'm glad you called me," I say.

"So am I. I don't know what I would have done without you here with me tonight."

"Get some sleep," I tell her, and she climbs into her car.

I wait until she is pulling away before I cross the lot to where I parked. As I'm approaching, I notice something tucked under my windshield wiper. I take the paper out and unfold it.

Back off the case or you're next

I resist the urge to ball up the note. Instead, I fold it again and head right back inside the hospital. The nurse looks up at me from the desk, and I see her eyes flicker to the doors like she thinks that something else has happened.

"Yes?" she asks.

"I need to speak to someone in security," I tell her. "It's extremely important."

It takes a while of me pacing through the waiting room again for a uniformed security officer to come meet me. His no-nonsense face expresses no emotion as he approaches me.

"Dan Wilder," he introduces without reaching out to shake my hand.

"Agent Emma Griffin," I tell him.

"What can I do for you, Agent?" he asks.

"I need to know if there are security cameras covering the parking lot," I tell him.

"There are cameras," he says. "They don't cover the entirety of the lot, but most of it. Why?"

I show him the paper I found under my windshield.

"I found this when I went out to my car. It is very significant to the case I am currently investigating. One of the victims is currently in this hospital. I need to see if the security cameras picked up who left this on my windshield."

"Come with me," he says.

We go to the security office, and I sit in a stiff-backed chair while he pulls up the footage from the time that I've been in the hospital. I go to his side and lean forward slightly to look at the screen. Images from several cameras fill it in little boxes, creating an almost dizzying black-and-white array.

"I'm parked in front of the emergency room entrance," I tell him, letting him narrow down the options for the cameras. Scanning the screen, I locate the row where I'm parked, but immediately, I notice that only half of my rental car is visible. I point it out. "Right there. Is there another angle that might have gotten more of the car?"

"Just this one," he says, switching to a different camera shot.

I can see part of the vehicle's front now, and we scroll forward until I see a quick movement near the car.

"Stop," I say. "Can you play that again?"

He goes backward a few seconds and plays the footage at regular speed. The movement is at the top corner of the screen, but it clearly looks like someone approaching the car. There's not enough of the figure to get any identifying features, which leaves me frustrated. This person keeps slipping right between my fingers, and it's infuriating.

"Thanks," I tell the guard.

"Sorry I couldn't be more help," he says.

I leave the hospital not at all dissuaded by the note. Rather than going back to Bellamy and Eric's house, I head for the police station. I'm not surprised when I find Detective Fuller there. He's changed clothes, which tells me he either managed to make it home for a little while today or he crashed on a couch somewhere and he keeps a change of clothes at the office the way I've known a lot of detectives do. It's much the same as the duffel bag of emergency essentials I keep stashed in my trunk just in case I find myself needing to stay at an investigation longer than I thought.

"I heard about Marshall Powell," he says when he sees me.

"I just came from the hospital," I say.

"How is he?" the detective asks.

"He's alive. But that's about the extent of what I can say about him. He was put under sedation, and they are running tests to see just how seriously he was injured. He was bludgeoned, just like Sabrina. But he managed to get away just before going unconscious," I tell him. "This needs to be investigated as part of the larger case."

"It is," he assures me. "That's why I'm here. I was finally home trying to relax, and they called me to tell me another of Ellis's employees had been attacked. At least I managed to get a clean shirt."

"Does wonders," I say.

"Yes, it does," he says with a slight laugh.

"What have you found out so far?" I ask. "I had a chance to talk to two of the responding officers at the hospital, but they didn't have much information. It seemed like they went to the hospital at the same time as Carla, so they were only able to tell me about the call to dispatch."

"That's about as far as we've gotten so far," he says. "A canvass of the neighbors didn't get us anything but some footage from a doorbell camera of a figure in dark clothes approaching the house and going around to the back. It's too far away to be able to see any details about the person. That's what we're working with right now."

"Not a lot," I say.

"Not really," he agrees.

"Did anything come through with that fingerprint from the car?" I ask.

"It didn't match anything in the database," he says.

"All right," I say, disappointed but not surprised. "Just give me a call if anything comes through."

"Go get some sleep," he says.

"Doubtful," I call behind me as I walk out and head back to my car.

It's not that I'm not tired. It's been a long day and an even longer night already. It's that I know there's more I need to do before I can even consider laying my head down to rest.

I get in the car and call Ander. It's late, but I highly doubt he would have already been able to get back to the house and sleep after the incident at the hospital.

"Hello?" he answers in a grumbling voice.

"Ander, this is Agent Griffin," I tell him.

"If you're calling about what happened at the hospital…"

"I'm not," I say, cutting him off. "That is what it is. I'm calling because I have a question for you. Gideon's computer had an unfinished email to Tracy Ellis about something going on in the company. There aren't any details, but it's obvious he knew something about a colleague and was going to expose it to her. I asked Tracy about it, and she told me that those kinds of reports are commonplace within the company."

"They are," Ander confirms. "It's part of proving your dedication to the ministry. And if Tracy finds out that you knew something was happening and didn't bring it to her attention, there can be consequences."

"Have you made any kind of report like that recently?" I ask.

"No," he tells me without hesitation. "I haven't turned anyone in for anything in a couple of years. I don't have the opportunity to interact with the other people in the company very much, so I don't get any information like that."

"So it isn't a matter of staying out of people's business, it's just that you don't personally know about these things," I say.

"If that's how you want to see it," he says. "But either way, I can't think of anyone whom I could have possibly offended enough to make them willing to kill my wife. Or anything I could have done. Other than just continuing to work for Tracy."

"Have you considered quitting now?" I ask.

"Of course I have. Being stubborn and keeping this job cost me my wife. I have started looking for something else, but I can't just quit. It's not like Sabrina and I had a ton of savings that I can live off of."

"I understand," I say. "Do you know anything about the email that Gideon was sending?"

"No, he didn't talk to me about anything like that," Ander says.

"All right, thank you. Try to get some rest."

"That's not going to be easy. If Marshall dies…"

"He's alive, Ander. I know he went through a lot, but he's alive. We just need to keep focusing on finding out who is responsible."

I end the call with a knot in my chest. Something is off about everything that happened tonight. I feel unsettled as I pull out of the parking space to start back to the house. I've barely gotten on the road when my phone rings again. I put it on speaker so I can answer it while driving.

"Agent Griffin," I say.

"It's Carla." Her voice is a tight whisper, but it sounds almost as panicked as when she called me earlier. "There's someone in my house."

CHAPTER TWENTY-FOUR

"CARLA? WHAT DO YOU MEAN THERE'S SOMEONE IN YOUR house?" I ask.

"There's someone here," she says. "I heard them come inside."

"Where are you now?" I ask.

"I'm barricaded in the bedroom. I'm so scared," she says.

"Call the police," I tell her. "I'm on my way."

Feeling an intense sense of déjà vu, I change directions and head for the Powell house. The police haven't gotten there by the time I arrive, and I take my gun out of the holster at my hip before climbing out of the car. Looking around carefully, I try to see into the shadowy areas around the house so I can see if anyone has come out or is lurking there being a lookout. I don't see anyone, and I race up the steps to the front door. It's locked, and I pound on it, then ring the bell.

"Carla!" I shout through it. "It's Agent Griffin."

There's no reply, and I run around the side of the house. I immediately notice a side door standing partially open, and I go inside. The door leads to a mudroom and then a laundry area before going out into the main house. I run inside, my gun still poised, calling out for Carla.

"Agent Griffin?" I finally hear her shout from upstairs.

"It's me," I reply, running up the stairs toward her voice.

I see the broken door of the master bedroom to one side and the bloodstained white carpet beyond it, so I turn down the hallway and find a closed door. I knock on it, and Carla opens it just as I hear sirens coming down the street. She's shaking as she cautiously steps out into the hallway. I put my arm around her and walk with her back down the stairs and into the living room.

The police knock on the front door, and I open it with my shield already out. I introduce myself and bring them into the room with Carla. She's curled up in a chair, her knees tucked close to her chest as she rocks slightly, tears falling silently down her face. I crouch down beside her.

"The police are here," I tell her. "Tell us what happened."

She lifts her head and sniffles. "I came home from the hospital and took a shower. I was hungry, so I made something to eat and watched some TV, just trying to unwind from everything. I was so tired, so I went upstairs to go to bed. I couldn't bring myself to go into my bedroom, so I went to the guest room to sleep. I couldn't fall asleep, and I heard the sound of the door opening down here. There's an alarm on the front and back doors, but the one on the side door broke, so it didn't go off. That's how I knew for sure it was the side door. I could hear someone walking through the house toward the steps, and I panicked. I locked the door and screamed that I was calling for help," she says.

"You didn't see anyone?" I ask.

"No," she says. "I didn't leave the room. But I know I heard someone walking down there."

"The side door was standing partially open when I got here," I say. "That's actually how I got inside. Was that door locked when you got home?"

"I'm pretty sure it was," she says. "We don't use it very often. But it's also a really old lock. We've been able to pick it to get inside when we've locked ourselves out before. We meant to replace it but just never thought about it. Maybe that's how whoever attacked Marshall got in tonight." Carla covers her face with her hands. "How could I be so stupid as to not check the locks? Why did I even come back here?"

"You have a lot on your mind," I tell her. "But everything is fine now. We're here. We just need to talk this through. You said you heard someone walking through the house. Did they say anything?"

"No," she says. "I just heard footsteps."

A knock on the front door makes all of us turn. I stand up and go to it. A nervous-looking woman in pajamas and a bathrobe is standing on the porch.

"Can I help you?" I ask.

"I need to talk to the police," she says.

"I'm an FBI agent," I tell her. "What do you need?"

"I saw someone," she says.

"Come in," I say.

We go into the living room where Carla is making her statement to one of the officers. The officer looks up from the notes she's writing and narrows her eyes at the neighbor.

"Bonnie?" Carla says, sounding confused.

"Who is this?" the officer asks.

"Bonnie Klein. She's my next-door neighbor," Carla says. "Bonnie, what are you doing here?"

"I thought I saw something, but I wasn't sure, and then when I saw the police back here, I knew I needed to say something," the shaky woman says. "I saw all the commotion that was happening here earlier tonight, and I didn't know what happened, but it really shook me up."

"Marshall was attacked," Carla says.

Bonnie's hands fly up to cover her mouth. "Oh god. Is he okay?"

"He's in the hospital. I'll know more tomorrow," Carla says.

"I'm so sorry. I was afraid it was something like that since I knew both of you worked for that Tracy Ellis woman and everything that's been happening. But I was hoping it was something else," Bonnie says.

"Please tell us what you saw tonight," I say, trying to move her along.

"I was just too anxious to sleep, so I was up in my sewing room, and I noticed a light go on outside. I looked out and saw that the motion-activated light on the Parrish house had come on."

"That's the neighbors behind me," Carla explains.

"I saw what looked like someone running out of your backyard and in between the houses to the next street over," she says.

It sounds very similar to what the neighbor described seeing after Sabrina Ward's murder.

"Could you see any details about them?" I ask.

"I'm pretty sure it was a man just by the way they moved and their size, but I couldn't really tell you how tall they were or anything. I wasn't able to catch any real details. I'm sorry. Maybe I'm not being as helpful as I thought," she says.

"No, we really appreciate you telling us this," I say. "I'm going to have one of the officers walk you back to your house, and I want you to make sure that all the doors and windows are locked."

She nods, and I look at the second officer, who stands.

Bonnie looks at Carla. "I'm so sorry about Marshall. Please don't hesitate to tell me if there's anything I can do for you. You can just stop by."

"Thank you," Carla says.

They leave, and Carla goes back to making her statement. I sit with her, but my mind is wandering. The events of the night aren't adding up. This situation feels too different from the others, but I don't know what to think of it.

"Do you want to stay here tonight or go somewhere else?" one of the officers asks after Carla finishes providing her formal statement.

"It would probably be best if you went somewhere," I tell her. "Just for your own peace of mind."

She nods. "Yeah, I don't think I'm going to feel safe here for a long time."

"I'll make sure she gets somewhere," I tell the officers. "Make sure that Detective Fuller gets her statement."

They agree and leave. Now that Carla seems calmer, I have the same question for her that I asked Ander earlier.

"It's come up in the investigation that it's expected that everyone who works for Tracy Ellis acts as sort of a watchdog and reports anything against the company's morality standards directly to her," I tell Carla.

"That's true," Carla says. "It's presented as a means of keeping the community close and holding each other accountable, so we're helping each other stay on the path of the truth. Tracy's favorite words."

"And if someone makes a report like that, the person who was turned in can face serious consequences, can't they?" I ask.

"They can be disciplined in a few different ways, all the way up to being fired. That's usually reserved for really egregious things or for people who refuse to accept responsibility for what they've been accused of and won't cooperate with other forms of discipline," she says.

"It sounds like dealing with children," I say.

"Discipline is important for everyone. Maybe even more important for adults than it is for children. How can we expect to raise the next generation of responsible, moral, strong people if they don't have that as their example? Besides, the people who work for Tracy know what they are getting into. They agree from the very beginning to act in a certain way or risk having others expose what they are doing. If they decide to go against those standards, then they should expect to deal with the consequences they were warned about," she says.

She doesn't defend Tracy Ellis's views or teachings, but I reluctantly know she's right about the reports. Regardless of how I feel about people being in a climate where they feel constantly judged and vulnerable to the people around them, fearing they could lose their livelihood for any perceived transgression, it is the reality of the company. No one forces anyone to work for Tracy Ellis. If these adults willingly seek employment by her and agree to the terms she puts forward to them, then they have made that choice for themselves. That doesn't change the impact the policy has.

"That could be a very pressing motive for retaliation," I point out to her.

"I thought that you were investigating this as someone who is acting against the ministry," Carla says, looking alarmed. "Are you saying you think this might be personal?"

"I'm saying I'm looking at the situation from all angles to make sure I don't miss anything. Have you or Marshall reported anyone to Tracy recently?" I ask.

She hesitates, her eyes locked in front of her like she's lost in thought. She jumps slightly as she seems to come back into the moment.

"Oh. I don't think Marshall ever has," she says. "He prefers to stay out of things. Not that I think he's ignored anything serious, but he's never told me about anything that he heard within the company that would warrant being reported…"

Her voice trails off, and I can tell there's something more to the thought.

"But what?" I ask, encouraging her to continue.

"Except for one situation," she says. "And he didn't make the report. I did. One person in a married couple making a report is sufficient for both people, according to Tracy, but it also works the other way. If one spouse knows something and doesn't say anything and the other doesn't either, both can get in trouble. So when he told me he'd heard someone in the outreach department talking about filing for divorce, I knew I had to say something so we wouldn't both have problems."

"Getting divorced is against the morality standards of the company?" I ask.

"Yes. Especially for people who deal directly with the public like the outreach team. They are considered the face of the company, and they are held to even higher expectations by Tracy. Which means happy couples," she says.

"What happened to the person you reported?" I ask.

"They were forced into company-mandated therapy," she says. "And were barred from attending public events with the company until further notice. Which means a major decrease in pay."

"I'm going to need this person's name and contact information," I tell her.

"It's Gloria and Vince Pryor," she says. "I have Gloria's phone number, but that's it."

"That will work," I say. She picks up her phone and goes to the contacts, reading me the number so I can jot it down. "Did this happen recently?"

"About two months ago," she says. "Neither of them works for the company anymore."

"They were fired?" I ask.

"They quit," she says.

"Do you know if they ever worked with Gideon?"

"He would have done security for events that they worked at," she says. "But I don't know for sure how well they knew each other."

"Okay, thank you for that. Let's get you packed for the night and somewhere safe. Where do you want to go?"

"I don't want to disturb anybody at this hour, so I'm just going to go to a hotel," she says.

"I'll escort you there," I tell her.

"Will… will you go upstairs with me while I pack?" she asks. "I don't want to face that room alone."

"Of course."

We go upstairs, and Carla hesitates before stepping into the bedroom. Her eyes drop to the blood on the carpet, and I put a hand on her back to gently guide her past it. She gathers a few things and we leave, making sure all the doors are locked before we go.

I follow Carla to the hotel and wait until she texts me that she is safely in her room before going back to Bellamy and Eric's house. A hot shower later, my head barely hits the pillow before I'm asleep.

CHAPTER TWENTY-FIVE

I GOT BACK TO THE HOUSE SO LATE LAST NIGHT THAT I'VE HAD VERY little sleep when my internal alarm jostles me awake. The sound of Bellamy and Eric downstairs getting ready for the day and the smell of cooking pancakes draw me to the kitchen, where I find Bebe happily playing with a doll and tiny play cookware. I kiss her on the top of the head and make a beeline for the coffeemaker.

"I woke up in the middle of the night and went to get a glass of water and noticed you weren't in your room," Bellamy says. "Where did you go?"

"Marshall Powell, another of Tracy Ellis's employees who got the threats, was attacked," I explain.

"Just attacked?" Eric asks. "He survived?"

"Yes. He's in the hospital and apparently suffered some pretty extensive injuries, but he is alive. He's under sedation, so I haven't been able to talk to him, but I'm really hoping that he'll be able to talk soon and can give me any information on who did this," I say. "I'm going to check on him this morning."

As soon as I'm done with breakfast, I get dressed and head for the hospital. I park at the general entrance and go inside to the information desk. Just as I'm asking about Marshall, the elevator opens, and I see Carla come out. She looks surprised to see me.

"Thank you," I say to the man behind the desk and go toward her.

"Good morning," I say. "How did you sleep?"

"I barely did," she says. "I kept waking up at every little sound. It was terrible. Eventually, I just got up. I was the first person down in the lobby for breakfast. I wanted to get here as soon as I could."

"How is Marshall doing? Are there any updates?" I ask.

"Things are looking better. The scans look good. The doctors are hoping to be able to bring him out of sedation later today or tomorrow depending on how everything goes, and they'll see how he reacts," she tells me.

I smile. "That's great to hear. I know it seems like a lot considering everything he went through, but it's really important that I'm able to talk to him as soon as he is possibly capable of it," I say. "The sooner he gives his statement, the better chance there is that he will remember helpful details."

"I understand," she nods. "I just don't know how much he's going to be able to remember."

"We'll just have to see," I say.

With Marshall still under sedation, there's no point in me going upstairs. Instead, I go back out to my car and dial the number Carla gave me for Gloria Pryor.

"Hello?" she answers with the wary tone of someone who doesn't recognize the number on their phone but isn't the type to just let it go to voicemail.

"Mrs. Pryor?" I ask.

"This is Gloria Pryor," she says. "Who is this?"

"My name is Special Agent Emma Griffin," I say.

"You're the FBI agent investigating the Tracy Ellis Ministry murders," she says before I can finish introducing myself.

I cringe at the media-spun description of the murders, but I push ahead.

"Yes," I say. "I need to speak with you about the investigation. Would you be willing to meet up with me to discuss a few things?"

She agrees and directs me to a coffee shop not too far away. We agree to meet in twenty minutes, and I head directly there. I get iced coffee and choose a table to wait. Sam calls me as I'm sipping the perfectly bitter brew.

"Hey, babe," I say. "Miss you."

"I miss you too," he says. "Where are you?"

"I'm sitting in a coffee shop waiting for a woman I'm interviewing for the case," I tell him. "There was another attack last night, and I found out that the wife of the man who was attacked reported this woman for a morality breach with the company."

"You think that she could have had something to do with it?" he asks.

"I think that it's important to get as many insights as I can. Someone has a reason to kill two people and try to kill two others, and it all seems to be centered on this ministry. But I'm not convinced anymore that there is some activist group targeting the ministry. I think there's something else going on," I explain. "There was something strange about how everything happened last night. Another employee was attacked, and then later there was an intruder at his house. But something was off."

"I'm sure you'll figure it out," Sam says.

His unyielding belief in me makes my chest warm, and I can't help but smile. He often worries about me when I'm out in the field, especially when I'm away from home for a long time, but he knows how important my career is to me. There was a time when I was considering walking away from the Bureau, retiring and settling into a quiet life. But I couldn't make myself do it. I was drawn back to the purpose that brought me into it in the first place. Sam understands, but that doesn't stop his protective nature from wishing I didn't take on dangerous cases and weren't as willing to throw myself into them. I've learned to appreciate both sides.

"The fact that no one is taking credit for the killings is bothering me," I say. "There are the messages on the walls, but there's nothing to link a specific group to any of this. I've had several people tell me that the ministry gets threats all the time, but those are just hate mail. No one has ever acted on it. I feel like that piece is missing. It's like the students on campus told me, it doesn't make any sense to lurk around in the shadows when you are trying to make a point."

"So what's the reason behind the threats?" Sam asks.

"That's where my brain is now," I tell him.

I see a woman walk through the door and look around. Thinking it must be Gloria, I wave, and she comes toward me.

"I have to go," I tell Sam. "I'll call you later. I love you."

I hang up and stand to shake Gloria's hand.

"Mrs. Pryor," I say.

"You can call me Gloria," she says, sitting down at the table.

"Do you want to go order something?" I ask.

She shakes her head firmly. "No. What's this about?"

"I wanted to talk to you about working with Tracy Ellis," I say.

"I don't work for her anymore. My husband and I both quit several weeks ago," she says.

"I know. I'm interested in what led up to that," I say.

She shifts uncomfortably in her seat. "We decided that the company wasn't the right fit for us anymore and decided to pursue other opportunities."

"That's it?" I ask.

"Yes," she says. "We both worked for her for a few years, but it ran its course."

"And how is your relationship with your husband?" I ask.

"My relationship with my husband?" she asks. "It's great. We're very happy. What does that have to do with anything?"

"Gloria, I heard that you were reported to Tracy Ellis for talking about filing for divorce," I say. "Is that true?"

Her face hardens, and spots of color appear on her cheekbones. "Yes."

"And she required you to participate in marriage counseling and restricted your activities within the company," I say.

"Yes." Gloria briefly ducks her head and tents her eyes with one hand. "I can't believe I'm even having this conversation. It's ridiculous that anybody is talking about my relationship and what did or didn't happen between us and the company we used to work for. This doesn't have anything to do with what's happening to the ministry now."

"How did you feel about the disciplinary actions taken against you?" I ask.

"I was embarrassed," she admits. "Just like I think anyone would be. I was angry that someone would report me for saying something really rash during a rough patch in my marriage. I know the guidelines of the company, but I made a flippant comment, and it turned into a massive ordeal. But at the end of the day, I'm grateful that it happened. It was humiliating, and it ended my career, but it really did turn out for the better.

"My husband and I went to a few sessions of the therapy Tracy set up for us before we decided to quit the company. It was actually our time in that therapy that made us realize that we needed the change and that it was time to start fresh together. After we left, we started going to a different counselor, and it has made all the difference in our marriage and our lives. We genuinely are doing great now. There are still hard days, but we're willing to work through it."

"Did you ever get any threatening notes?" I ask.

"No," she says. "I honestly waited for one to show up. I figured it would."

"Why is that?" I ask.

"Because it was very known that we were pretty well disgraced within the company, and I thought the threats sounded like someone who would go after that within the ministry," she says. "But it never happened."

I sift through my notes and pull out the list that Tracy Ellis gave me.

"Do you know if any of these people also faced any kind of discipline after being reported to Tracy?" I ask.

"Grant Pruden," she says. "I don't know what he was reported for, but he was restricted from public events for almost two months. I heard that Mila was also called into Tracy's office a few times to discuss a personal matter, but I never got any more details about it."

Grant Pruden is one of the people I called early in the investigation. The call I got back a couple of days later wasn't very illuminating, but now I have a different perspective. I feel like I've found a thread. I just have to pull it.

"Thank you for meeting with me," I say to Gloria, starting to stand up.

"Can you tell me something?" she asks.

"What?" I ask.

"I heard on the news this morning that Marshall Powell was attacked in his home last night," she says.

"He was," I say.

"Since I'm sure you've interviewed her, can you tell me if it was Carla Powell who reported me to Tracy?" she asks.

"I can't comment on details of the investigation," I say.

This doesn't really fall under that umbrella, but I don't feel like it's my place to disclose the identity of someone who made a report while assuming they would be able to remain anonymous.

She nods, the look on her face saying that even though I didn't confirm it, she knows that's the situation.

"That's interesting," she says.

"What is?" I ask.

"It's interesting that Carla would go around making judgments like that against other people with what I've heard is going on in her marriage," she says.

"What do you mean?" I ask.

She shrugs. "It's all rumors. But I've heard there's a story behind them leaving the company."

CHAPTER TWENTY-SIX

GET A CALL FROM DETECTIVE FULLER AS I'M DRIVING AWAY FROM
the coffee shop asking me to come into the station, so I turn in that
direction. As I'm driving, I call Carla.

"I just spoke with Gloria Pryor," I tell her. "I didn't tell her that you
were the one who reported her to Tracy, but she made the assumption
herself. Then she said she thought it was interesting that you would make
a report like that when there was something going on in your marriage."

"She said what?" Carla asks, sounding stunned.

"Apparently, there were rumors of a story behind why the two of
you were leaving the ministry," I tell her.

"I told you why we decided to leave," she says. "We are moving and
starting a new chapter in our lives. There's no more story to it than that.
It sounds like she's just angry with me for talking about her to Tracy. She
wants to make Marshall and me look bad."

I pull into the police station parking lot and end the call, a prickling
feeling along the back of my neck as something inside tells me that I'm

starting to unravel a little more. I know I have to move faster. The looming weight of something else possibly happening is pressing down on me, reminding me with every passing hour that there are several other people who have received threats. The same horrific scene could play out again if I don't find the person responsible and stop them.

As soon as I walk into the station and find Detective Fuller in the investigation room, I find out I was almost too late.

"A woman named Mila Taylor called dispatch about ten minutes ago reporting that someone broke into her house. She said it needed to be brought to your attention."

"Mila Taylor is one of the employees of the ministry that received threatening notes," I say. "I talked to her right after Gideon was murdered. Is she all right? Was she attacked?"

My heart is racing in my chest as I think of another person falling victim to an assailant who is getting bolder and leaving less time in between his strikes.

"No, she wasn't home when it happened. Do you want her address?"

"Yes."

I'm out the door in seconds, already driving as I program my GPS. The directions bring me to a small apartment complex not too far from the ministry headquarters. I see two police cars parked near the apartment number Fuller gave me, and I jog up to the door. I knock, and Officer Massengill answers.

"Agent Griffin," he says. "I thought I might see you here."

"Where is Mila?" I ask.

He lets me into the apartment, and I immediately see the stark block letters across the living room wall.

You won't be spared again

A frightened-looking woman is sitting on the beige corduroy couch, hunched over so her stomach is pressed to her knees and her arms are wrapped around herself defensively. Officer Trammel is sitting beside her with a notepad. They both look up when I approach.

"I'm Agent Griffin," I tell her. "We spoke on the phone."

"They came for me," she says.

"Tell me what happened," I say.

"I took the day off work because I wasn't feeling well this morning. But then I started feeling better, so when my sister called wanting me to go shopping with her, I decided to go. She picked me up. I was gone for less than three hours, and when I got back, my door had been pried open, and I saw that written on the wall," she says.

"Who knew that you were supposed to be home today?" I ask.

"Anyone who looked at my social media," Mila says. "I posted there this morning. Someone saw it and thought I was going to be here. They probably even saw my car in the parking lot." She lets out a shuddering breath. "I could have been killed."

"Is there anywhere you can stay for a few days?" I ask.

She nods. "I've already called my sister. I'm going to stay with her."

"Good," I say. "While the officers are still here, I'm going to go talk to your neighbors, but then I'll stay with you until your sister comes."

"Thank you."

I leave the apartment and cross the breezeway. No one answers the door, and I move on to the one beside it. Again there is no answer. I'm about to walk away from the final door when a man comes up the steps and gives me a questioning look.

"Can I help you?" he asks.

I point at the door. "Is this your apartment?" I ask.

"It is," he says.

"Have you been away all day?" I ask.

"Since early this morning," he says. "Are you police?"

"FBI," I tell him. "But you did see police cars in the parking lot. They are in that apartment." I point to Mila's door.

"Did something happen to Mila?" he asks.

"No, she's safe. But there was a break-in at her apartment just a little while ago. I wasn't able to get any answer at the other apartments on this floor. Do you know if they would be home right now?" I ask.

"I doubt it. They aren't ever home during the day. What happened at Mila's place? Who broke in?" he asks.

"That's what I'm trying to find out. Have you seen anything unusual recently around her apartment or the building? Any cars that you didn't recognize?" I ask.

"I wouldn't really know a strange car from somebody's guest," he says. "But come to think of it, I did see someone a few days ago who I didn't recognize. They were walking around behind the building, kind of looking around. I was up here, so I didn't get the best look at them. It could have just as easily been someone visiting somebody in the building or maybe someone who just moved in. I just got a strange feeling from them though."

"I know you say you didn't get a good look at them, but is there anything about them that you can remember?" I ask.

"Their head was down, and they were wearing a hat," he says, "but I saw some blond hair sticking out from the bottom of the hat. I didn't see their face from the front, but I'm sure it was a man."

"Thank you," I say.

Going back into Mila's apartment, I don't see her sitting on the couch. Officer Massengill nods toward the back of the apartment.

"She's in her bedroom getting some things together for when her sister gets here," he says. He steps closer to me and lowers his voice, saying, "This is the same person as the others, isn't it?"

"It looks like it," I say. "It seems like they thought they were going to catch Mila at home, and when she wasn't here, they issued another threat."

Mila comes back into the room with her bags and sets them on the floor next to the door. She looks at the evidence of it being forced open and shudders.

"I called the superintendent, and he's going to make sure the door gets fixed while I'm gone. But I don't know if I will ever be able to feel safe here again," she says.

It's the exact same sentiment as Carla's, and the words sit heavily in my chest.

The officers get another call and have to leave, but I stay with Mila for a short while longer until she gets a text saying her sister is waiting downstairs. The crew has already arrived to fix her door, so she's able to leave without worrying that her home is just sitting open. I walk her downstairs, and her sister comes running up to throw her arms around Mila, hugging her tight.

"I'm so glad you're okay," she says. "This is scaring the hell out of me."

"Me too," Mila admits. She steps back from her sister and looks at me. "Are you going to be at the memorial tonight?"

"What memorial?" I ask.

"Tracy is hosting a gathering tonight at the headquarters. She wants to give everybody a place to feel united and pay respects to the victims. Gideon didn't even have a funeral, and Ander said the services for Sabrina would be out of state with her family. So we're doing this," she says. "It's at five."

"I'll be there," I say.

The timing of the gathering means that most of the people in attendance have come straight down from the offices to the large conference room. They're still in work clothes, clutching their travel coffee mugs and totes, looking more like they are going to happy hour than to a memorial for two murder victims.

Large pictures of Gideon and Sabrina flank a podium at the front of the room. Several people are gathered around the pictures, huddling together as they speak in hushed tones. I notice some wiping away tears. I take my position at the back of the room. I'm here to observe. I want to see how people are reacting to the situation as it has unfolded. Mila walks in with her sister, and I nod a greeting to her.

A few minutes after I arrive, Tracy and Ander walk into the room. He stands to the side of the podium, and even from the distance, I can see the remnants of the brawl at the hospital on his face. He shifts his weight on his feet, looking around the room like he's not sure if he's here as security or as a grieving husband. His eyes go to the picture of Sabrina, and for an instant, his head hangs. A few people walk over to him, squeezing him on the arm and leaning their heads close to speak to him. He offers weak smiles, and I can see on his face he wishes they would leave him alone.

Tracy stands behind the podium and swings her gaze over everyone who has gathered in the room.

"Good evening, everyone," she says. "Thank you so much for coming tonight. I know that you could have gone home after you got off work, but you chose to stay and show your solidarity with the rest of the community, and that means so much. We are coming through a very difficult week. There has been another murder. Though Sabrina Ward didn't work for the ministry, her husband has been an integral part of my security team for several years, and I had the pleasure of meeting Sabrina on several occasions. She was a beautiful, caring woman who shone with truth and commitment. I know life will never be the same for Ander, and I ask that you be there for him as he finds his new way.

"In addition to her death, there has also been a brutal attack. You've already heard that Marshall Powell was assaulted in his home but mercifully survived. I can tell you, there were forces more powerful than us watching over him. Keep lifting him up in your hearts as he works toward healing.

"But even as we grapple with these unfathomable events, we can't forget to look around us and see what else is happening right in our midst. As I've struggled this week to come to terms with the evil that has befallen us, I've also had to sit by as several members of our ministry family chose to walk away. The fear affected them so deeply they couldn't withstand it any longer and decided to leave. I've also just learned that the group who had previously welcomed me to speak in a couple of days' time has decided to cancel my appearance. They believe it could put those who come to hear me in danger and don't want to risk anything happening.

"There is a great sense of loss surrounding us. I mourn, but I am also angry. And I ask you why I shouldn't be. If you think that anger doesn't have its place in this moment, then you aren't understanding what is truly happening. Lives have been horrifically cut short, people have been cast off their paths to truth, and I have been told to stay quiet. But I won't be silenced. For all of the victims, I will keep going. This will only make my message stronger. I will come through this, we will all come through this, more powerful than before."

CHAPTER TWENTY-SEVEN

L ISTENING TO TRACY ELLIS SPEAK, FOR THE FIRST TIME I FEEL LIKE I may believe in something that she's saying. She's right. Now is the time to feel angry. She might be thinking largely of herself and the impact this is having on her ministry, an impact that goes against what she initially thought it was going to do for her, but the sentiment is there. People are nodding their heads, expressing their own fury at the brutality and torment being doled out around them with seemingly nothing they can do about it.

Those who have been on the receiving end of the threats look afraid, wondering if they're going to be next. Those who didn't get the notes are on edge, waiting for the next horror to come. They're grappling with whether to stay at their jobs, wondering what is going to come of the company they've devoted themselves to. The energy in the room is heavy but tingling, full of tightly wound anticipation that feels ready to snap again at any second.

Tracy finishes talking and steps down from the podium so she can mill around among the people gathered in the room. I make my way over to Ander. Another employee is standing with him, offering his condolences, and Ander thanks him, patting him on the shoulder as he walks away before turning his attention to me.

"How are you doing, Ander?" I ask.

"You know, I don't even know how to answer that question anymore," he mutters.

"I'm sorry," I say.

He shakes his head. "No, it's not your fault. I just honestly don't know how I'm doing. It feels like maybe the big reality of it all hasn't actually hit me yet. Going back to work so fast and everything, I haven't taken the time to just sit with it and realize what it means. There have been a couple of times when I've checked my phone to see if she's texted me or I've thought to call her and see what we're having for dinner. Just those little things that you do a hundred times a day and don't think about."

"I know what you mean," I say.

"I know it's going to all come down on me eventually. I'm just waiting for that moment to come. I decided to go back to the house. It was good to stay with Mom for a couple of days, but I can't hide forever," he says. "A couple of friends got things cleaned up for me, so I didn't have to face any of that when I got back."

"I'm glad to hear that," I say. I point to his bruised face. "How is all that feeling?"

He touches his fingertips to the injuries. "Not too bad. It looks worse than it is."

"Ander?" Tracy calls from across the room.

"Excuse me," he says.

I watch him walk toward her and notice a slight hitch in his step like he's stiff and sore. Mila comes over to me as I'm starting to walk toward the exit, deciding to leave them to their memorial without my interference.

"Hi, Mila," I say. "How are you?"

It's not as loaded a question as it was when I asked Ander, but it still hangs in the air between us.

She nods and gives a half shrug. "Still shaken up, but I'm feeling better. It's going to be good to be with my sister for a couple of days so I don't have to feel completely freaked out all the time."

"I think she should just move in with me," her sister says, looking at Mila through the side of her eyes. "She doesn't need to go back there and feel like she's not safe in her own home."

"I have to go back eventually," Mila says.

"No, you don't. You're never going to be able to walk into that place and not think about what you felt like when you saw the door broken and the message written on the wall. It's always going to be there for you, and I don't want you to have to face it. You should just stay with me and find a new apartment when you're ready."

"Maybe I will," Mila says. She looks back at me. "I wanted to know if you found out anything else. I know you talked to some neighbors and stuff. Did anyone see anything?"

"I actually only got a chance to talk to one of your neighbors. The other two on the floor weren't home. But your next-door neighbor got there while I was at his door. He told me that he saw someone he didn't recognize walking around the back of the building a few days ago. He didn't get a good look at them, but he said it was a man with long blond hair wearing a baseball cap. Did you see anyone like that?" I ask.

She purses her lips as she thinks. "I didn't see anybody behind the building, but I did see someone driving really slowly past the building a couple of times. I noticed it because I was out getting the mail. The box is at the end of the block, so I was seeing it from a distance. I watched them go by really slowly and look like they were pulling out of the complex, then come back around and drive by again. I didn't really think much of it because it looked like someone who was lost and just couldn't find the right building, but now it seems strange."

"Can you describe the car?" I ask.

"I don't really know anything about cars, so I can't give you a make or model or anything. It was dark blue. Not a truck or van. Just a normal-sized car. Not in great condition, looked older," she says.

That sounds very familiar.

"Do you remember what day you saw it? Was it near when Sabrina Ward was killed?" I ask.

"Come to think of it, I think it was that day. Because I remember watching the news and finding out that she'd been murdered," she says. "Does that mean something?"

"It might," I tell her.

It sounds very much like the same rental car that dropped the note off at Ander's house came by the apartment to scope it out, and the mysterious man in the blond wig walked around the apartment building to get a better view, meaning the attempted attack on Mila might have happened on that particular day because she was home from work, but it was planned well ahead of time.

As I'm leaving the memorial, I get a text message from Carla. She lets me know that the doctors think that Marshall is responding well to his treatments and that they are planning on gradually taking him off sedation starting this evening. She tells me they say he should be ready to talk to me tomorrow morning if all goes well. That's great news, and I message back that I'll see her in the morning.

I've barely had the chance to get to my car when my phone rings. It's Detective Fuller.

"Hey, Detective," I say, pinning the phone between my ear and my shoulder as I get into the car.

"Are you busy right now?" he asks.

"I'm actually just leaving a memorial Tracy Ellis is holding at her headquarters. It turns out her belief that her zeal and fortitude during all this was going to rain down extra rewards on her isn't quite turning out that way. Several more people have quit the company, and the appearance she was getting ready for was canceled. She's not handling it particularly well," I tell him. "Why? Do you need something?"

"There's someone up here at the station who wants to talk to you. She says she has some information she thinks might be valuable to the case," he says. "Can you come talk to her?"

"Sure," I say. "Do you have any idea what it's about?" I'd like to know what I'm getting myself into before I go.

"Not specifically. She just said she has some information that she wants to share about one of the people involved in the case. She wanted to speak directly to you, so I have her waiting in one of the conference rooms just in case you were able to get here," he says.

"Yeah, I can come. Just tell her to sit tight. I'm on my way. It shouldn't be more than about ten minutes," I say.

I toss my phone into the passenger seat and head for the police department, wondering what this person could know that would have to do with the investigation. So much has been spread out through the media coverage, but there are also details that I've managed to keep close to the case, giving me some leverage if there's a question about whether this person is being authentic with what they have to offer.

Getting to the station, I grab my notepad so I can jot down anything that could be of value and go inside. Detective Fuller meets me in the lobby and brings me back to the conference room.

I'm intrigued by the well-dressed woman sitting at the table with her legs crossed, her manicured nails deftly typing on the tiny keyboard of a tablet she has propped on the table in front of her.

"Mrs. Harris?" Fuller says.

The woman looks up, and I extend my hand to her.

"I'm Agent Emma Griffin," I say.

"Caroline Harris," she says. "Thank you for coming out here to meet with me."

"Of course," I say. "Detective Fuller tells me you think you might have information that could be useful for the investigation?"

"I'll leave the two of you to it," the detective says and backs out of the room, closing the door behind him.

"I do," she says. "And I appreciate your understanding that I wanted to speak directly to you rather than to the detective. This information is fairly sensitive in nature, and I'm hoping you'll be able to treat it with discretion."

"I will do my best to respect your privacy, but I can't promise that whatever you tell me won't come out during the course of the investigation if it really does have significance. It might end up being discussed in open court. You need to understand that."

She nods with a slight sigh. "I figured that is what you would say. I really hesitated to come forward to talk to you because I didn't want to be dragged into anything, but I decided I couldn't just sit by and not say anything. It might mean nothing. I might be dredging all this up for no benefit, and it's going to turn around and bite me in the ass, but I'd rather risk that than think that I could have made some kind of difference."

"What is it that you need to tell me?" I ask.

"Ander Ward isn't the person you think he is."

CHAPTER TWENTY-EIGHT

T HE WORDS ECHO IN MY HEAD.

The woman sitting in front of me doesn't look flustered or upset. She's perfectly calm and put together, making me even more interested in what she has to say.

"All right," I say. "What do you mean by that?"

"I've been following this case really closely and watching all of the news coverage of his wife's murder. He's being presented as this devastated widow grieving the loss of his beloved wife. And then the neighbor said that Sabrina Ward was pregnant when she was killed and how that made the whole situation so much sadder because they would have made such a beautiful family," she says.

"Yes," I say. "You have reason to believe that isn't true?"

"Very much so," she says.

"What is it?" I ask.

"I was sleeping with him. And I'm probably not the only one," Caroline says.

"You were having an affair with Ander Ward?" I ask.

"I preferred not to call it an affair. I think of an affair as a relationship that involves feelings and a deeper connection. That's not what was going on between us. It was sex, plain and simple. But that's not the most important part. Ander and I met on Secret Keepers," she says.

"What's that?" I ask.

"It's a website designed to help married people who are looking for something casual with other people to find each other and connect," she says.

I take a second to let that sink in, churning over every interaction I've had with Ander in my head and seeing every second of it differently now.

"Ander Ward was on an adultery site?" I ask.

"Was and very likely still is." She leans toward me. "Look, I'm a married woman. I've been with my husband for almost twenty years. We have two teenage children. I have a career. A big life. It isn't like I just woke up one day and decided I was going to start cheating on my husband. Whatever you might think of me or what I'm doing, I do love him. I want to be married to him. But things just started getting extremely predictable and routine.

"Everything in our life was prescribed down to the minute, it felt like. What we ate. Where we spent our leisure time. The shows we watched in the evening together. Everything. My husband is perfectly fine with that. He likes the routine and feeling like everything is settled. We talked about it over and over, and he always said that's just what being grown-up and married is all about. You figure out what works for you, and you stick with it.

"That just wasn't enough for me. I needed more excitement and adventure in my life. I needed to feel that thrill of being desired. Really desired. I didn't need more romance or affection. My husband is a very caring man who makes sure I know he loves me. He's just not been willing to try anything new or go outside of our little rhythm that we've established. I never thought about starting up a relationship with anyone else. It's not like I have flings with people at work or anything like that. But I heard about Secret Keepers, and it stuck with me. I didn't just jump on it. It took a few months for me to even look at it and then even longer for me to make a profile. I just wanted to get back that feeling of being really alive."

"How long after you joined did you meet Ander Ward?" I ask.

"He was one of the first connections I made. I saw his picture and thought he was really attractive, so I sent him a connection request, and he accepted it. We started talking on the site, and it all went from there," she says. "I didn't come to tell you this just because he was cheating on his wife. It's more than that. The site has you fill out a questionnaire with all kinds of details about who you are, your lifestyle, what you're looking for. That kind of thing. It just ensures you connect with other like-minded people and minimizes the chances of things going wrong."

"And I imagine the risk of that is very high with something like that," I say.

Caroline nods. "That's part of the reason I was so drawn to the idea of a site specifically dedicated to married people wanting discreet, casual connections. I've heard plenty of horror stories of people starting affairs with people they've met in bars or other places online turning into obsessive stalker situations because one person ends up wanting much more than the other. I didn't want anything to do with that.

"The site makes sure that everything is laid out clearly, so you know what you're signing yourself up for when you make connections with people. Ander's profile described him being bored in his marriage and feeling trapped, like he had gotten himself tangled up in a net when he was too young to recognize it and now can't cut himself out of it. And he was extremely blunt and upfront with the fact that he does not and will not ever want children. That was actually something we talked about when we first started communicating. He said he couldn't fathom why anyone would want children, and it was something he and his wife agreed on before they got married. They weren't ever going to have them."

"But he never did anything about it? He never got a vasectomy to make sure?" I ask.

"He said he wasn't interested in getting surgery. It was too invasive, and he was worried about the potential side effects. So it was all on his wife. She had an IUD. There's no way he's in deep mourning for a possible baby," she says.

I'm stunned by the revelations and feel a hot ball of anger building in my belly.

"When was the last time you met up with Ander?" I ask.

"It was several weeks ago," she says. "We'd kind of cooled things off. It wasn't as exciting anymore."

"Did it end on a negative note?" I ask.

"Not at all. Again, we didn't have feelings for each other. There was nothing deep or meaningful about what was going on between us. We liked talking to each other, met up sometimes for sex, and then it was done. It's that simple," she says.

"Would you be willing to show me the communication between the two of you on the site?" I ask.

"Sure," she says. "I can pull it up on my tablet."

It takes her a few seconds to get the site open, then she turns the screen toward me. I'm faced with a message thread between her and Ander that leaves absolutely nothing to the imagination. Within the first couple of exchanges between the two, the intention is obvious, and there's no question as the communication continues about what is going on. Bold details about their liaisons lay bare a torrid relationship happening completely unbeknownst to the unsuspecting Sabrina Ward.

"Can you show me his profile?" I ask after getting my fill of the salacious conversation.

She clicks a few commands, and the screen fills with several images of Ander as well as a descriptive bio and the answers to several prying questions. If it wasn't for the fact that this woman had met up with Ander in person on multiple occasions, I would be tempted to think that this was all crafted by someone else. It's so completely against everything that Ander presented himself as being.

"I really appreciate you coming forward with this," I tell Caroline.

We stand up, and she shakes my hand again.

She lets out a heavy sigh. "I guess it's time to go home and talk to my husband," she says. "I don't want him to find out about this for the first time on the news."

"I'm going to do my best to keep it discreet for as long as possible," I tell her. "But it's a good idea to tell him. Thank you again."

She leaves, and Detective Fuller comes into the room. The look in his eyes tells me he was watching the entire interaction on the feed from the camera mounted in the corner of the room.

"Did she just tell you that she's been sleeping with Ander Ward, the pious security guard wracked with grief over the loss of his pregnant wife?" he asks.

"That would be what she said," I tell him. "And by the messages I just read between them, she's not exaggerating. I think I need to go have a chat with him."

"I wanted to let you know that I put in a request for Marshall Powell's phone records. They said we should be getting them possibly tomorrow."

"Great, thank you," I say.

I call Ander from the car.

"I need to talk to you," I tell him. "Are you still at the memorial?"

"No, I'm at my house. What's wrong?" he asks.

"I'll be there in fifteen minutes."

Ander's eyebrows are knit together, his expression concerned, when he opens the door to me at his house. There's still a lingering smell of industrial-strength cleaners in the air, and I can see the damage to the paint on the wall where the permanent marker was scrubbed away. We walk into the living room where I sat with him and Sabrina as I interviewed them about Gideon, and I feel a tightness in my chest.

"Do you want to sit down?" he asks.

"Not particularly," I say. "When were you planning on starting to be honest with me?"

He looks confused as he lowers himself into his chair. "What do you mean? I have been honest with you."

"No, you haven't. Do the words 'Secret Keepers' mean anything to you?" I ask.

He looks stunned for a second, then his head drops into his hands. "Shit."

"Strong word for someone so committed to the ministry and the way of the truth," I say. "Of course, that's nothing compared to what was going on through that website, is it? And before you try to twist and concoct anything, I have already seen it and know the details. So please don't waste my time by pretending to not know what I'm talking about."

Ander lifts his head. "I'm not going to. I'm just so embarrassed."

"I'm sure you are. And you should be. But that's really not what you should be worried about right now. Your wife, who was carrying your child, was murdered, and you've been maintaining a profile talking about how trapped you felt in your marriage to her and that you never wanted children. That you agreed to that before you got married and couldn't even imagine ever wanting them. Do you understand how that looks?" I ask.

His face goes red, and he jumps to his feet.

"Agent Griffin, I admit I was doing something horrible. I went behind my wife's back, and I sinned against her. I broke my marriage vows and violated the trust that she put in me from the day we met. I can't deny that, and I'm going to have to live with that for the rest of my life. But I didn't know she was pregnant until I saw it on the news. She must have told Annette, but she never told me. I said things on that site that I am not proud of, and I can't change them, but you can't possibly think that I killed Sabrina. I would never be able to do something like that.

"I was on that site for entertainment. It was a wrong decision, and I own that. We got into a slump, and I just wanted to feel that rush again.

But even if you don't believe me about that, you have to remember that I was at my mother's house when she was killed. There are probably a dozen police officers, firefighters, and neighbors who can tell you that. I was unfaithful to my wife, but I didn't murder her. I would have no reason to."

CHAPTER TWENTY-NINE

W ITH NOTHING LEFT TO SAY TO ANDER, I GO BACK TO BELLAMY
and Eric's house. I take out all my notes and spread them out on
the coffee table in the living room so I can look over them.

"Wow," Bellamy says, coming into the room with a cup of tea. "I
wish I had a piece of butcher paper and a wall to offer you."

"That would be great," I tell her. "I've got to figure out a way to make
those transportable."

This process really would be easier if I was at home and could plaster the wall with a giant piece of paper like I usually do during investigations. There's a lot to be said for being able to step back and look at all the notes and webs at the same time. Sometimes something doesn't occur to me until I see it right up there in front of me. But since I can't do that here, I'm resigned to having everything as spread out on the table as I can and rereading everything until it feels like I could recite them verbatim.

I'm driving myself crazy going over everything about Sabrina Ward's death, trying to find anything to answer the suspicion crawling up the back of my neck. I know Ander has a strong alibi. He wasn't exaggerating when he said there were at least a dozen people who could vouch for his whereabouts at the time his wife was murdered. And because of the fitness tracker I pointed out to Detective Fuller at the crime scene, we know the exact moment when her heart stopped beating—a moment when Ander couldn't possibly have been in the house with her.

I can't stop thinking about the adultery website and the double life Ander was living. Just because he was cheating on his wife obviously doesn't make him a killer, but the extent of the lies and depth of the betrayal to not just Sabrina but everyone who looked at him as a pinnacle of what the ministry stands for has my fingertips tingling.

"It wasn't just her," I mutter.

"What?" Bellamy asks. She settles into a recliner, coiling her legs under her and bobbing the tea bag in her mug as she eyes me with a curious expression.

"Oh, I was just thinking about Sabrina Ward's murder. Her husband has an airtight alibi. He was literally standing there with law enforcement a whole town over at the moment his wife was killed. But he was living this whole double life that was so far removed from everything he pretended to believe before and even after she was killed. Something about that whole situation is really bothering me. But then I have to remind myself that she's not the only victim. She's not even the first victim. Gideon Bell was murdered and Jesse Kristoff was attacked days before she was killed, and the threats had been going out long before that. And then there was Marshall."

I stop myself as I'm looking at the notes I took about my conversation with Marshall and then later after his attack.

"And his wife, Carla." I look at Bellamy. "They were both supposed to be home at a given time and weren't unexpectedly, and in that time, their spouses were attacked. Sabrina was killed, and Marshall barely survived."

"You think something might have been going on between the two of them?" she asks.

"Ander was active on a website for married people looking to cheat on their spouses. It's not that far of a leap to think that he possibly brought that inclination into the real world and was having an affair with Carla," I say.

Even as I say it, the unfolding thought isn't fully sitting right with me.

"But I don't know how that could have worked out. I saw Sabrina's body and the damage done to her. I highly doubt a woman Carla's size could have done that to her. And when Carla's apartment was broken into, she seemed genuinely terrified."

I brush my hand back over my hair and push a breath through my lips.

"I'm going up to the hospital in the morning to see if I can talk to Marshall. I'll have to talk to him about this."

Bellamy stands up and hands me the mug. "Here, you take this. I'm going to make another cup. We're going to ignore everything on the table for an hour and watch some TV that requires absolutely no thought. How does that sound?"

"Wonderful," I tell her.

She walks out of the room, and my eyes drop back to the notes on the table. There's something here. Something that links Gideon's murder, Jesse's attack, and the attempted attack on Mila to Sabrina and Marshall. I keep going over everything until Bellamy is back and she turns my attention to the TV.

Even as we're laughing our way through the show, my mind is still racing. I have to figure this out. The threat to Mila written on her wall wasn't hollow. There could be more bloodshed if I don't bring this to a close.

The next morning I call Carla as I'm drinking my coffee.

"How is everything going with Marshall?" I ask, not giving away any of my thoughts from last night.

"He woke up and is doing really well," she tells me, sounding relieved. "I told him that you want to talk to him, and he said that he's ready to talk whenever you want to come to the hospital."

"That's great to hear," I say. "I'm going to get ready and make my way over there. It shouldn't be more than an hour. Will you still be there?"

"Yes," she says.

"Good. I need to talk to you," I say.

There's a beat of silence on the other end of the line.

"Did you find out something?" she asks.

"I'd rather talk to you about this in person. I'll be there soon," I say.

I get off the phone and finish my coffee before having a quick break-fast and getting dressed. The drive has become familiar, and I find myself in the hospital lot without even thinking about it. With the threatening note I found on my windshield in my mind, I park closer to the entrance to the hospital and go inside. The elevator brings me up to the floor where Marshall's room is, and when the doors open, I see Carla standing in a small room set aside for families to wait. She's on the phone, her head tucked down as she talks in hushed tones. She looks up when the doors ding open.

"I have to go," she says. "I'll call you back. Bye."

She ends the call and holds the phone up as she walks out of the room.

"Updating Marshall's family on how he's doing. They wanted to come out here, but they couldn't make it work out. They're going to come next week though, so they can be with him when he's at home."

"That's good," I say. "Even if he's recovering well, the support will mean a lot to him."

She gestures toward the hallway. "I can show you to his room."

"Actually, I want to talk to you first," I say.

"All right," she says hesitantly.

"It would be best if we were somewhere private," I say. "Let's go back in here."

I walk into the small room, and she comes in after me. There's no door to close, but at least we're alone in here.

"I need you to be honest with me about something very important," I say.

She nods. "Of course. What is it?"

"What is the nature of the relationship between you and Ander Ward?" I ask.

Her mouth falls open slightly. "Me and Ander? I know him from work. We've done a few double dates and hung out during work events and things."

"And that's it? There's nothing else going on between the two of you?" I ask. "And there never has been in the past?"

"I can't believe you're even asking me that," she says. "Is this because we've been talking on the phone recently? We've both just been through something horrific. You ever heard of trauma bonding? That's exactly what it is. He called me after Marshall was attacked to see how I was doing. It was comforting talking to someone I knew about it because I'm having to be the strong one here for Marshall by myself. Our fami-lies aren't here. Our friends have stopped by, but everybody is so afraid because of the whole situation that they don't want to hang around me. It's like I'm cursed. But Ander has been someone to talk to about what I'm going through, and I've been letting him vent."

"What were you doing the morning that Sabrina Ward was killed?" I ask.

"Are you serious right now?" she asks.

"I am," I tell her. "I'm digging into everyone who was anywhere near these murders, so you aren't unique. But I need to know all the connections, and that means I need to know where you were."

"That morning I baked a couple of loaves of bread for a bake sale at our church. Then I went to a morning yoga class with, oh, I don't know, about twenty-five other women. If you don't want to believe them, the classes are live streamed, and you can access replays of them on the school's social media. I was at the front of the class with a bright-pink mat. I'm sure you'd be able to see me," she says. "Hopefully, that's good enough for you. Now, are you here to talk to my husband or to accuse me of being an accomplice to murder?"

She whisks out of the room visibly offended and upset as I follow her to Marshall's room. Her reaction doesn't bother me. I don't have the luxury of time or delicacy when it comes to investigating these murders. What matters is finding who is responsible and stopping any other killings or attacks.

Carla forces on a smile before stepping into the room.

"Hey, honey," she says as I walk in after her. "I just talked to your sister. She says your parents are going to be here on Wednesday. She'll be here Friday."

"They don't need to do that," he says. "I don't want them going out of their way just to come here and see me like this."

Carla leans over and kisses her husband on the forehead. "They love you and are worried about you. They want to make sure that you're all right and be here for you while you're recovering. Besides, maybe we can rope them into helping with some packing while they're here."

He chuckles, but it looks painful. His head is still bandaged, and one eye is swollen shut. I can see bruising along one arm, and I imagine there are many other injuries I can't see.

"Hey, Marshall," I say, stepping further into the room.

"Hi, Agent Griffin," he says. "How's it going?"

"I'm the one who should be asking you that," I point out. "How are you feeling?"

"Not the best I ever have, but I'm alive. I'm glad for that," he says.

"I am too," I tell him. "I'm not going to stay here for too long. I know you need your rest."

"Stay for as long as you need to," he says. "I want to find out who did this. I managed to survive, but Gideon and Sabrina didn't. I want to see the guy pay."

"So do I. I need you to tell me everything that happened that night. Everything you can remember."

"All right. Well, Carla and I were at home. We were planning on having just a night in, but then she got a call that she needed to help with an event she's organizing for her charity work. I was disappointed because it was already getting kind of late in the evening, and I was really looking forward to just spending some time with her. But I knew how important the event was to her, and I could hear how frantic Sarah was on the phone, so I knew she needed to go.

"She told me not to watch the show ahead, so I switched over to something else. I haven't been sleeping very well with everything that's been going on, so I was tired and ended up nodding off on the couch. I woke up to someone hitting me with something. I don't know what it was, but it was hard. The rest is kind of a blur. I know I managed to get off the couch, and I tried to fight back, but I had taken my contacts out, and my glasses were knocked off when he first hit me. I could barely see, and I was disoriented from the first blow. He got some good hits in, but I know I came in contact with him a couple of times too. I managed to grab a knife from the kitchen and got him in the leg. He hit me again and knocked the knife out of my hand.

"I can't believe I'm saying this because it sounds so ridiculous, but I hit him with a skillet and managed to get away from him. I had my phone in my pocket and called 911 while I was trying to get up the stairs. He caught up with me and hit me a couple more times. I don't remember anything after being about halfway up the steps. The next thing I knew, I was waking up here. They told me I managed to somehow make it to the bedroom and lock myself in there. Then I passed out."

"I don't understand why you didn't just run out of the house," Carla says.

"You know how when you're watching a horror movie and you're yelling at the characters because they're doing stupid things, thinking you would never do something like that?" he asks. "You do them. That's the only thing I can say. I don't know what I was thinking at that moment. Something just told me to go upstairs."

"You never know how you are going to react to a situation until you are actually in it," I say. "You might think you know exactly what you would do, but people always surprise themselves. All that matters is you survived. What can you tell me about your assailant?"

"Not much. It was definitely a man. He was wearing a black ski mask and gloves. Long sleeves. He was totally covered. The lights were off in the house, so the only light was coming from the TV, and I remember thinking he looked like a shadow," Marshall says.

"Did he say anything to you?" I ask.

"Not to me. When I was on the phone, I heard him yell for Carla. I was so glad she wasn't home," he says.

"Did you recognize the voice? Was there anything about it that stood out to you?" I ask.

"I didn't recognize it. It sounded deep and gravelly, almost like the guy was trying to force it to sound intimidating."

"Like it wasn't his real voice?" I ask.

"Or just that he was trying to make it sound bigger and more aggressive than it actually is," he says.

"I'm so sorry I wasn't there," Carla says, taking his hand. "I wish I had been there."

"I'm so glad you weren't," he repeats. "If he was coming after you, I'd much rather it have been me. I'm just sorry there isn't more I can remember."

"You did great," I say. "Thank you for talking to me."

CHAPTER THIRTY

LEAVE THE HOSPITAL AND GO TO THE POLICE STATION. DETECTIVE Fuller is in the conference room and looks up at me in surprise when I walk in.

"Hey," he says. "I was just about to call you."

"You were?" I ask.

"Marshall Powell's phone records came in." He picks up a stack of papers from the desk and hands it over to me. "It doesn't look like he talked to anyone the night he was attacked. Other than the 911 call, he didn't make or receive any calls or send or receive any texts for at least six hours. And before that, there was a message from Carla asking if he wanted her to make pasta for dinner."

It reminds me of what Ander said about losing Sabrina and the little things that wouldn't happen anymore, like talking about what they were going to have for dinner. The thought makes the back of my neck tingle. I'm convinced Carla wasn't involved with Ander, but there's still something that isn't fitting together.

Crime scene pictures of the threatening messages on the walls of Gideon and Sabrina's homes are sitting on the table, and I stare down at them. I started this investigation so focused on the threats and what kind of entity might have wanted to not only send them but act on them. But now my feelings have shifted. This feels personal. Without any group or fanatical person claiming responsibility for the crimes, the threats feel random and almost arbitrary. There's no real reasoning for who got them and what they say.

I start to sift through the phone records, noticing that Marshall seems like one of those people who doesn't use his phone very often. Carla's number appears over and over with a few others scattered in the list. I've gone back a few pages when a number pops out at me. It's there only once, and it says the call lasted less than five seconds, but I can't take my eyes off it. I recognize that number. I've dialed it, and it has shown up on my phone screen.

Jesse Kristoff.

I look at the date of the call and realize it is a few weeks before the first reports of the threats came in. I think back on the conversation I had with Marshall and Carla right after Gideon died when they told me that they were preparing for a big move—plans that had been just getting started right before this all started. I can't prove it just from this, but I know in my gut, I was right—I just had the wrong person.

Grabbing that sheet from the records and shoving it into my bag with the rest of my notes, I start out of the conference room.

"You're leaving already?" Detective Fuller asks. "You just got here."

"I know," I say. "But there's something I have to do."

For the second time today, I make the drive to the hospital and park in the main entrance lot. I jog to the door and hop on the elevator to get to Marshall's floor. The door to his room is closed when I get there, so I knock, and he calls out for me to come in. There's a doctor standing alongside Carla by the side of the bed, and she looks annoyed at the interruption.

"Can I help you?" she asks.

"This is Agent Griffin. She's the FBI agent investigating my case," Marshall explains.

"This is really going to have to wait. We're discussing some important issues about Mr. Powell's condition and preparing to run some additional tests," she says.

"That's fine," I tell her. "I just need to have a word with Carla."

Carla looks surprised. She glances at Marshall, who nods.

"It's all right. Go ahead. I'm not going anywhere," he says.

Carla gives him a little smile and leans down to kiss him again. "I'll be right back."

She follows me out of the room, and I lead her directly back to the alcove where we talked earlier.

"Are you here to accuse me of something else?" she asks bitterly.

I ignore the swipe and hold out my hand. "Can I have your phone please?"

"My phone?" she asks. "Why do you need my phone?"

"Information has just come to light, and I need to make a comparison," I say.

"I don't have to give it to you," she says.

"No, you don't. But I'll just get a warrant and look through your phone records. Or you could save me a lot of time and hassle in trying to find out what happened to your husband and just give me the phone," I say.

"What are you looking for?" she asks, taking the phone out of her pocket and handing it over to me.

"I want to see just how many times you've called a certain phone number."

Her hand comes down over the phone in my hand as she lets out a heavy breath. I look into her face and see tears in her eyes.

"You don't need to look," she says. "I've erased all the times his number was on my phone. And all the texts."

"Whose number, Carla?" I ask, needing to hear her say it to confirm my suspicions are correct.

"Jesse Kristoff," she admits.

I let out an exasperated sound as I slam the phone back into her hand.

"So you stand there, right in front of me, and act like you are so deeply offended by the suggestion that you are having an affair with Ander Ward, only for me to find out you're actually sleeping with Gideon Bell's roommate," I say. "How long has this been going on?"

"About a year," she says. "Gideon brought him to a work party, and we talked. Then we ran into each other at the grocery store a couple days later and then again while we were jogging at the park. It was funny that we just kept seeing each other, and we decided to grab some coffee just to chat. We hit it off. I didn't expect it to turn into anything. I really didn't. It's been over for a while."

"I'm assuming since right around when his number showed up on Marshall's phone records?" I ask.

She nods, a tear coming down her cheek. "Even before that, I was feeling really guilty about the affair and knew I couldn't keep it up. Jesse was pushing for me to divorce Marshall and be with him, and I couldn't see myself doing that. I don't know how to make it make any more sense. It was just like a splash of cold water, bringing me into reality again. Then Marshall got suspicious. He saw the number on my phone before I was able to delete it and called it. I was able to explain it away, and I really think he believed me, but that was it for me. I couldn't do it anymore.

"I told Jesse that the affair was over and I didn't want to hear from him again. I asked him to respect that I was recommitting fully to my marriage and there was nothing he could say that would change my mind. Marshall had already started talking about the possibility of moving, and after that happened, I decided that was best. I told him I thought it was a great idea, and we really started planning. It brought us closer together than we've been in so long. We have been in a great place since then."

"How could you not tell me about this?" I demand. "People are getting threats about being wicked and vile behavior, including you, and you didn't think it might be important to tell me that you were having an affair?"

She presses the fingertips of one hand to her forehead, squeezing her eyes closed as more tears flow out of them.

"I'm sorry," she says. "I really didn't think that it was. I didn't think that it could have any impact. If anything, I thought it would just confuse things and make it harder. Things were over between Jesse and me. We hadn't spoken in weeks. He was really upset when I broke things off with him, and I insisted that we couldn't even be friends. There was no way we could carry on being in each other's lives anymore. So we cut each other off. Then when Gideon died, Jesse was attacked too. And so many people got the threats. I didn't think my bad choices mattered. They didn't have anything to do with it. Gideon wasn't doing anything wrong."

"No, but he was about to turn in someone who was," I say.

CHAPTER THIRTY-ONE

JESSE LOOKS STARTLED WHEN HE OPENS HIS APARTMENT DOOR and I push past him to get inside.

"Agent Griffin," he says. "Is everything all right? What's going on?"

"You were sleeping with Carla Powell," I say angrily.

His face falls, and he takes a step back, his head hanging for a second before he looks back at me.

"You found that out," he says.

"Yes, I fucking found that out," I snap. "I had to find it out myself rather than either of you coming clean and telling me even while I was in the middle of investigating your roommate's murder and a near-fatal attack on her husband."

"Wait," he says. "You can't think I had anything to do with those. I admit I was having an affair with Carla. Neither one of us planned it, and I definitely didn't plan on it lasting as long as it did or getting as intense as it did. But it happened. And then it ended. Before any of this happened, it was over. Besides, you'll remember that I was attacked when Gideon was murdered. I got stabbed in the back. And the night Marshall was attacked, I was on the phone with you. Then I talked to my brother for a while because I was still worked up about Gideon not getting the same attention as Sabrina. You are welcome to check my phone records and have them look at the cell towers, or triangulate it or whatever. I was nowhere near Carla's house."

I realize he's right. The call from Carla the night Marshall was attacked came minutes after I got off the phone with Jesse and the attack had just happened. He couldn't have been there. Still filled with fury, but with nothing to say to Jesse, I storm out of the apartment and get back in my car. My mind is spinning. Pieces are falling into place, but there are details that still aren't making sense. I start the car and drive back to Sabrina and Ander's neighborhood.

Annette Chambers looks less wary when she opens the door.

"Hi, Annette," I say. "I need to ask you about something you told me the day Sabrina Ward died. You said she told you that she was pregnant, or that she was pretty sure that she was."

"Yes, she was thrilled," she says.

"Right. It was something she'd been wanting for a long time. Did she happen to tell you how far along she was?"

"Not very. Just a few weeks," she says.

"Okay, thank you."

I'm on the phone with Detective Fuller before I start my car.

"I need to know Sabrina Ward's doctor's name," I say.

"I'll call you back."

He takes less than ten minutes to call me back with the information.

"It looks like all of her doctors were within the same practice. Women and Family Medical Associates," he tells me.

"Perfect."

I type the name into my phone and see that the office is still open. I get there as quickly as I can and walk up to the check-in desk with my shield.

"Agent Emma Griffin. I'm with the FBI. I need to request access to the medical records of Sabrina Ward," I say.

Though the Privacy Act protecting access to medical records persists even after a person has died, this doesn't apply when the person is the victim of a crime. Law enforcement can request the records even without a warrant, meaning I can access the information I need without wasting any time. The nurse behind the desk nods and hands me a form to fill out with the formal request. She reads it over and sucks in a breath.

"Sabrina," she says. "I thought that name sounded familiar. I can't believe she was murdered. Do you really think there's something in her medical records that could be helpful?"

"I hope so," I say.

She nods and goes to her computer, typing in a few commands. "All of our records are digital now. We don't maintain any paper files. But I can give you the access details to her online records," she says.

"Thank you."

She writes down the information, and I leave with the note tucked into my bag. Back at Bellamy and Eric's house, I take out my tablet and input the information into the log-in fields. All the details about Sabrina's recent health and her visits to the doctor appear on the screen, and I find the date I was looking for.

Opening the appointment record, I read the notes. It's exactly what I was expecting to see. I'm getting ready to close the site when I notice a notification on the section about medical record requests. It's too soon to have me listed on the site, so I click on it and read the request. Letting out a breath, I allow the solemn, painful reality to wash over me.

Sabrina Ward had gone to the doctor and had her IUD removed. She wanted a baby even though she knew her husband didn't. Whether it was something she had always wanted and just made the agreement not to have children because she didn't want to alienate Ander and thought he would change his mind, or this was something that had only recently developed in her, she decided that she wasn't going to give up on her dream to be a mother. I obviously don't know for sure what she was thinking or how she was planning on explaining it to Ander when she revealed that she was pregnant. Maybe she would tell him that it just fell out and she didn't notice. I'll never know the full plans she had. But I know she was trying to get around the agreement she made with Ander to never have children.

She wasn't anticipating him going to her doctor and asking for information about her recent appointments. There's a release right there on file showing her giving the doctor's office permission to share information with her husband upon his request. All he needed to do was make a request, and he found out what she had done.

From there it doesn't take much digging to uncover that Ander has already called the insurance company to make a claim on the sizable life insurance policy Sabrina has been carrying. I now have no doubt that the persona Ander has been portraying is concealing a man who wanted his wife dead. A man tired of his marriage and enraged by the thought of being saddled with a child he didn't want, but also aware that a simple divorce would never be an option, so he decided it would be better to get rid of her.

I spread out my notes and read through them again, trying to piece together a timeline of everything that has unfolded since the beginning of the case. The protest at the hospital comes back into my mind, the sight of the enraged people gathering at the emergency room entrance compelled by the disgust Tracy's live post stirred up within them. I can see Ander in my mind, standing in front of them with his arms outspread, shifting his weight as he tried to hold them back from going inside. And then the sudden violent fight that broke out on the sidewalk.

It was so unexpected, such a rash and unnecessary reaction to how far the situation had escalated. But as I'm looking over everything in front of me and letting it all process through my mind, I know why he did it. And I know exactly what happened.

"This could be really serious. I think that something is going on at the Tracy Ellis Ministry headquarters that could put everyone in danger. I need you to meet me there in an hour. You know the entire building and are trained in security. This could be instrumental to the case."

I hang up without waiting for Ander's reply and make sure I am ready before going to the headquarters. With enough time to get there and make sure I'm inside first, I leave the house.

The headquarters parking lot is dark except for small pools of light coming from recessed bulbs near the building entrance. I park where I know my car will be readily visible, clearly indicating I'm already here, and wait for a few moments until I know everything is going according to how I arranged it.

Getting out of the car, I cross to the door and input the code I got from Tracy into the keypad. The electronic locks disengage, and I go into the building, going to the alarm console to put in the next series of numbers she texted me earlier this evening. With the alarm deactivated, I make my way to the conference room where the first company meeting I attended was held. I leave the lights off and take my place just out of sight next to the door.

Everything is still and silent throughout the building. Adrenaline has my heart beating in my temples as I wait. I watch the screen of my phone. I've linked it to the security footage of the cameras at the front of the building. They don't show enough of the parking lot to have helped those who got threatening notes on their windshields, but they clearly show anyone who is entering the building. I watch until a dark figure appears approaching the door. They move swiftly, their head ducked down, but even with their faces turned away from the camera, it's clear to see they are wearing a ski mask.

Once they've opened the door and come into the building, I put my phone back into my pocket and anchor my spot in the shadows by the door. I wait. I know he's moving through the building looking for me. But he's not going to call out for me. And I'm not going to call out for him. He'll know I'm here when he finds me.

It takes several long minutes before I see movement at the end of the hallway. There's just enough light coming from the emergency lights at the edge of the ceiling to show the masked man coming toward me. There's something in his hand now. Either he had it pressed to his side when he walked inside, or he drew it out of the unseasonably long sleeve of his shirt when he came in. He looks into each room as he goes past, and I remain absolutely still as he approaches the door to the conference room. He looks inside but doesn't see me, and he moves on down the hallway.

I step out from behind him and raise my gun.

"Looking for me?"

CHAPTER THIRTY-TWO

H E WHIPS AROUND TO LOOK AT ME, THEN DARTS INTO THE EMER-
gency stairwell at the end of the hallway. I run in after him, listening
for the sound of his feet on the steps. I hear nothing and search for
a light switch on the wall next to the door, but I don't find one. There
are only small red emergency lights in the stairwell, which give very little illumination and don't break the shadows beneath the last flight of
steps. Taking out my phone, I shine the light of the screen under the
stairs and don't see anything.

Putting my phone away, I start up the stairs, climbing cautiously as
I look ahead of me into the darkness to see any kind of movement. I've
reached the landing to the second floor and am considering whether
to proceed on this floor and continue to search when something dark
suddenly drops from the overhang of steps above me to land on the
stairs behind me. Before I can turn all the way around, a hard blow to
my hip makes me stagger. I grab on to the handrail to keep from falling
completely. The club comes at me again, but I swing a swift kick to block

it and throw my assailant off balance. Another kick to his gut forces him down the steps.

He lands hard on the floor, and I come down on him, pressing my knee to the center of his chest as I train my gun on his head. I reach with my free hand and wrench the ski mask off, pulling the blond wig with it.

"Doesn't that feel better, Jesse?" I ask. "I think it's a little too hot for all this."

He struggles on the floor, but the combination of the fall and my pin keeps him from getting up.

"Don't worry, you aren't the only one. Officers should have already gotten to Carla's house to arrest Ander. She called him over there to see her tonight because I told her to. I knew when I called him to come here, it would give the two of you the opportunity you've been waiting for. When I was found dead at the headquarters after receiving one of the threatening notes, the police would look at my phone and see Ander's number. But Carla would give him an alibi. And I'm sure he's making sure that there is some kind of time-stamped recording or some other evidence to back it up. He'd explain that I called to tell him I thought something was going on at the headquarters, but he had already committed to going to Carla's house and didn't think he should be involved in my investigation. Leaving you to come here and stop me from getting any closer," I say.

I hear heavy footsteps coming toward us, and I shout to them, "In the stairwell!"

The door opens, barely missing Jesse's head, and four officers swarm in. They've been waiting in the back parking lot, giving me just the amount of time I asked for before they came inside. I move away from Jesse and let them flip him over and cuff him before yanking him to his feet.

"Be careful. My leg," he complains.

"He fell down the steps pretty hard," I tell them. "You're going to want to have him seen at the hospital."

They drag him out, and I follow, encountering Detective Fuller in the hallway.

"Exactly like you said it was going to happen," he says.

"Yep," I say. "The two of them have been working together from the beginning. When Carla broke up with Jesse right around the same time that Ander found out his wife had gone behind his back to take out her IUD and might already be pregnant, it created the perfect storm. They met through Gideon and somehow ended up finding kinship in their misery as their lives spiraled out of control. They already knew that people had major problems with Tracy Ellis and her ministry. She received death threats and hate mail regularly. All they had to do was latch on to that.

"With Gideon figuring out the affair between Jesse and Carla, he knew he would have to go. But it would be far too suspicious for Gideon and Marshall to both be killed as well as Sabrina Ward. There would be easy links between Ander and his wife, and Jesse and his roommate and lover's husband. It had to look like there was no possibility they were involved. So they worked together. They concocted the plan to send out the threats and wait for a while to act on them. Then Ander killed Gideon and cut Jesse so that he was obviously not the one who did it. That was the only attack that involved a knife.

"Then Jesse lit Ander's mother's shed on fire and killed Sabrina while Ander was very visible to a variety of law enforcement. Ander attacked Marshall while I was on the phone with Jesse. I believe he would have attacked Carla too, if she had been home. I don't think he would have killed her, but the fact that she wasn't home saved her from being injured to further the narrative. The planned attack on Mila was to shift the focus away from that group. I believe they could have killed others just to keep their tracks covered. Including me."

The detective puts out his hand to shake mine. "Thank you, Agent Griffin. I'm glad you were here."

"I have to admit, they were pretty meticulous in their planning," I tell the family as I sit down on the couch beside Sam and rest my head on his shoulder. "They really paid attention to details to make sure that people saw the crimes the way they wanted them to. Like Ander knowing his wife had the fitness tracker bracelet that she always wore. He knew that would record her heart rate and pinpoint the time of her death, which would completely exclude him. No one would be able to suspect that he could have killed her before he left the house to go to his mother's if they had proof she was still alive until a time when he was talking to police in the next town over.

"Then making sure that he was seen on his camera picking up the mail after the note was dropped off. They checked the fingerprint on the seat adjuster, and it came back to Jesse. He cleaned off every other surface in the car but didn't think about that one little knob."

"And the wigs," Dean says, reaching toward the coffee table to swirl a carrot stick in a container of hummus.

"That was a pretty ingenious detail. Both men are very similar in size and build. They knew if they could make a defining feature really obvious, people who happened to see them would report it when they were asked. They went with blond wigs so that it would look like a man with long blond hair. It probably didn't occur to them that fibers would fall out of the wigs in the apartment and in the car. But honestly, it was the protest at the hospital that really pieced it all together for me.

"Ander didn't anticipate Marshall to fight back so hard. He thought he would be able to get the best of him pretty easily and then knock him out so he could kill him without a lot of difficulty. But Marshall did fight. He managed to get in a couple of good blows, including stabbing his assailant in the leg during the attack. That's what really saved his life. Then Tracy Ellis called Ander to come with her to the hospital after she did her live stream. He couldn't get out of it, so he wore a hat and stayed outside. He started a fistfight with one of the protestors and purposely let the guy get a couple of good punches in to cover up the effects of the attack on Marshall.

"Later, Marshall told me about stabbing the assailant in the leg, and it occurred to me that I saw Ander shifting his weight a lot at the hospital and during the memorial at the headquarters. His leg was hurting, and he was trying to take pressure off it.

"I had been suspecting for a while that the threats were a ruse. No entity was taking responsibility for them. There weren't any specific calls for action against Tracy Ellis. It just seemed too neat and tidy, as far as death threats can go. It felt like it had to be personal. They tried really hard to make either of their involvements look impossible. Just not hard enough."

"Well, that's another case solved," says Sam. There's a twinkle in his eye. "Wanna click on the live stream and see what Tracy has to say about all of this?"

I gag. "Absolutely not. I've heard enough out of her for a lifetime."

EPILOGUE

Two weeks later...

DESPITE THE SHADE OF THE MASSIVE UMBRELLA SHIELDING THE lounges, the cement pool deck is sizzling hot beneath my feet as I take off my sandals. I look around and see people wearing brightly colored, rubber-soled water shoes and wonder if I will ever be the type of person to take that step. I doubt it. I like the feeling of the water cooling off my burning feet and my toes wiggling beneath the surface too much, even if that means having to bear the burn for a bit to get to it.

Sam didn't learn any lessons the last time we were here and takes a tube of sunscreen out of my bag to slather it over his shoulders and chest. He hands me the tube and turns his back to me. I don't mind rubbing the lotion into his skin, even if I am already well coated. I wipe my hands with one of the towels and let my cover-up fall from my shoulders so I can drape it on the back of the chair.

The community center pool opens early, and we're there when the gate is unlocked. It's a vibrantly sunny morning that I'm sure will lead to a day of everybody in town packing into the pool to try to find some relief. I wasn't planning on coming out here today. The newspaper clipping is still sitting on my desk at home, the image taunting me as I try to make sense of it and the question I was asked just a few days ago.

Does anyone really know Terrence Brooks?

I can't stop thinking about it, but Sam is actually taking a few hours away from both the sheriff's office and his campaign this morning. The promise of some time with him and the draw of the pool finally brought me out of the house. I'm trying not to be distracted. I want to be present in this moment and enjoy the occasional soft breeze and the image of my husband preparing to dive into the deep end. He disappears beneath the surface and then breaks through again, shaking the water out of his hair and smiling over at me.

"Are you just going to sit over there the whole time?" he asks. "I thought we came here to swim."

I stand up and take off my sunglasses, dropping them down onto the chair. Rather than going to the diving board, I walk down the steps of the ladder into the moderate-depth section of the pool.

Sam meets me at the bottom, sweeping me into his arms.

"I thought we just came here to relax," I say.

"We could sprawl out in the shade at home," he says. "I want to swim. And swimming is so much better with you."

I smile. "Maybe a few laps."

He knows it's all teasing. The water is one of my favorite places to be. It might have been a while since I went down one of the giant slides at a water park, but if the occasion came up to haul a raft up to the top of one with Sam and the others so we could ride down together, I definitely wouldn't turn it down. For now I'll be satisfied with just slowly swirling around in the water in Sam's arms.

We've been swimming long enough for my muscles to relax and the chill feeling to have set in when I climb out of the pool to stretch back out on the lounge. Sam comes with me, spreading out a towel on his own chair and plopping a large hat down over his face. I'm pretty sure he's asleep within a few seconds. The sound of my phone ringing in my bag wakes him up.

"Tell him no, whatever it is," Sam grumbles.

I take my phone out of the bag and see that it actually is Eric calling.

"Hey, Eric," I say.

"Where are you?" he asks without greeting.

"You caught me at the pool again," I tell him.

"You need to go home and make sure your house is secure, then see if you can stay at Xavier's place in Harlan for a while," he says.

There's a sense of urgency and intensity in his voice that tells me he's very serious about this.

"What's going on, Eric?" I ask.

"A dangerous inmate that Greg put away escaped from prison last night. He's accused of murdering a guard during the escape, and there's reason to believe he's on his way to you."

AUTHOR'S NOTE

Dear Reader,

Thank you for choosing to read *The Girl and the Lies!* With each book release, I wait with bated breath for your feedback. Whether through reviews, messages on social media or emails, it is always exciting to hear your thoughts. The incredible reception and feedback you shared on the previous book were both energizing and motivating. Knowing that these stories continue to resonate with you and evoke such a range of emotions is incredibly rewarding!

I am eager to hear what you thought of this book, so please take a quick moment to leave a review. Your voice and enthusiasm have been instrumental in shaping the direction of this series, and I am deeply grateful for your continued support. Thank you for being such a vital part of Emma's journey and for helping to make these books come alive!

In the next engaging installment, *The Girl and the Inmate,* Emma is thrust into danger when she unexpectedly receives a call from an escaped inmate seeking her help. A man, last seen fleeing a bloody crime scene. As Emma races against time to uncover the truth, a simple misunderstanding leads to many deaths. Brace yourself for a suspenseful journey where trust is a rare commodity…

While you eagerly await the next Emma Griffin book, I invite you to join Ava James as she follows her instincts to narrow down the suspect list in *The Housewife Killer.* With tensions running high and the case becoming more personal than ever, the thrilling face-off will answer the question: Who could be the elusive predator that is killing young women and dressing them up as a 50's housewife?

Yours,
A.J. Rivers

P.S. If for some reason you didn't like this book or found typos or other errors, please let me know personally. I do my best to read and respond to every email at mailto:aj@riversthrillers.com

P.P.S. If you would like to stay up-to-date with me and my latest releases I invite you to visit my Linktree page at *www.linktr.ee/a.j.rivers* to subscribe to my newsletter and receive a free copy of my book, Edge of the Woods. You can also follow me on my social media accounts for behind-the-scenes glimpses and sneak peeks of my upcoming projects, or even sign up for text notifications. I can't wait to connect with you!

ALSO BY
A.J. RIVERS

Emma Griffin FBI Mysteries

Season One
Book One—The Girl in Cabin 13*
Book Two—The Girl Who Vanished*
Book Three—The Girl in the Manor*
Book Four—The Girl Next Door*
Book Five—The Girl and the Deadly Express*
Book Six—The Girl and the Hunt*
Book Seven—The Girl and the Deadly End*

Season Two
Book Eight—The Girl in Dangerous Waters*
Book Nine—The Girl and Secret Society*
Book Ten—The Girl and the Field of Bones*
Book Eleven—The Girl and the Black Christmas*
Book Twelve—The Girl and the Cursed Lake*
Book Thirteen—The Girl and The Unlucky 13*
Book Fourteen—The Girl and the Dragon's Island*

Season Three
Book Fifteen—The Girl in the Woods*
Book Sixteen —The Girl and the Midnight Murder*
Book Seventeen— The Girl and the Silent Night*
Book Eighteen — The Girl and the Last Sleepover*
Book Nineteen — The Girl and the 7 Deadly Sins*
Book Twenty — The Girl in Apartment 9*
Book Twenty-One — The Girl and the Twisted End*

Emma Griffin FBI Mysteries Retro - Limited Series
(Read as standalone or before Emma Griffin book 22)

Book One— *The Girl in the Mist**
Book Two— *The Girl on Hallow's Eve**
Book Three— *The Girl and the Christmas Past**
Book Four— *The Girl and the Winter Bones**
Book Five— *The Girl on the Retreat**

Season Four

Book Twenty-Two — *The Girl and the Deadly Secrets**
Book Twenty-Three — *The Girl on the Road**
Book Twenty-Four — *The Girl and the Unexpected Gifts**
Book Twenty-Five — *The Girl and the Secret Passage**
Book Twenty-Six — *The Girl and the Bride**
Book Twenty-Seven — *The Girl in Her Cabin**
Book Twenty-Eight — *The Girl Who Remembers**

Season Five

Book Twenty-Nine — *The Girl in the Dark**
Book Thirty — *The Girl and the Lies*

Ava James FBI Mysteries

Book One—*The Woman at the Masked Gala**
Book Two—*Ava James and the Forgotten Bones**
Book Three —*The Couple Next Door**
Book Four — *The Cabin on Willow Lake**
Book Five — *The Lake House**
Book Six — *The Ghost of Christmas**
Book Seven — *The Rescue**
Book Eight — *Murder in the Moonlight**
Book Nine — *Behind the Mask**
Book Ten — *The Invitation**
Book Eleven — *The Girl in Hawaii**
Book Twelve — *The Woman in the Window**
Book Thirteen — *The Good Doctor*
Book Fourteen — *The Housewife Killer*

Dean Steele FBI Mysteries

Book One—The Woman in the Woods*

Book Two — The Last Survivors

Book Three — No Escape

Book Four — The Garden of Secrets

Book Five — The Killer Among Us

Book Six — The Convict

Book Seven — The Last Promise

Book Eight — Death by Midnight

Book Nine — The Woman in the Attic

ALSO BY

A.J. RIVERS & THOMAS YORK

Bella Walker FBI Mystery Series

Book One—The Girl in Paradise*

Book Two—Murder on the Sea*

Book Three—The Last Aloha*

Other Standalone Novels

Gone Woman

* Also available in audio

Made in the USA
Middletown, DE
29 August 2024

59998853R00123